THE GREATEST LOVE

E M Richmond

This book is a work of fiction. The names, characters and incidents are products of the writer's imagination or have been used fictitiously and are not to be construed as real. Any resemblance to persons, living or dead, is entirely coincidental.

Leanne Warr (t/a EMR Books)

Palmerston North

New Zealand

The Greatest Love

978-0-473-56407-0

Cover art by Carol Fiorillo

First edition. Published by Leanne Warr. 2021

Email: leanne.warr.nz@gmail.com

Deanna has spent her life trying to please everyone. Then Richard Carter asks her to marry him and she accepts … because, why not? He's smart, good-looking and, sure, there are a few red flags, but he claims to love her. The marriage is against her father's wishes but she's tired of sacrificing her own desires for her father's sake.

She slowly begins to realise her husband's charming exterior hides a monster beneath. She escapes her abusive marriage and falls for another man - her husband's former best friend. He's kind and thoughtful - sure, he may not be as good-looking but he's a good man and he makes her laugh. She loves him but knows it's not enough. Ultimately, she must decide if this new love is what she really needs.

She has to move on from the past and learn to love herself.

Dedication

For all those who have gone through similar experiences.

For Kat and Jenny, who continue to provide unwavering support. And Carol and Mary Ellen for their friendship.

Acknowledgements

Laurence Pollwade for his invaluable editing skills
www.ghostwritingspot.com

Carol Fiorillo for her consistently stunning cover art
www.carolscoverdesigns.com

Chapter One

Deanna Carter breathed deeply, fighting the butterflies which had suddenly decided to use her insides to practice their take-off and landing skills. Her breath came out a little shaky as she stood on the threshold of the hotel ballroom, gazing at the crowd of people laughing and chatting like old friends.

She recognised no one. Then again, why would she? This was not the world she was used to. The product of a middle-class upbringing, she was not accustomed to, as her father used to call them, "the rich and shameless." It was a world that was almost alien to her.

What am I doing here? she thought, not for the first time.

The rings on her finger felt heavy. She flexed her hand, her thumb twisting the bands as if that would help ease her anxiety. Where was Richard?

He had called earlier that day, telling her he was going to meet her at the function instead of picking her up at home. His cool response to her anxious request for a reason implied that he considered her grown-up enough to drive down to the city and find her way to the charity fundraiser. She didn't need him to hold her hand, he had told her.

That was all very well, she thought, but he also needed to remember that she didn't know anyone and had no idea how they were going to react to her.

His mother had not been happy when Deanna had met her. As far as Julia Carter was concerned, no one was good enough for her son, and for him to marry a young woman she had not approved of, or chosen herself, was just unacceptable.

The way she had wrinkled her nose and looked like she was sucking on a lemon when Dee had shyly introduced herself had been difficult enough. When she had refused to shake Dee's hand, her expression akin to someone about to dip their hand in something disgusting, it was proof that the older woman was determined not to like her new daughter-in-law to-be.

Now, here she was, forced to enter the lion's den alone. Dee smoothed down the skirt of her cocktail dress. It tapered down, following the shape of her lower body, the hem reaching to just below her knees. The waist slightly bulged. For all the exercising and calorie counting she had done before her marriage, she had been unable to shift the last few kilos that appeared to amass at her middle.

The assistant in the shop where she had bought the dress had guided her to some new shapewear which she had promised would flatten the bulges and give her figure a more flattering shape in the dress. Dee just felt like a blimp, barely able to breathe for fear of popping something.

The dress was ... okay, she thought. It was navy blue lace over a silk lining with long sleeves and a knee-length skirt. The neckline was a modest V-neck, showing little in the way of cleavage. Her husband had never approved of her showing off too much of her figure.

The assistant had assured her the dress was appropriate for the occasion. Since she had never been to a charity event before, she had no idea if the assistant was right. She had never been a fan of reality television shows that told women 'What Not to Wear,' and social events for those with money was something she had never experienced growing up. She might have watched dramatised versions of them on television, but even those hadn't told her what to expect.

She caught her reflection in the glass of the door that was wide open and locked against the wall with a strong hook. She had gone to a hairdresser, asking them to create an up-do. Richard had criticised her lack of skill in hair styling. She had always worn her dark-blonde hair either short or shoulder-length but, after they had got engaged, he had persuaded her to grow it out. The length was still reasonably short, but the hairdresser had made a good job of styling it to look fuller, leaving short pieces around her ears to frame her face.

Dee briefly touched her hair. It was sticky and hard from the styling gel and hairspray in it. She supposed it looked good but she wasn't the best judge where that was concerned.

That was another thing her husband often criticised her for. She had always lacked self-confidence. Being rather shy and insular, she had never been the type of person who enjoyed being the centre of attention. It wasn't that she didn't consider herself attractive. It was more that she would rather downplay that attractiveness. She had been told far too many horror stories from friends who had been hit on by creepy, strange men because of their apparent attractiveness.

She stepped further into the room, half-paralysed by her anxiety. While she had tried to make as quiet and unobtrusive an entrance as possible, it felt like every pair of eyes in the ballroom turned to look at her.

Swallowing hard, she decided to bite the bullet and continued walking.

A waiter intercepted her before she could make it to the bar.

"Ma'am?" he offered her … He was holding a silver tray where several crystal glasses were balanced on top. Some of them were filled with orange juice while the others she assumed were filled with champagne.

She looked at him questioningly before taking a glass of orange juice. He nodded and turned away to serve the next guest.

Thankfully, once she had taken the glass, the rest of the guests appeared to ignore her. She assumed that the initial looks were to gauge if she really belonged here. Once she had been served a drink, they felt free to continue conversing with their companions.

God, what am I doing here? she thought. There was still no sign of Richard. He had told her two days earlier that he had to go on a business trip and hadn't expected to be back until tonight. He hadn't told her exactly what time he would be arriving nor had he trusted her with his flight information.

She didn't have the nerve to confront him. As his wife, she felt she had every right to know when he was coming home, especially considering the fact they were expected at this function tonight. That didn't seem to matter to him.

She sighed as she sipped her drink. They had been married six weeks, and this was not how she'd imagined it would be when she'd agreed to his proposal. She couldn't help thinking about the way it had all happened. She had grown up reading romance novels, never thinking for a second that they were a true reflection of reality. In many ways, romance fiction was like a modern-day fairy tale, where boy would meet girl, they would discover some obstacles to be overcome and then they would live happily ever after.

Having witnessed her parents' miserable marriage, Dee was under no illusion that love could solve any problem. As far as she knew, her parents, Jack and Linda Hargreaves had married for love. Yet they just couldn't seem to work together to resolve the issues that would often come up. If it wasn't financial problems, it was work. Or it was her mother's ambition to be anything other than a secretary.

Jack had always been the kind of man who felt that certain people were born to a certain class and they should never aspire to be anything but what they were. Jack Hargreaves lacked ambition and thought he could control his own daughter by refusing to support her dreams.

It wasn't that he didn't consider her smart. She had, after all, achieved above-average marks in school. Jack had, at least, been savvy enough to realise that girls were not limited by their gender. He was a child of the late '60s when the feminist movement was just taking off. Yet he was still rather old-fashioned in many ways.

Dee wondered if part of her father's problem had been fear. Fear that she would walk away from him, the way her mother had done. Linda had finally had enough when Dee had been a teenager. She had packed a suitcase and walked out of the family home, leaving her husband to pick up the pieces. She had gone off to 'find herself.' It wasn't that she hadn't wanted to take her daughter with her, Linda had explained when Dee had gone to stay with her several months later. At fifteen years old, Dee had known enough about divorce to realise she had nothing to do with her mother's leaving.

There had been no custody battle, no court order forcing either parent to give up their time with their child. Linda had simply chosen not to uproot her from her school, where she was in her third year of high school, and it was the first year where her end-of-year exams would decide her future.

She didn't blame her mother for leaving her with a man who really had no idea how to raise a child to be independent. He thought being a parent meant doing everything for his daughter; the result being that by the time she was old enough to be doing everything for herself, she had no idea how.

At eighteen, Deanna had left Petone Girls' High School with nothing but her newly-acquired exam results. With no experience, she couldn't get a job in anything except for unskilled work. Forced to work in fast food, she did her best to consider it a blessing in disguise. At least there she wasn't under her father's thumb.

The only problem with working in such an environment was that two of her coworkers believed that was their lot in life and claimed they had no dreams beyond getting into the management programme. One of them was her manager, who quickly proclaimed that Dee could also become a manager if she worked hard enough.

The last thing she saw herself doing was getting into management in what was essentially a low-wage job, even if their management training programme was considered one of the best in the industry.

She had always wanted to become a photographer. Dee had a restless nature. Being stuck living in the same town - about half an hour's drive from Wellington on a good day, or at least an hour in peak traffic - never venturing further, was something that didn't appeal to her. She wanted to travel the world.

Jack, who had grown up in the town and had never even had a passport, would never have approved. He had been firmly against it when she had told him she wanted to move away to a city about two hours away; to take up a course at the local tertiary institution while working part-time. Even at twenty-one, the powers-that-be, in their infinite wisdom, had decreed that she could not be considered independent and still had to get her parents' approval before she could apply for any kind of support while studying.

Forced to put her own dreams aside to please her father, Dee had continued to work in the restaurant for another year, secretly putting some money aside so she could save for the day when she could leave for good.

She was stunned when her father told her one day that he had found her another job, as an executive assistant to the general manager of a technology company that had its biggest branch in the town. Headquarters was in the city north of Petone.

Her father had been so excited about the job. Having worked in I.T. himself for nearly thirty years, he had built himself a network of contacts and had heard through the grapevine that the role was coming available. He had talked her up to his contact who had, in turn, talked to the man. Given that her only experience had been in fast food, the man who would be her prospective employer had been a little unsure that she would be the right fit, but she had agreed to attend the interview and had secured the role.

Robin Daly had taken a chance on her and Dee had found (to her surprise) that she did enjoy her work. It was more challenging than managing the restaurant but, soon enough, she realised she was more than ready for that challenge.

She had been there a year when Robin told her that he needed her to go with him to a meeting with the company's owner. He very rarely came down to the branch office, relying on his employees to run things efficiently.

Dee had been expecting an office in one of the buildings in the central city. What she hadn't expected was to be driven out of town into one of the city's newer suburbs. Or for the man's office to be in a separate wing of what could only be described as a two-storey mansion.

The house sat on a hill about ten minutes' drive out of the city centre. It had huge plate-glass windows which overlooked a sweeping view of the city. As she followed her boss to the wing where they would be meeting with the owner, she could see a light haze over the city. While it wasn't as expansive as some cities in New Zealand, and the buildings were not tall skyscrapers, the vista was still impressive from the house.

The maid, or whoever she was, led them to a room with double doors which swung inward when open. A man, about ten or so years older than her, was sitting at the desk but rose from his chair to greet them.

Robin introduced her, and she studied the older man as she stepped forward. He was extremely good-looking with dark blond hair, greying at the temples. The flesh around his eyes was slightly crinkled at the corners, indicating a man who smiled often.

"Hello, Deanna. It is Deanna?"

"Most people call me Dee," she replied.

He smiled, taking her hand in his. She was quick to notice his hands were almost twice the size of hers and were warm, where hers were cool.

"I'm Richard," he said.

When the meeting began, she sat down and began to take notes; the main reason why Robin had brought her to this meeting. She couldn't help noticing the occasional glance Richard would send her way and she felt an odd … chill, no, not chill, she thought. A shiver, she amended silently; up and down her spine.

The more glances he sent her way, the more disconcerted she felt. Dee knew she was attractive, but. certainly not beautiful. Having lived under what she supposed was the controlling thumb of her father, she was unused to such attention from men. Especially a man who was a fair few years older than herself and surrounded by wealth.

They broke for lunch after about two hours. The maid brought in what looked like homemade pumpkin soup and club sandwiches made with the softest bread Dee had ever tasted and fillings so fresh it was as if the vegetables had been just picked and the eggs laid that morning.

Richard sat next to her. "How are you enjoying the sandwiches?" he asked.

"They're delicious," she replied.

"The bread is baked fresh each day," he told her. "My housekeeper bakes it every morning." She blinked at him, not sure what to say. He smiled at her. "You seem a little … surprised."

She swallowed the bite of sandwich. "No, it's not that. It's just … well, I would have …"

He appeared amused. "You would have thought my lunch would be something like caviar and pâté?"

The thought had crossed her mind, but she wasn't about to voice that thought, considering the man was her boss's boss.

"I'll let you in on a little secret about most rich people. Or at least the ones I know. We can't stand the stuff. Of course, I can't speak for the Hiltons and the Rockefellers of this world since I don't personally know them and don't care to. And we do put our pants on one leg at a time."

Dee had the impression that Richard was laughing at her innocence. Since she had never really been around wealth before, she knew she came across as naïve and unsophisticated. She couldn't help it.

As Robin was a keen gardener, he went out to explore the gardens, while Dee stayed indoors, checking emails, and going over her meeting notes.

Richard placed a glass of iced tea in front of her.

"Tell me about yourself," he coaxed.

She looked up at him over the steel rims of her glasses. She had worn glasses for over ten years and was so used to them that she barely noticed them on her face, but she was momentarily surprised at the blurred view of the man standing almost over her.

"Um, there's really nothing to tell," she remarked.

"Oh, I would have to disagree with you there," he replied with what sounded to her like a drawl. "I know what Robin's told me about you. Now I'd like to hear it from you."

She told him about growing up in the town, her parents' divorce and the last few years living with her father. She was careful not to talk about the way he had tried to control her life. Whenever she had mentioned it to a coworker in the past, they'd quickly changed the subject, as if they didn't want to hear about it. Her father had always had a reputation as a decent man, and she had very quickly realised that no one wanted to hear anything that might contradict that.

"So, what is an attractive young woman such as yourself doing working in the tech. industry?"

She shrugged. "It's a job."

"You don't like your job?"

"I do, to a point, I guess."

"Is there something else you wanted to do instead?" Richard asked.

She found herself telling him about her once-held dream of being a photographer and travelling the world. Like her mother, Deanna wasn't happy living in the same place she had grown up in, without the prospect of being able to go anywhere she wanted.

She would occasionally ask him questions about himself, but it seemed he was only interested in talking about her. Dee found that a little odd, but since he was her superior, she decided not to push her luck with him.

He seemed nice, if a little condescending of her lack of knowledge of his world. Dee had always looked at her job as a place to work, not to get involved in the personal affairs of any of her colleagues. She had one close friend with whom she shared many of her frustrations, but they never discussed their respective jobs. Work was always left at work.

Robin returned from the garden and the two men began a conversation that didn't include Dee, leaving her to continue working on the laptop, writing up notes and replying to any urgent messages.

The meeting went on for another two hours and it was dark by the time they got back into town. Dee finished writing up her notes and sent them off to her boss the next morning.

She was surprised, a few days later, when a package arrived for her from the city. When she looked at the return address, she realised it was from Richard. The package contained a book of photographs by someone she had mentioned to the older man as a photographer she had admired.

'Enjoy. Richard,' was all that was written on the accompanying note.

Over the next few weeks, another two packages arrived for her. One was a box of her favourite chocolates. Dee wondered how he knew that since she was sure she had never told him what she liked. She shared the chocolates with her colleagues, not missing the looks of envy from them when they learnt who the sweet treats were from.

Richard would occasionally call to speak to Robin, but would talk to her for a few minutes, asking about her week and what she had been doing outside of work. She had to admit she was flattered at the attention, if a little concerned.

She had mentioned going to see a film that had been adapted from a stage production and wasn't surprised when Richard sent her a ticket to a stage show currently touring the country. The only problem was that the show was only going to be in a venue at least two hours south of the city where Richard lived, and about half an hour or so from town if she took the train.

She wanted to refuse the ticket, assuming that he had reserved the other seat for himself. He called her office two days before the show.

"I think you'll enjoy it," he told her. "And I refuse to take no for an answer."

"But I … I don't know if I can …"

"Of course, you can." He told her that, since he was driving down himself, he could pick her up. She tried to protest, telling him it was a little out of his way, but again he refused to take no for an answer.

She waited nervously in the living room of the house she shared with her father. It wasn't huge, being only two bedrooms. He, of course, had the bigger room, whereas the second bedroom was just big enough to accommodate a single bed and dresser. The walls were bare since the house was a rental. The landlord refused them permission to hang up artwork.

While her parents had owned their own home, when they had divorced, it had been expected that her father would pay her mother out for her share of the house. Instead, he had sold it, clearing the hefty mortgage, and rented a property to move into. Or so she'd been told.

Dee had dressed in a simple skirt and blouse, similar to what she would wear for work, not knowing what she should wear to the theatre. She'd slipped high-heeled shoes on her feet, hoping they were good enough to pass. She'd bought them at the local charity shop, thinking they would be good enough for work.

She was glad her father had told her he would be going out to the local pub after work instead of coming straight home. She didn't want to face any questions he might have. Like: who was this Richard and why was he taking her out to the theatre?

She fidgeted as she sat on the lumpy couch. Jack had also gotten rid of most of the furniture when they had moved and furnished the new house with random pieces from the local Salvation Army thrift shop. Dee had managed to convince him to get some blankets to cover the couch, which was old and not very clean. There had been an odd smell coming from it when the couch had first been installed and it didn't seem to matter how much she tried to clean it, the smell lingered.

She got up and began to pace restlessly across the carpeted floor, looking out the window on each pass to see if any car had pulled up outside. She had no idea what kind of car the man drove.

She hadn't even looked up a bio on him, not wanting to get any preconceived ideas. She supposed that made her naïve since most of the women she worked with often looked up the social media accounts of the men they were going out with just to see what they were like.

It was ironic that Dee, the daughter of a man who had worked with computers for longer than she had been alive, had little interest in social media and didn't even have her own online profile.

A car pulled up outside. It was just light enough that she could see the car as it stopped on the road beside the house. Knowing little about cars, she could only guess that it was an expensive model. It seemed more or less like any other four-door vehicle, except perhaps slightly sportier in looks.

Not that I would know, she thought with a sigh. Her education was lacking.

She grabbed her bag and keys and went out to greet the visitor. Richard's face had that amused expression he always adopted when she did or said something that screamed of her innocence.

"A woman usually waits for me to come to the door," he remarked as she approached his car.

"I'm not *most* women," she responded, thinking she should at least try to cover her naivety.

"No, you're not," he replied, opening the passenger door for her. "I find that most refreshing actually," he added, as they both got in the car.

The car had a smell that reminded her of new shoes and an odd memory popped into her head. If there was one thing her father had never skimped on, it was shoes. When she was about to enter high school, he had taken her shopping for a new pair of school shoes. Instead of going to the local discount shoe store, they had ended up going to one of the higher-end stores.

"Your Grandma used to tell me that she could always replace cheap clothing, but to never buy cheap shoes," he'd told her.

She'd frowned at him. "Why not?"

"Because a good pair of shoes is good for your feet. Do you remember last year when your mum bought you those silly shoes and you got blisters?"

She nodded. The shoes had been for a party but, while pretty, they hadn't fitted well and had been made of imitation leather. After a few hours' wear, Dee had got blisters so bad they became infected. It was one of the few times her father had ever spent a certain amount of time with her where they were not arguing.

"This is a nice car," she commented as Richard drove off, hoping it would at least break the sudden tension between them.

"It's a Porsche," he replied. "I've only had it a couple of weeks." He stopped the car at an intersection, waiting for traffic to clear before turning onto the highway. "I bet you think it's pretentious."

"Um, I wasn't thinking anything of the sort, actually. It's just ... nice."

"Just nice?" he repeated, sounding almost incredulous. "You do realise how expensive this car is!"

"When you say it like that, yeah, that sounds pretentious," she said. "I thought you said you didn't like showing off?" she added, recalling one of their first conversations.

He grinned at her suddenly. "I didn't think you were paying attention."

"And yet, somehow you avoid the question."

"Okay, so sue me if I want to indulge myself in a nice sports car," he replied, returning his concentration to the road.

"There's nice and then there's ... holy crap!"

He laughed again. "That's what I like about you, Deanna. You have a unique perspective on things."

She wasn't sure how to take that.

***

Watching the musical performed live was obviously going to be a different experience than seeing it in the movie theatre. The usher led them to one of the box seats, high above the auditorium. It was obvious Richard had paid a lot of money for the seats. They were given what she could only guess was the 'special treatment,' reserved for those who had paid for higher-priced tickets.

A bottle of wine was already waiting for them as they were shown to their seats. Dee didn't drink a lot of wine and what she did drink was hardly the same kind she assumed Richard was used to. He poured her a glass. It was a white wine and seemed rather dry when she tasted it.

"Not to your liking?" he asked, clearly having seen her expression.

"It's a little drier than I'm used to," she remarked. "It's fine."

"Of course. You'd be used to the sweeter wines."

She couldn't tell whether that was meant to be condescending or diplomatic. Richard was an awfully hard man to read, she thought.

The lights went down, and they settled down to watch the performance. She again felt that sense of a shiver up and down her spine - like she felt when she had first met him. She had no idea what it meant, except that she liked the look of him. He was an extremely attractive man.

She was acutely aware of those feelings as she sat next to him, trying to focus on the action on the stage below them.

Eventually, she was able to immerse herself in the performance, ignoring the odd tingle in her body.

It was pitch-dark when Richard drove her home. He said little, not even commenting on the shabby condition of the streets. Being so late, only a few of the houses still had lights on.

The porch light was on and Dee could see moths flying around the shade, attracted to the heat of the bulb. Richard got out of the car and came around to the passenger side to open her door.

She stood on the grass verge, gazing up at him, wondering what next.

"Well, it was good. Thanks. Did you enjoy it?"

She nodded. "I did. Thank you."

He answered with a nod of his own. "Great. Well, I should get going. Rather late."

"Sure," she said, stepping up to the path and watching as he went back around to the driver's side. He paused, looking as if he wanted to say something, but got in the car without saying anything.

So, that's that, she thought as he drove away. She doubted she would see him again.

She was surprised when, just a few days later, a bouquet arrived for her at work. There was a note from Richard, mentioning their evening and wanting to do it again.

Robin came out of his office and stared at the flowers.

"Those are nice. From Richard?" he asked.

She stared at him, wondering what he knew. When she queried it, he shrugged.

"He just mentioned he took you to a musical the other night. Are you going out with him again?"

"I … I don't know. I mean, he suggested dinner," she added, waving the note, "but …"

"If you want my advice, you should go. I mean, a girl like you … well, that sort of opportunity doesn't come your way very often."

What on Earth did that mean? she asked silently. Was Richard trying to woo her?

"Richard's a nice guy," Robin was saying. "And he likes you. I can tell. He's been kind of lonely since his wife divorced him."

He'd been married for about two years before his wife left him, citing 'irreconcilable differences,' whatever that meant. Dee knew at least that much about the man. He had mentioned her once but hadn't said anything beyond the fact that she had chosen to leave. He had said it rather matter-of-factly instead of saying something that could be construed as hurtful to his ex-wife.

She agreed to go to dinner with the man, but still wasn't certain what he wanted from her. The conversation was again mostly one-sided. He wanted to know more about her but when she asked him questions about himself, he was almost evasive, his answers short and with little detail.

She did manage to learn that his mother lived in a city in the South Island and that she was married to her fourth husband. His father had died when he was ten, and she had been divorced twice.

The dinner was good, although a little rich for her taste. Richard had taken her to a French restaurant which was known for its expensive dishes. Dee had not been impressed with the restaurant's menu or its décor. The lighting was a little dim, making it difficult for her to read the menu. Her eyesight had always been poor but trying to read the small print in what was barely brighter than candlelight was an exercise in futility.

Richard had taken pity on her and ordered for her. She knew enough French to understand some of what he was saying and was relieved he chose not to order something she would normally not eat. She wasn't a fussy eater, but there were still some things she disliked and would never order for herself.

The wait staff seemed friendly and welcoming, but she couldn't help noticing a slight undertone whenever the waiter spoke to her. Maybe it was her imagination, but she thought she detected a tone of superciliousness when she was addressed, and deferential when talking to her companion.

It was again dark when he drove her home. Before she could gather her wrap and bag, he was opening the door for her and holding his hand out to help her out of the car. The Porsche was rather low to the ground and she had difficulty getting out in high heels. At least, with any sense of dignity. She stood on the kerb, her spike heels digging into the soil, making her feel a little unbalanced.

"Thank you for dinner," she said quietly.

"You're welcome," he replied.

She hesitated as he continued to stand beside the car, making no move to return to the driver's side.

She started to step onto the grass to walk up the path to the front door when his hand on her arm stopped her. She looked up at him. Richard was as tall as her father, who was just over 1.8 metres, but he appeared to tower over her. Dee was about a head shorter.

She fought the urge to bite her lip as he leaned closer to her, pressing his mouth to hers. She hadn't been kissed by men a lot, but this kiss was hardly what she would call fireworks-inducing. It was almost like kissing a relative, she thought. There was no heat, no fire - nothing close to what she would call passion.

He drew back and looked at her quizzically.

"All right?" he asked.

She nodded. "I'm fine."

He shivered. "It's cold," he said. "You should get inside."

"Yes," she returned, not knowing what else to say. He gently pushed her in the direction of the house. "Go," he ordered. "I'll call you tomorrow."

Chapter Two

She was suddenly pulled back to the present with the sound of a deep voice.

"You look a little lost."

Startled out of her memories, Dee looked up and stared at the dark-haired man smiling down at her.

"Excuse me?" she queried.

His brown eyes crinkled at the corners in what she took to be amusement.

"You looked miles away."

She realised she had barely touched her orange juice and had probably been standing in one spot for about five minutes or more.

"I'm sorry," she said.

He shook his head. "Don't apologise. Whatever had you so deep in thought is probably more exciting than anything these bozos can come up with."

She raised her eyebrows. "Bozos?" she asked.

He laughed. "Well, what else would you call a bunch of social snobs who do little else but spend money sunning on the beaches of St Tropez," he returned in what sounded like a snooty tone.

She bit back a laugh, amused by the man's brief diatribe but still very unsure of herself.

"Wow!" she exclaimed! "And I thought I was cynical."

"I'm Phillip, by the way," he told her.

"Dee. Well, Deanna, actually, but …"

"I know who you are," he replied with a nod. "Richard's new wife."

"It's that obvious?" she asked.

"Well, you do kind of stand out," he said. "Not that it's a bad thing by any means. It's rather refreshing to meet someone who isn't impressed by any of this."

"By this, you mean …"

"The utter pretentiousness of the rich and shameless," he returned with a smirk. "Take Bella, for instance," he added, pointing to a thin woman with snowy white hair. She was aged somewhere in her seventies and had full-face makeup. She wasn't smiling and appeared almost stone-faced.

"She's had so much Botox that if she smiled, I'm sure her face would crack."

Dee bit her lip to keep from laughing at Phillip's description of the older woman.

"Don't get me started on her 'cosmetic enhancements'," he continued.

"Oh, please, let's not fall victim to political correctness and call it what it is."

"Ah, yes, that constant battle to keep ten steps ahead of that disease known as ageing."

He pointed to someone else. A man about 50 years old with a hairstyle that flopped over his forehead and a paunch around his middle. A woman about Dee's age stood beside him. She looked like a model, except her chest was unnaturally big and her waist was tiny as if she was trying to be the real-life version of a Barbie doll.

"Now, there's a prime example of a man in his … uh, prime. He's on his third, or is it fourth wife now? He went through a mid-life crisis when he turned 40, left his wife for his mistress and now trades them in like cars. He's so convinced of his attractiveness that he thinks they marry him because they can't live without him. More like they can't live without his money, but who are we to judge, hmm?"

She couldn't stop the laughter that bubbled up at Phillip's audacity. It would probably sound cruel to make fun of them, but he spoke in such a way that she did find it rather funny.

He was in the middle of telling her a story about a couple's wild adventure in a jail in Italy after they had been caught skinny-dipping in Lake Como when she felt a hand on her arm.

"Why am I not surprised to see you here?" Richard said gruffly. "And flirting with my wife!"

She stared at him, confused, and wondering why he thought they'd been flirting. They had just been chatting, hadn't they?

"But … we weren't," she began. "He was just …"

His grasp on her arm tightened.

"I'm sure it was all innocent, right, Mason?"

Dee frowned at her husband, wondering why he was acting so jealous. They had only been talking.

"I was merely keeping your wife company until you arrived, Richard." His look was scathing. "Maybe if you had been here on time, your wife wouldn't have looked so neglected."

"Are you criticising my marriage?" Richard accused, practically baring his teeth at the other man.

Dee wondered if the two men were about to come to blows. She touched her husband's arm.

"Richard, please. He was just keeping me company until you came. Don't make a fuss."

He turned on her and hissed. "Don't tell me what to do, Deanna!"

She stared at him, taken aback by the threatening tone. She had little chance to reply, or even think of something suitable to say that would calm the situation as he pulled her away, his grip on her elbow hard enough to bruise.

She decided her best course of action was not to argue with him and ignore his outburst. She let him pull her to the other side of the room. The ballroom had several sets of French doors which opened out onto a balcony.

Richard let go of her elbow and went out through the French doors. The balcony appeared to have been installed along the entire width of the building. Several people were smoking, standing beside the glass barrier or sitting at tables with their drinks.

Her husband lit a cigar and she crinkled her nose.

"I wish you wouldn't," she said. She hated the smell of cigars. When she had been little, in primary school, her parents had taken her with them to a meeting at a teacher's home. The man had smoked cigars and his house had reeked of them. Dee had felt ill for hours afterwards.

"I'll smoke if I want to," he returned waspishly.

"You're acting like a child," she admonished him.

He glanced at her but continued to smoke. The one consolation she had was that he chose not to blow the smoke in her direction, knowing how she felt about them.

She sighed and looked out over the city view. The hotel was in the city centre and while it wasn't as lavish as the hotel they'd stayed in one weekend not long before they had got married, it was certainly more opulent than some hotels she'd been in since they'd begun dating.

If dating was really the word, she thought, reminded once again of those early days when he would call her up and tell her he was taking her out. There was never any opportunity for her to refuse.

Their relationship had changed as the year wore on. Winter became Spring, which then became Summer, and the outings changed from tickets to a play, or dinner, to concerts in the park. Richard would always drive her home, commenting on the condition of the houses surrounding hers without directly criticising them. Yet she could tell he disliked her living conditions.

He had met her father once, although he had never actually spent any time in the house in which she had spent the last nine years. Jack had just arrived home when Richard had driven up to take her to dinner. It was obvious the two men disliked each other on sight. Whether it had been because of what she had already told him about life with her father, or something else, she didn't know.

Her father, of course, had asked her later about it.

"Is this what you've been doing the last few months?" he asked. "Dating a man behind my back?"

She frowned at him. "Behind your back? What am I supposed to do, Dad? Stay at home and do nothing?"

"He's too old for you."

"He's thirty-five, Dad. Ten years is not too old."

"I don't approve!"

"Well, I'm an adult and you don't get to dictate who I go out with," she told him defiantly.

"The man is far too mature. And he owns a Porsche!"

She was confused. "Meaning I'm too immature for the likes of him?"

The argument continued with him trying to shoot down every one of her responses.

Dee hadn't been so sure about continuing to see Richard, but for the first time in her life, she decided to rebel against her father's wishes.

Looking back, she later realised it was not so much the man's age he disapproved of. It was his money. As far as Jack had been concerned, she did not belong in Richard's world. He claimed he didn't make a lot of money in his job and seemed to be permanently stuck in the mindset that they would always be middle-class.

The next week, instead of the usual outing, Richard told her to pack a bag. He was taking her away for the weekend to Queenstown. They would be flying out of Wellington airport Friday evening.

The resort where they were staying was surrounded by beautiful scenery. They were in a part of New Zealand that included national parks and ski fields. Surrounded by mountains and lakes, it was a popular destination for tourists.

They were taken to a studio which Dee estimated was about half the size of her father's house. She looked around, realising there was only one bed. Which meant …

Richard waited until the man who had shown them to their room had gone before he wrapped his arms around her.

"I know this is the first time we've spent a weekend together. I want you to know that you're safe with me."

She bit her lip. She had slept with one man before him and that had been an utter disaster. She had been twenty-one and had only been going out with the young man for a month. He had been more intent on getting what he wanted from the sex, rather than ensuring she was comfortable. She had liked the young man a lot but, once he had slept with her, he'd dumped her; his last words involved telling her that she was just not good enough for him. Whatever that meant.

They ate dinner in the restaurant. Dee knew her lack of sophistication was showing as other couples sent curious looks her way and all she could do was drop her gaze coyly. She felt like they were judging her, for her clothes, her looks and her shy nature. She listened to the buzz of conversation around her while she quietly ate dinner with her companion but couldn't make out what they were saying.

When they returned to the room, she faced him, her nervousness causing her to tremble almost violently. He told her to go and take a shower to calm herself.

She gaped at the huge bathroom, which was at least twice the size of the bathroom at home.

She mentally berated herself, glad that Richard had not been there to see her wide-eyed surprise at signs of a life of luxury that she had never known until she met him. For a man who claimed he was not pretentious, he certainly enjoyed the finer things in life, she thought.

She showered quickly. Dee had never been one to waste time in a shower. She preferred to get in and out quickly. That was unusual for a young woman.

Richard cocked an eyebrow at her when she emerged ten minutes later, wearing a nightgown and kimono robe. He looked amused.

"My ex-wife, bless her, could spend hours in the bathroom," he said.

She shrugged. "I guess I'm just unusual."

He kissed her. "That's one of the things I like most about you," he said. "You defy the conventions of the gender."

She raised her eyebrows at him. "That's rather a generalisation, isn't it? I've heard that men hate it when women do that to them."

"Oops," he said, pretending to be sheepish. "You're right. That is a generalisation."

He let her go, moving over to what she assumed was the bar, taking out two glasses and a bottle of what she realised was brandy.

"Nightcap?" he suggested.

"Not for me," she said. "I don't really like brandy."

"Suit yourself," he replied with a shrug. He poured himself some of the brandy and went over to the door, sliding it open.

Dee pulled back the bedcovers and got in. She lay back against the pillows, shifting back and forth until they felt more comfortable. Meanwhile, Richard had lit a cigar and was smoking while he drank his nightcap.

Thinking about what was to come, her anxiety returned. She began reading a book she had brought with her, hoping it would help calm her nerves. Richard came back inside and left the glass tumbler on the bar before disappearing into the bathroom.

He emerged a short time later wearing only boxer shorts. She tried not to be obvious as she looked him over. He had an athletic build, his torso long and slim, although lacking what she imagined was called a six-pack. He was not fat, but his body wasn't completely perfect either.

"All right?" he asked, having caught her gaze.

She nodded, not knowing what to say.

He pulled back the covers and got in bed beside her.

"What's that you're reading?" he asked.

"Um, nothing. Just a crime story."

"I see. You like crime fiction?"

"It's all right. It depends on the author."

"What else do you like to read?"

"Biographies. I like reading about people's lives. Learning why they did the things they did." She hesitantly asked him the same question.

"I don't like to read," he answered. "I have a hard enough time reading company reports."

"Maybe you should hire someone to read the reports for you and just give you the cliff notes," she teased hesitantly.

"Now, there's an idea," he drawled. He reached for her, a hand on her waist as he pulled her close to him. He took the book from her hands and tossed it toward the chair beside the bed. It just missed the mark and fell onto the floor. Dee was not impressed with his casual mistreatment of her belongings but said nothing.

She let herself be swept away by his lovemaking. Richard was a skilled lover, knowing just how to elicit the right kind of reaction from her. Yet she could not help but feel that something was missing. Almost as if he were going through the motions. She felt little to no emotion from him. No passion.

The next morning, they breakfasted on the patio. Dee was quiet, thinking about what had happened the night before. She sipped her orange juice and gazed at the scenery.

"You're very quiet," Richard said. "Something wrong?"

She glanced at him, wondering if she should broach the subject with him. He appeared impassive, making her think that no matter what she replied, it would make little difference to him.

She decided it was a subject best left alone.

"Just thinking about my dad," she said.

"Oh?"

"He doesn't think I … he doesn't …"

"He doesn't like me. He thinks I'm too old for you, or that you don't belong in my world. Does that cover it?"

"How did you …" She stared at him. "I've never …"

"I know," he said. "But Petone is a small town and people talk. Your father was complaining to one of his friends in the local pub and word got back to Daly." He smiled in amusement. "Your father seems permanently stuck in the twentieth century."

"I guess he is."

"And, frankly, it's none of his business why a man of my age and … station …" (he seemed even more amused by this) "chooses the companionship of someone like yourself."

"Then why?" she asked.

"Because you're so very different from every other woman I've known. Yes, you're very sheltered. That's your father's fault. But there's something about you. Something I find very attractive." He paused for a long moment. "Deanna, I have been married before and my wife … ex-wife, rather, was from the same background as myself. While we were dating, she seemed to be everything I thought I wanted in a wife. To give her credit, she was a gracious hostess whenever I threw a party. She knew everyone in our social circle. She was good at wooing potential business contacts, I'll give her that. But for all that, we had nothing in common. She didn't likc to go to the theatre. Or outdoor concerts."

He pulled his chair closer to her. "I was attracted to your innocence, but as I got to know you, I began to realise that you were just as lonely as I was. I loved your enthusiasm for everything, from watching a musical on stage to a drive in the countryside. Watching your face as you experienced all those things, your joy as you discovered something new and wonderful, was what made me fall deeper and deeper in love with you."

She blinked. He was in love with her?

"I know we've only known each other a few months, Deanna, but I want to marry you. If you'll have me.

*****

Dee was once again brought back to the present with the announcement that dinner was going to be served. She looked up at her husband who had finished smoking his cigar and appeared to have been waiting for her.

She turned away and began to head indoors, intending to follow the other guests. He grasped her arm. Thankfully not the one he had already bruised.

"I'm sorry," he said. "For my behaviour earlier."

She studied him but didn't reply.

"Phillip Mason is a business rival. I'm not even sure what he's doing here." He looked out at the city for a moment. "I thought ... well, it doesn't matter what I thought."

"Nothing was going on. He could just see I was feeling a little like a fish out of water and was trying to make me feel more comfortable, that's all."

He nodded. "I just didn't like it. Again, I'm sorry. I had a hell of a day and I didn't mean to take it out on you."

"What happened?" she asked, genuinely concerned for him.

"Just business stuff," he said. "It's nothing you need to worry about," he added, almost dismissively. He grasped her arm again. "Come on. We should go into dinner."

Chapter Three

At first, sitting down for dinner was about as comfortable as she expected it to be. Like the night in the Queenstown resort restaurant, Dee found herself the subject of stares and probably conversations as well.

She tried to ignore the looks from the other guests. She noticed some of them sent friendly smiles her way, but others appeared to be looking down their noses at her. One woman - the one Phillip had pointed out earlier who did indeed look as if she had a lot of cosmetic surgery - glared at her from another table.

She wanted to return the glare in an act of defiance but decided someone had to take the high road. These people might have a lot of money, but they were no better than anyone else.

Richard nudged her. "Stop it," he said.

She frowned at him. "Stop what?"

"You're fidgeting."

"People keep staring at me," she told him.

"So, stare back at them," he returned. "You're my wife and if they don't like that, it's their problem. Not yours." His tone told her in no uncertain terms that he would not tolerate her acting like a child.

She took the mild rebuke without correcting his assumption. She didn't think she was acting like a child, but that didn't seem to matter to her husband. He turned away from her, ignoring her obvious discomfort to talk to a tall, dark-haired woman who was closer to his age than hers. They appeared to know each other well, judging from their conversation, she thought.

The woman was stunningly beautiful. Her makeup was subtle enough to look natural and Dee was sure that, even without makeup, the older woman would be stunning. She could have been a top model with her high cheekbones and full, pouty lips.

Dee turned away from them while wishing, not for the first time, that she could be anywhere else. There were more than a hundred people in the dining room and the volume of chatter was almost deafening.

Resigned to enduring the torture, she began studying the room. She counted at least twenty round tables, with three couples seated at each. All the tables had been covered with white linen. Dee felt a twinge of sympathy for whoever would have to clean up afterwards, knowing there would be more than a few tablecloths which would be badly stained at the end of the night.

When they had been chatting, Phillip had cynically told her that most of these events were just excuses for some people to get as 'merry' as they wanted, with no recrimination. Who cared? he had told her. They didn't have to drive, since some of them would be staying in the hotel, or others had their own driver.

She spotted him at one of the other tables. He was alone, obviously not having brought a date with him. He caught her gaze and lifted his wine glass with a sardonic smile.

The chatter died down to whispers and she looked for the reason. There was a stage at one end of the dining room. A podium had been set up with a sound system and microphone stand. A man wearing a formal dinner suit stood on the podium, looking over the guests.

There was a slight squeal of feedback as he began to speak.

"Ladies and gentlemen, if I could have your attention, please."

Some guests complained at the squeal and he shifted slightly.

"Is that better?" he asked. There was no feedback that time. There were murmurs of assent from those watching.

"Ladies and gentlemen, thank you for coming tonight. As you know, we hold a silent auction every year to raise money for child cancer research." He pointed to a corner of the room where Dee saw for the first time some items which had been offered in the auction.

"We have recorded the bids on each piece, and we'll announce the winning bids very soon. In the meantime, the staff will be out shortly with the first course. Again, thank you for your patronage and please enjoy the rest of your evening."

There was a short wait before the servers came out with trays of dishes. Dee looked down at her place setting and saw a slip of paper advising the menu for the night. The starter was going to be seared scallops with a pea puree, served with a small salad.

She bit her lip as a server approached their table and began placing the dishes in front of the guests. While she ate almost anything, she had never had scallops before and had no idea what to do or what the etiquette was.

She watched the guest opposite, copying their movements, from the way they placed their napkin on their lap to the cutlery they chose. She hesitantly took a bite of the scallop and found to her surprise that it was not as bad as she thought it was going to be. The taste was sweet and buttery and similar to crabmeat.

"How do you like your scallops?"

She looked up. An older woman at the table was smiling at her. She appeared to be about forty, with greying dark-brown hair which was cut in a layered bob and arranged in such a way that the grey looked more like highlights. Like Dee, she wore glasses, which made her look rather bookish, but the style suited her.

"It's delicious," she said.

"Yes, the chef here is rather good," the woman replied. "You have to be careful not to overcook scallops or they tend to taste rubbery."

Dee wrinkled her nose in distaste at the thought. "Oh. That wouldn't be very nice."

The other woman smiled. "I didn't get your name."

"It's Deanna. Deanna Ha … Carter," she amended, glancing at her husband, who was ignoring her in favour of his neighbour. They appeared to be chatting quite animatedly. Almost flirtatiously, which was a little hypocritical on his part since he had just yelled at her for apparently doing the same thing not more than an hour earlier.

"My name's Carol. Carol Foster." She glanced at the man next to her, who was chatting to his neighbour, a man aged in his early 50s. "That's my partner, Stewart."

He looked up, confused. "Did I hear my name?" he asked.

"Go back to your gas-bagging, dear," she told him tartly.

Dee laughed. It was odd hearing the term from someone she assumed had grown up surrounded by wealth.

Stewart scowled at his partner.

"Men do not 'gasbag'," he replied haughtily. "We wax philosophical, we …"

"Gas-bag," she returned, winking at Dee. She flapped her hand at him. "Go on. I'm not talking to you."

For a moment, Dee thought the older woman was being rude to her partner, but he just rolled his eyes and turned away, but not before she caught a grin from him.

Carol leaned her elbows on the table and laced her fingers together, propping her chin on her hands.

"So, you and Richard, hmm? We heard he'd got hitched again. I must say, you're much prettier than his mother told us."

"You know Mrs Carter?"

Carol made a face. "Unfortunately. The woman is a complete battleaxe, and nuts to boot. Completely off her rocker."

"Really?" Dee didn't get that impression when she had met the woman. Then again, she had barely spent a day in the woman's company. Other than the wedding, that was.

"Don't let the woman fool you. She hates everyone who comes within a metre of Richard. No one is ever going to be good enough for her 'precious baby'."

"Telling tales about me again, Carol?" Richard cut in.

She shot him a look. "Perish the thought." She nodded at Dee. "You better look after this girl, Richard, or you'll have me to answer to." Dee laughed silently at the way Carol seemed to have instantly adopted her. The woman's tone was playful, but her expression was hard.

Richard put an arm around her shoulders and pulled her close.

"Oh, I intend to," he replied. Dee caught an edge to his words. As if it was an act of defiance, rather than reassurance.

She continued chatting to the other woman, who reminded her a lot of her mother.

Linda had come to the wedding, pleased that her daughter had found someone who could look after her.

Jack, however, had refused to even show his face. When Dee had agreed to marry Richard, they had gone to talk to her father together. His response was: "Over my dead body."

It was ironic that her mother, who had left because she wanted freedom from the confines of her own marriage, was more supportive of the marriage than her father, who had once told her that the only reason she needed to work was so that she could find someone who could take care of her. She supposed he would have been happier if her future husband had been 'their' type of people, rather than a man who owned a multi-million-dollar company.

*****

As the servers took away the plates, another man got up to talk about the research and where the money raised from the evening's auction would go. Dee listened intently. While she wasn't close to anyone who had lost a child to cancer, she had once had a friend whose aunt had experienced such a loss. The friend never really spoke of her cousin, who had been diagnosed with leukaemia at age five.

While they waited for the next course to be brought out, Dee found herself telling Carol about her friend. The other woman nodded.

"That's why we came to this," she said, glancing at her partner. "Stewart's daughter had a brain tumour when she was twelve. She survived, luckily, but not every child is as fortunate."

"I'm so sorry," she said, not failing to notice the way Carol had mentioned the daughter.

"It's all right. They had a difficult time for a while, but Helen is an incredible young woman. She now heads up a non-profit organisation herself."

It was obvious Carol was extremely proud of the other woman.

The main course was brought out and Dee saw to her relief that it was a dish she recognised. At least, partially. She had never had Chicken Roulade before but again was pleasantly surprised to discover she liked it.

The final course was some kind of fruit pudding with pears poached in brandy.

Once the dinner was over, the master of ceremonies stood at the podium and began listing the auction items and the companies and artists who had donated them.

"Now, of course, we shall announce the winning bids."

Dee tuned out a little as the names were called out. She was surprised when she heard Richard's name. The emcee was holding up a painting. She recognised it as a painting she had admired in a gallery a month or so earlier when they had taken a drive along the coast. It was a photo-realistic painting of the coastline.

"This fine piece was donated by an artist from Kapiti," the man was saying. "Richard's bid of $5000 was the top bid, which makes him the proud new owner."

She looked at her husband as he stood up to acknowledge the applause. He smiled at her when he sat down again.

"I got it for you," he said. "I knew you liked it."

She nodded. "I did. I … thank you."

He shrugged. "Consider it your wedding present."

Dee was surprised at his generosity. There were times when she didn't understand her husband. He could be sometimes arrogant, sometimes brooding, but then he would turn around and do something for her that was so kind and thoughtful that it seemed almost out of character.

The evening came to a close shortly after. As they were leaving, Carol approached her, business card in hand.

"Here's my number," she said. "If you ever need to chat, or even go out for a coffee."

Dee smiled at the older woman. "Thank you. It was so nice meeting you."

"And you, Deanna." She leaned forward. "Don't be afraid to stand up to him if he bosses you around too much."

Dee frowned, wondering what the woman meant by that. She didn't have a chance to ask her as Richard took her arm.

"Let's go," he said.

Chapter Four

They were staying at the hotel overnight, returning home in the morning. Dee resented being almost dragged out of the ballroom and up the stairs to the fourth floor. A dress and high heels were hardly appropriate clothing to be climbing stairs. Even if it was only three flights. Richard huffed almost scornfully.

"It's not as if you don't need the exercise," he had commented.

The words grated. It wasn't the first time he had remarked on her figure and she guessed it wouldn't be the last. She wasn't that overweight and what extra weight she did carry wasn't overly obvious, apart from the slight bulge at her waist. Being slightly above average height for a woman, she had the kind of frame that appeared to distribute the weight more evenly.

The first time they had slept together, he hadn't even mentioned it. The second time, he had made an offhand comment that she supposed had been meant to sound like it was out of concern but was slightly offensive.

She had turned down his proposal the first time, unsure if she cared enough about him to marry him. It wasn't just the casual way he treated not only her but anything she cared about, but the thought of tying herself to someone she had barely known a few months was another, and she felt more valid reason.

She hadn't been able to quash her niggling doubts about him, even as he proposed twice more. When they were together, he was attentive but, even then, he didn't appear to be the kind of man who lavished affection on someone. Even someone he claimed to be in love with.

The deciding factor, in the end, had been an argument with her father. He had criticised Richard at every turn, even going so far as to tell her that she would be of little use to a man like Richard anyway, since she couldn't cook, and certainly couldn't take care of herself. She had responded by telling him exactly why that was. After all, ever since her mother had left, he had refused to let her lift a finger, even when she had told him she wanted to learn to cook.

That weekend, she went to stay at Richard's place. A simple dinner was served. He had once explained that he preferred simple meals rather than gourmet dinners when he was at home.

They had been sitting on the terrace, looking out over the river. It was an extremely warm night and she could hear the chorus of cicadas in the trees and bushes below. They always tended to be quite loud, but not loud enough to drown out the traffic moving across the bridge.

Richard was smoking a cigar. She hated any kind of smoking, regardless of whether it was cigarettes or cigars, and had told him as much. He had promised not to do it too much around her, but there were times when he appeared to either forget or ignore her protests.

"What's wrong?" he asked her.

"It's just my dad," she told him. He looked half-annoyed. She knew it was a constant excuse, but while she did bring him up when she was trying to avoid telling Richard her true feelings, this time it was genuine.

"He seems to think that I'm pretty much worthless to someone because I can't cook, and I don't even do housework."

The man snickered, clearly amused. "Deanna, I didn't ask you to marry me because I wanted a woman to cook and clean for me."

"Why did you, then?"

"Because I love you. How many times must I ask before you'll accept me?"

"It's just … he's always acting like I'm not good enough. For anyone. He's so determined to control me and everything I do … you know he got me the job at Carter Tech."

"I'm aware of that," Richard said, no longer amused. "Why do you keep listening to him when it's obvious he doesn't have your best interests at heart?"

"He's my father," she said with a sigh.

"Yes, your father. Not your keeper." He leaned forward, placing a hand on her knee.

She tried not to flinch away from the cigar in his hand, but he appeared to notice her recoil and put the cigar out in the ashtray beside him. "I apologise," he told her. "I know you don't like it." He glanced away for a moment before turning to look back at her. "Deanna, I care about you, not where you come from. It is the twenty-first century, after all."

"But … won't people think I'm …"

"A gold-digger?" He snickered. "For one, you would have accepted my first proposal if you were. Second, you hardly look the part."

"What does that mean?" she asked.

His gaze swept over her. She suppressed an involuntary shudder at his expression. It seemed almost predatory as if he considered her to be his prey

"Don't mistake me," he said. "You're a very attractive woman, but you're unlike any other woman I have been involved with in the past. You choose to be more natural. As I believe I told you, I find that very refreshing."

She gave in.

It wasn't long before the rumour mill began circulating at work. Dee happened to be in the kitchen when she overheard a conversation between two of her younger coworkers. The rooms had been built so the dividing walls didn't quite reach the ceiling, allowing voices to drift.

"You know he's only marrying her because she won't cheat on him." Dee frowned, wishing she could be anywhere else but there, listening in to the woman's gossiping. Gina Markwell was well-known for being the office gossip. She had also made it clear on several occasions that she thought she was far more qualified for Dee's job.

"I mean, you've seen her, right?" Gina continued. "It's not like any other man is going to be panting after her. We're talking plain Jane. She doesn't even wear makeup, for God's sake. And that figure ..." She snorted. "I barely see her eat anything, yet she's so chubby."

Dee couldn't make out who the other coworker was as they spoke much more quietly as if they were aware their voice could carry. Gina didn't seem to care.

"Well, you know what happened with his first wife, don't you? She cheated on him."

She wanted to give the woman the benefit of the doubt, but the more she listened, the clearer it became that Gina was talking about her. Knowing she couldn't hide in the kitchen forever, she decided she had to bite the bullet. Taking her coffee with her, she left the room, walking past the two women without even bothering to look their way. From the gasp from Gina's friend, she decided her guess had been correct.

Her father, while not completely disparaging, had made his disapproval of the engagement very clear.

"Don't come home crying to me when it doesn't work out," he told her.

She decided not to tell Richard about the gossip, but it seemed it was unnecessary. Word got back to him and he turned up at the offices late one morning about two weeks following the engagement, calling for an office-wide meeting.

The branch offices of Carter Tech had been built in a converted factory. Most of the executive suites were on what had once been the mezzanine floor where management would be able to watch the staff working on the factory floor. That main area was divided into two sections. The back section included pods where most of the staff worked, from those in research and development to other administrative staff. The front section was a large reception area which could easily hold the hundred or more employees.

Dee made her way downstairs, following her boss. As he started toward Richard, he turned to look at her, then returned to her side, guiding her forward. She frowned at him, wondering why he was pushing her toward her fiancé.

Richard smiled at her and took her hand.

"Don't look so worried," he said. "It's not going to be the Spanish Inquisition."

She laughed shakily. It was an old joke. They had been watching an old movie on television one night and one of the characters had said almost the same thing. Richard had told her his father had been a Monty Python fan.

All the employees had gathered by now, chattering to each other, and she tried to shrink into the background, feeling that they were all staring at her. The din was almost deafening. Robin ordered them all to quiet down and Richard began to speak.

"It has come to my attention that there are rumours around the company about myself and Miss Hargreaves. Well, the rumours are true." He turned to her, lifting her hand to kiss it.

"This charming young lady has agreed to become my wife." His gaze swept over the room as it began to buzz. It appeared some of the employees were congratulating themselves on having managed to figure it out before the official announcement.

"It has also come to my attention that some of my employees have made disparaging comments regarding my future wife. Such comments will not be tolerated and, henceforth, any further remarks will result in immediate termination. Is that clear?"

There were rumblings and judging from the expressions on people's faces, not all of them were positive. Gina shot her a disgruntled look before pushing through the crowd leaving the area to march up to them.

"Congratulations," she said coolly. Yet her expression said something else entirely.

"Thank you, Gina," Richard replied, his tone icy, which left Dee in no doubt that he knew exactly what the woman had said about her. Ignoring the woman, he turned to her. "Darling, I thought I'd take you to lunch. That okay with you, Rob?" he asked Robin.

"Of course, it is. Have fun, you two lovebirds."

Dee looked at her fiancé, telling him she needed to get her bag. He shook his head.

"You don't need it," he told her. She had no choice but to let him push her out the door and into his car, which he had parked in one of the two handicapped spaces.

For a man who claimed not to care about his money, he certainly seemed to like throwing his weight around, she thought. He had told her more than a few times he parked where he pleased. He had once threatened to sue a towing company after the said company had towed his car for illegal parking.

At lunch, he began lecturing her about being more assertive and standing up for herself.

"I shouldn't have had to come down here and threaten the entire company with dismissal," he berated her. "When we're married, I expect you to behave accordingly."

"And how is that?" she asked, wondering exactly what he meant by that. Did he expect her to act arrogant and walk all over people?

He scowled. "For one thing, you should have put Gina in her place the moment she stepped out of line." He looked her over. "She was correct on one thing. You need to lose some weight. I have hired a personal trainer for you."

She stared at him. "I'm not …"

"People in my social circle have certain expectations," he told her.

"Meaning I don't meet their standards?" she returned, disgusted at the attitude.

"I can't have them thinking you're unsuitable now, can I?"

She sighed. "I suppose."

"This is for your own good, Deanna. Tell me you understand."

What choice did she have? She sighed and nodded meekly.

The date of the wedding was at least six months away. Richard, of course, had made every decision where that was concerned as well. He hired a wedding planner who coordinated everything from the ceremony, which was going to be a formal affair in a local church. Since they had both been baptised under different denominations, the All Saints church had agreed to hold the ceremony there.

Dee found it rather amusing that Richard was so adamant they get married in a church, considering he had told her he had never even gone to Sunday School.

She resented that he had taken over everything, even when he assured her that he was only trying to make it easier for her. Weddings were stressful enough, he told her.

She sat through meetings with the wedding planner, unable to even contribute any of her own ideas. Every time she even opened her mouth, Richard would shoot her a look - as if to tell her that whatever she wanted to say wasn't important.

Yet he somehow managed to make it look like she had full approval on everything.

They had met with the woman one Friday afternoon, about two months before the wedding.

"I have a wonderful idea," the planner practically gushed. "We release one hundred white balloons as you come out of the church."

Dee frowned. The original idea had been for doves, but apparently, they were too difficult to get hold of and the local animal welfare groups wouldn't approve of it. Nor would the city council. Richard's name and money only got him so far.

"Balloons?" Richard turned to her. "Darling, what do you think?"

She started to shake her head, but he ignored her and turned back to the woman. "It's a little tacky. A little too low-brow."

Dee almost snorted at his choice of words. God forbid they do anything that his social circle might frown upon, she thought. She did agree that it was inappropriate to release balloons, considering the damage a hundred of them could do.

The planner quickly crossed off the idea and moved on to the guest list. She had sent out invitations months earlier and all but about a dozen had RSVP'd. Richard didn't appear too concerned at the lack of interest in what was supposedly going to be the biggest event of the year in their part of the world.

She had few guests to invite. Of course, she had already told her parents and only her mother had responded, saying she would be delighted to come to her only child's wedding.

As they left the meeting, Richard pulled her aside.

"Did you bring a bag with you?" he asked.

She frowned at him, wondering for a few seconds what he meant. She normally stayed with him on weekends now, rather than spending the weekend at her father's house.

"Oh. Yes, of course. Why?"

He asked her what clothes she had brought. She usually brought only a pair of jeans and something slightly less casual which would be suitable for any occasion. She had a few items of clothing in one of the wardrobes at Richard's place.

"What's wrong?" she asked when he pronounced that her usual choice of outfit would never do.

"We're going to see my mother this weekend. I must warn you. She's very particular; not the kind of woman who likes to see women in jeans. She prefers tailored pants or modest dresses or skirts."

He went on to tell her that his mother was going to be holding a cocktail party at the house she shared with her husband and they were expected to attend. Dee understood. She was being presented for inspection by the matriarch of the family and lord help her if she failed to measure up to Julia Carter's standards.

He left her at the local shopping centre to buy a suitable outfit, telling her he needed to pick her up in an hour so they could get to the airport. Their flight would leave in just over two hours.

She managed to find a fairly simple dress in black silk that would at least hide some of her flaws. Richard had complimented her on the weight she had already lost but had then turned around and suggested she work a little harder to lose more before the day of the wedding.

It was something she saw a lot in her future husband. He could be very charming. But he often paid backhanded compliments. When she queried his behaviour, he told her it was nothing. She could never understand it, or predict what he would do from one moment to the next.

The flight was a nightmare. It wasn't unusual for the city to have high winds and they were buffeted as the plane took off from the airport. They continued to be battered as they flew over the Cook Strait, the aircraft dipping with alarming frequency, forcing some of the less secure passengers to grab onto the seat in front of them with each shudder.

It started to level out as they flew south, landing in Christchurch. Passengers disembarked, chattering about the horror flight as they left. Richard guided her to the waiting area so they could sit and wait for their connecting flight, which was at least another two hours away. Since they had that long to wait, he suggested they go and have dinner in a restaurant that was part of a complex of eateries within the international airport. It was hardly a four-star restaurant, he told her, but it would do them.

It was late when they landed in Nelson, a small city on the east coast of the South Island. The city was a well-known tourist spot, known for its arts and crafts and the Annual Wearable Arts Competition.

Richard explained that his mother had moved there many years earlier. Dee got the sense he was rather relieved that she had chosen to live there rather than stay in the city where he had opted to build his business.

A taxi was called, and they were driven to a hotel in the city centre. Of course, it had to be a luxury hotel. Nothing else would do. The night manager greeted them cordially and confirmed their details. He looked apologetic.

"Sir, I was unable to reserve a king-size bed for you and your lovely fiancée."

The man, who was probably only a year or so older than Dee, shrank back at the way Richard glared at him.

Richard looked annoyed. "What do you mean, no king bed? I asked for one when I called in the reservation."

"And as was explained to you over the phone, Mr Carter, we can't guarantee availability. Especially when it's such late notice."

Dee spoke up quietly. "Dear, it's fine," she said.

He turned to glare at her. "No, it's not fine. It's incompetence!"

She returned the glare. "How is it incompetence when there's even a sign saying they'll do their utmost to fulfil requests but can't provide a guarantee?"

"I'm paying good money …" he began to rant.

"And you don't have to take it out on the nice man. He's just doing his job! Leave him alone!" She turned to the man and smiled apologetically. "I'm sorry," she said. "We'll take whatever you have available."

Richard fumed by her side, even as he handed his credit card over. Dee refused to look at her fiancé. He had been out of line and she was sure he knew that. The question was, how was he going to deal with the matter once they were out of earshot of staff.

They were shown to their room, a large suite on the top floor. There were two queen size beds in the bedroom. Once they were alone, Richard grabbed her arm, hard enough to bruise.

"Don't ever contradict me like that again!" he told her.

She tried to pull away, staring at him in shock. He had been rude and rather arrogant but had never spoken to her in such a way before.

"I was trying to get you to calm down!" she returned, trembling a little from the verbal attack.

"When I pay good money to stay here, I expect to get what I want."

She pulled at his fingers, releasing his tight grip on her arm. "Well, we don't always get what we want!" she told him. "Don't ever touch me like that again!"

She pushed past him and picked up the key card where he'd tossed it on the dresser before going to the door.

"Where are you going?" he asked, his tone still angry.

"For a walk," she shot back over her shoulder, refusing to look at him. "And don't follow me!"

"It's nine o'clock," he said in protest.

"So it is!" she snapped, opening the door. She left without looking back.

She had no idea where she could go this late at night since she didn't know the city and didn't want to get lost. She returned to the foyer. The manager was still at the desk, working on the computer when she passed him.

The hotel had a bar and restaurant, so she decided to relax with a drink. Fortunately, she still had her purse with her and was prepared to pay for her own drink instead of putting it on the room tab.

The woman on the bar smiled at her. She had crooked teeth that showed white against her dusky brown skin. She looked about twenty years older than Dee, who was not the best judge of age. "What can I get you?"

"Um, just an orange juice, please?" she said.

"Sure. What room are you in?"

"Oh, no, I'd rather pay in cash," she replied.

The dark-haired woman nodded and picked up the pump dispenser, filling a glass with orange juice.

"That's three-fifty," she said. Dee put five dollars on the bar. The woman took it and put the money in the till putting two coins down on the bar. She peered closely at Dee. "Are you all right, miss?" she asked.

"I'm fine," Dee said with a shrug. She wasn't, but the other woman didn't have to know that.

The bartender was quiet for a few moments, but Dee felt the woman's gaze on her. She suppressed the urge to cross her arms over her chest and concentrated on sipping her drink. More customers came in and the bartender was kept busy serving them. After about five minutes, there was a lull in customers, and she came over.

"You should leave him," the woman said.

Dee stared at her. "Excuse me?"

"The man who put that mark on your arm. That's where it starts, you know."

She frowned. "Starts what?" she asked.

"First it's the grabbing of the arm, then it's the excuses, like 'I didn't mean to' and 'You just make me so mad sometimes,' then it's the casual put-downs, the things he says that sound like a compliment but are just subtle insults. Before you know it, he's hitting you and you think it's all your fault."

Dee blinked, not knowing what to say. Richard wasn't really like that, was he? He wouldn't hit her!

"Take my word for it," the woman said, introducing herself as Gail. "I should know."

"He wouldn't …" she replied. "He's not like that. He just gets stressed."

"I told myself that, too. Even when my friends tried to point out the way he was behaving wasn't okay. We'd barely been married a month before it started. I stayed with him for fifteen years, and every time I ended up in the hospital, I kept asking myself, 'is this going to be the last time? Or is it next time when he kills me?' I knew when I began asking myself that question more and more that I had to leave. For my kids. For me."

Dee nodded. The woman had been through hell and had made it her mission in life to help others she suspected were in the same situation. It just didn't sound like Richard, she thought.

"Darling, there you are. You were gone so long I thought you'd gotten hurt or something."

She turned and looked at her fiancé. He did look worried. Gail walked further down the bar to serve a new customer but kept watch.

Richard sat next to her. "I'm sorry," he said. "You were right. I was out of line. With the manager and with you. I shouldn't have spoken to you like that." He looked at her arm, wincing. "Or grabbed you like that. Again, I'm very sorry. Will you forgive me?"

She could see Gail shaking her head, but he looked so contrite that she couldn't help it.

"Yes," she said. "As long as you tell me what's got you so tied up in knots."

"It's my mother," he replied with a long sigh. "It's not just the summons, it's … You've heard of a movie called Monster-in-Law?"

She nodded. "Of course." She hadn't seen it but knew enough about it.

"Well, that's my mother. No one is ever good enough to meet her standards. Even me," he added wryly. He took her hand. "Come on, darling. It's late and we're both tired."

"All right," she said softly.

That night he was gentle and loving and it did seem that he was remorseful about his earlier behaviour. She slept that night in his arms thinking that Gail had been completely wrong about him.

Chapter Five

They left the hotel just before lunch the next day. Richard's mother had made it clear she wanted them there for lunch and she wasn't taking no for an answer. Dee quietly felt that must be where Richard got his tenacity from, considering how he had refused to take 'no' from her.

Julia Carter lived in a luxury apartment with an amazing view of the bay. As they pulled up in the car Richard had hired, Dee could see the clear, blue water. It was a sunny day which made it appear as if the sky and the water were almost the same colours.

"Wow!" she said, shielding her eyes as she looked around. "This is beautiful!"

Richard just smiled and locked the car before heading up the path to the glass doors. Dee followed him, hurrying her pace a little to keep up with his long-legged strides. He grabbed the long handle and pulled the door open, ushering her inside.

She realised they were in a sort of lobby. Along one wall was what she assumed were postal boxes. Each one was numbered. On the other side were two elevators. A door at the end of the hallway looked like it led to a corridor, which Dee thought must be where residents went to use the building's facilities, like the gym and indoor pool. The building was fairly new, with construction having been completed in the last six months or so, according to Richard. None of the apartments had been priced under a million dollars, he proclaimed.

The elevators seemed to be operated with a security key system. Richard was already on his phone, presumably calling up to the apartment so they could be let in.

She tried not to fidget as they waited, but even Richard began to look annoyed as the minutes ticked by. He would glance at his watch, shift his feet, before resorting to pacing the floor. Just as he took out his phone to dial a number, the elevator dinged, signalling someone was about to exit.

He appeared relieved as a man aged about sixty-five came out, clearly there for them.

"It's about time!" Richard snapped rudely. "What the hell is she doing, she can't come downstairs to greet us?"

The man shrugged. "You know your mother." He turned to look at her with a smile of welcome. "Hello. I'm Al," he said. "Julia's husband."

She nodded. "I'm Deanna. Most people call me Dee."

"Mother isn't most people," Richard told her, practically shoving her into the elevator car.

With a sigh of resignation, Al followed them in. He again looked at her and rolled his eyes in exasperation. Dee grinned back at him, ducking her head to avoid her fiancé seeing her reaction. She liked the older man. He seemed sweet and not at all like Richard had told her he was.

According to him, his mother had only married Al for security. While she had her own money, it wasn't enough. She always wanted more. Al was reasonably well-off, although apparently not wealthy enough for Richard's satisfaction.

Julia had married Richard's father when she was barely eighteen, but Dee had been told that Alan Carter had been the love of her life. Hence her continued use of her first married name rather than changing her surname back to her maiden name or taking her husband's name. In many ways, people of

Julia's generation were still more traditional in the sense that when they married, they took the husband's name, but Julia appeared to be the exception.

Dee had no idea what she would be facing as the lift made its way to the fourth floor of the building. Like her son, Julia had refused to settle for anything less than an apartment on the top floor. She had heard enough about her fiancé's family to know they weren't close. Richard often described his mother as difficult. While Dee couldn't exactly call her own family picture-perfect, it was certainly less dysfunctional than the one she was marrying into.

They left the elevator and it felt as if someone had been watching out for them as a door immediately opened and a woman with hair so blonde it was almost white came out to greet them. She pulled her son into a hug, exclaiming how wonderful it was to see him and how long it had been since his last visit. Dee took advantage of the distraction to look the woman over. She was in her fifties but, at a distance, she could look in her early forties. She was slim and lightly tanned. It was obvious she had her hair set regularly as it was styled as if she had just walked out of a hair salon. Her makeup was even perfect.

"So," Julia said. "Introduce me."

Dee walked forward and held her hand out shyly. The older woman immediately made a face. Dee had heard the expression 'sucking on a lemon' before, and the woman's sour face reminded her of the phrase.

"I'm Dee," she said.

Julia raised an eyebrow. "Dee? Oh, no, that will never do. What is your proper name?"

"It's Deanna," Richard told her.

Mother and son looked at each other and their expressions were almost identical as non-verbal messages passed between them. Even Dee, who knew little about body language, could tell that the older woman didn't approve, while Richard was stubbornly telling her that she would have to like it or lump it.

The next hour or so was almost torture. Julia addressed every question to her son and acted as if Dee didn't exist. When the pair disappeared outside, so Richard could smoke a cigar, she heard part of the conversation. Julia wasn't one to keep her opinions to herself and she chose to share them, at almost full volume. As far as she was concerned, her only child was not going to marry 'that woman.'

To his credit, Richard told his mother he was not a child and wasn't going to allow her to dictate to him how to live his life. He certainly wasn't going to stand there and let her talk about the woman he loved in such a manner.

Julia scoffed. "Love? What on Earth do you know about love? You should have stayed with Miranda."

"She cheated on me, Mother. I caught her with someone else."

"What does that matter? If you had been a decent husband, then she would not have strayed."

Dee turned away as the woman began to criticise her son. It was little wonder the man hated his mother, she thought. Especially if she treated him like that.

"You will marry that woman over my dead body," Julia snapped at her son.

"That could easily be arranged, Mother," Richard returned.

Dee suddenly felt a chill up and down her spine at her fiancé's words. Would he really arrange to have his mother hurt, or even killed if she didn't accept the marriage?

She started at the hand on her shoulder. Al, who had disappeared into another room after lunch, had returned.

"Don't take them too seriously," he advised. "Richard can be a bit of a hothead, but he wouldn't really do anything to Julia. My wife, on the other hand," he added with a sigh, "is just the kind of woman to throw a tantrum if she doesn't get her way. He's just as stubborn as her, though."

"What should I do, then?" she asked quietly.

"What you are doing," he responded.

She was confused. She hadn't done anything except go along with what Richard wanted. She had sat quietly through lunch, being polite with the older woman and ignoring her jibes.

Maybe that was what Al meant, she thought. Refusing to respond to the woman's criticism of her was probably the best way to deal with it.

They returned to the apartment that evening for the cocktail party. Dee was surprised to discover that Julia was a charming hostess, circulating the room and chatting to guests as if nothing had happened that afternoon. She gushed about her son's future bride to anyone who would listen, putting an arm around Dee's shoulders like they were the best of friends as if she hadn't been screaming earlier about refusing to let her son marry some 'gold-digging tart who wasn't fit to walk in his shadow.'

Dee did her best to keep her distance from the woman. Having witnessed her earlier tantrum, she would rather not deal with the apparent two-faced behaviour of her future mother-in-law.

She chatted politely to the guests, thankful that most of them seemed very happy she was marrying Richard. One man - she had forgotten his name - told her she was much prettier than his ex-wife and would be just the ticket to keep Richard in line. She doubted it, but smiled and nodded in agreement.

By the end of the night, she was exhausted from trying to smile and make nice with people she probably wouldn't have anything to do with if she had never met Richard. By the time they got back to the hotel, she was ready to just fall into bed as soon as she had showered and changed into her nightgown.

Her fiancé got in beside her, wrapping his arm around her waist and pulling her closer. She lay still, too exhausted for anything and just wanted to sleep. He didn't make a move, which was unusual for him, since he always liked to assert dominance over her, especially in bed.

"Thank you," he said quietly.

She turned her head to look at him. "For what?" she asked.

"For today. I know you heard what my mother was saying. I appreciate the fact you didn't call her on it," He sighed. "What I told her about Miranda was true. She did cheat on me. But I suppose my mother was right on one point. If I had been a better husband, she might not have left. Then again, if she hadn't, I never would have met you." He caressed her bare arm. "I want you to know I'll be a good husband to you. I never want to give you cause to leave me, like Miranda did. And for the record, I don't think you're a gold-digger."

"I'm sorry that happened," she said. "That she cheated on you."

"That's one of the things I love most about you, Deanna." He didn't elaborate further. His light snores a few minutes later told her he'd fallen asleep.

For the next few days, Richard was not only more attentive, he was more loving as well. She arrived at her desk one morning about a week after the trip to find he had sent her flowers. Not just any flowers, but her favourites. White and red chrysanthemums wrapped in beautiful, expensive gold paper.

She had once told him a friend had taught her about flowers and their meanings. They had been out for a stroll and passed by a florist. He had stopped and pulled her into the shop, obviously intent on buying her some flowers. She had paused by the chrysanthemums, mentioning they were her favourites. Richard had stroked the blooms.

"So, what do these mean?" he asked.

"It depends on the colour. Mostly fidelity and long life, but if you go for red ones, they mean love and white ones mean loyal love."

He nodded. "Is that why you like them?" he asked.

"Well, yes and no. I mean, we're supposed to love roses, but it seems kind of ironic to me that roses have thorns. It's like saying, 'I'm beautiful but untouchable'."

"I see. Interesting. So, if I were to give you red and white ones of these, what would that say to you?"

She chewed on her lower lip. He told her he loved her, and they were engaged, but there were times when she doubted his feelings for her.

"Well, I think you'd be promising faithfulness and long-lasting love."

"Well, that's easy," he said, gazing at her meaningfully.

She smiled with the memory, stroking the delicate petals. Despite all of her doubts about marrying him, she was impressed that he remembered that conversation and what it all meant. Robin came out of his office and stared at the bouquet.

"Those are nice," he said. "Richard?"

She nodded. "Mmm."

"So, what'd he do?"

She stared at her boss. "Nothing. Does he have to do something wrong to give me flowers?"

Robin laughed wryly. "Try telling my wife that. She claims the only times I ever give her flowers is when I'm feeling guilty about something. She might have a point."

Richard took her out for dinner that night. He behaved like a complete gentleman. Dee even noticed he was being nice to the server. Normally he treated servers and anyone else in the service industry as if they were beneath him, but he was courteous, soft-spoken and would respond in a friendly way to their questions. More importantly, he allowed Dee to choose her own meal from the menu instead of making the selections for her as he usually did.

She was surprised at his sudden change in attitude. She liked it but was nonetheless surprised. As much as she wanted to ask him about it, she didn't want to rock the boat.

After dinner, he took her for a stroll through the Square, a large block of green space in the city centre. She had learnt in high school that the railway line had once run through the Square, but it had been moved to the outskirts of the city long before she was born. Now the green space was used for local art festivals and events.

They paused on the bridge over the duck pond. Richard turned her around, so she was leaning against the guard rail.

"What's wrong?" she asked as he gazed down at her. She wasn't short by any means, but it felt like her height was diminished slightly by the angle she was at.

"Nothing's wrong," he said. "I wanted to ask you … Deanna, I want you to stop working for Robin."

She frowned. "What? Why?"

"So, you can move in with me. You'll have to move in eventually," he said reasonably. "The wedding is less than two months away."

It was tempting. Her father had lately been saying all kinds of things to try to convince her not to go ahead with the marriage. The quarrels had escalated into fights where she had accused him of trying to control her, trying to keep her dependent on him. He had even tried to put his foot down when Richard had signed her up for driving lessons not long after they'd got engaged. He was equally furious when Richard had bought her a car.

She looked at her fiancé. His eyes were pleading with her.

"Darling, I know you're hesitating because of your father. You are a grown woman and he doesn't control your life."

"I know. It's just … he's so angry lately."

"It's his way of manipulating you," Richard told her. "He has controlled you for your whole life and now … Darling, don't do this. Don't let your father make you feel guilty for wanting a life of your own."

He was right, she thought. She had been feeling guilty all the months she had been seeing Richard and now they were getting married, her father's belligerence had just compounded that guilt. As if she somehow felt responsible for Jack.

If there was one thing she had learnt from Richard's relationship with his mother, it was that she wasn't responsible for her father's happiness. Especially since his need to control every aspect of her life made her so unhappy.

Yet, she couldn't help the niggling doubt about her future husband's behaviour. The past week he had been wonderful. Everything she had assumed a loving partner should be. Why then did she feel as if she was expecting the bubble to burst?

She looked at her fiancé once more. He kissed her briefly, pulling her into his arms and holding her close, stroking her hair.

"I'm probably being too pushy," he said.

She shook her head. "No, you're not. I just … I don't know why I'm hesitating."

"It's a big change," he told her, huffing so she could feel a light breeze through her hair. "I just thought it would be easier to move in now."

She lifted her head and smiled up at him. "It's not as if I have much in the way of stuff," she replied.

"That's another thing we need to talk about," he said slowly. "My solicitor wants to draw up a prenuptial agreement."

She frowned at him, wondering why he had sounded so reluctant to bring it up.

"I don't care," she said. "Tell him to draw it up. I'll sign it."

He studied her. "You really don't care, do you?"

"Richard, I didn't agree to marry you for your money. Just like you didn't ask me to marry you because I'm a great cook."

He laughed as he turned and wrapped his arm around her waist so they could resume walking.

"You're right. I didn't fall in love with you for your mad cooking skills," he responded cheekily. "I still get indigestion from that breakfast you tried to cook."

She elbowed him. "Hey, you said you were never going to bring that up again."

He laughed again, his hand on his stomach as if he were experiencing indigestion all over again. Dee joined in the laughter. She had been trying to learn to cook, especially since she'd been on a diet.

One Sunday morning, Dee had decided to try her hand at cooking some pancakes for brunch. She'd tried following the recipe to the letter but, in her clumsiness, she had dropped some eggshells in the bowl, put in too much flour and forgot to add the raising agent, so the pancakes had ended up stodgy. Richard had bravely tried to eat them anyway, only to pronounce them inedible.

The matter of her moving in was dropped for the moment, but the decision was made the next week when her father once again tried to convince her to not go ahead with the wedding.

"He's no good for you," Jack told her as she packed for yet another trip with her fiancé. This time they were going to stay for a few days at a lodge near Lake Taupo.

"You mean, I'm not good enough for him. Isn't that what you meant, Dad?"

Her father made a disgusted sound. "Look at you. I don't even recognise you anymore. What happened to the clothes I got you?"

She made a face at him. He had gone through her wardrobe and tossed out most of her clothes, especially the ones that had fitted her new, slimmer figure, replacing them with baggy tops that were either too old for her or too young. Even the trousers he left her had sagged around the back.

He complained she wasn't eating enough and losing too much weight. She had stuck to the diet the personal trainer prescribed for her and, along with exercise, it had helped her lose weight steadily, so she was now at a good weight for her height. Her father had tried to sabotage her efforts there as well, throwing out the healthy food she had bought and refusing to let her cook her own meals. Fortunately, she had been able to enlist the help of a friend.

He continued to rant and rave, telling her that if she went through with it, he wouldn't be there for her when it all went to hell.

She paused, a woollen jumper in hand as she looked up at him.

"When have you ever been there for me, Dad?" she accused.

He stopped mid-rant and stared at her. "What?"

"When Mum left and I cried for days, what did you tell me?"

"I told you to stop acting like a child."

"I was fifteen, Dad! Technically, in the eyes of the law, I was a child! You told me to get over it. That you didn't care if I was hurting. Remember when I came home with high marks on my school exams? Remember how I got that 98 per cent in English? What did you do? You asked: 'What happened to the other two per cent?' Remember that? Nothing I did was ever good enough for you!"

"I've done everything for you!" he told her. "And you stand there and …"

"What?" she asked with a glare at him. "I'm ungrateful? Is that what you're going to say? Yes, you did everything for me. So, I don't know how to do anything for myself! You tell me I'm acting like a child, but you treat me like one, instead of a grown woman. I'm old enough to decide what's best for me."

"I know what's best for you," he told her.

"No, you don't, Dad. You just want to control me."

She turned and resumed packing, throwing the rest of the clothes she planned to take into the bag. He continued to stand in the doorway, watching her, his body posed as if he intended to stop her leaving.

She zipped up the bag and picked it up, moving to the doorway. He remained where he was, refusing to move.

"Get out of the way, Dad."

"No. You're going to listen to me."

She heard the purr of the Porsche engine and knew Richard had arrived to pick her up.

"That's Richard," she exclaimed. She glared at her father and he shifted his stance. It was clear he realised he was fighting a losing battle.

She went to the front door. Her father huffed noisily.

"You walk out the door now, don't even think of coming back here."

Dee opened the door before turning to look at him. He hadn't moved from his spot by her bedroom door. "Don't worry. I don't plan on it. I'll send for my things." She hesitated. "On second thought, I won't bother. There's nothing here I want."

When she told Richard what had happened, he seemed to smirk, as if he had won. He made the right sympathetic noises, of course, but Dee could not help thinking he'd seen her battles with her father as a sort of competition.

They had a quiet few days at the lodge. She was thankful for the respite, giving her the time to come to terms with what had happened. She still loved her father, despite his behaviour. His over-protectiveness had been suffocating at times, but she understood why he acted that way. Her grandmother had told her long ago that her father had a little sister. When she was six, she disappeared on her way home from school. Just two days later, her body had turned up on the banks of the river less than a kilometre from where he lived. She had been raped and strangled. When the police caught the man who did it, they learnt he had been watching the little girl for weeks and had snatched her off the street.

A psychologist would have probably determined her father's over-zealous need to protect her stemmed from the loss of his sister and his own failure to protect her, even though none of it had been his fault. He had been sixteen at the time and, like many older siblings, didn't want the extra burden of having to walk his sister home from school. He clearly still blamed himself.

Moving in with Richard wasn't the chore she initially thought it was going to be. Leaving her job, however, was a lot harder, emotionally, than she expected. Her colleagues threw her a farewell luncheon, wishing her luck in her new life.

Of course, Gina was the only one who didn't offer her congratulations or wish her luck for the future. The woman stared daggers at her throughout the farewell. Dee had been told by someone who worked closely with the other woman that she was jealous, wishing it had been her that Richard had chosen.

Time passed and, before she knew it, Dee was getting married. Her mother had returned home from wherever she had been, full of tales of her adventures teaching children in Vietnam, building schools in African villages, and helping women start their own businesses in remote villages in India. Dee was envious of Linda's adventures but also saw that she was far happier than she had ever been with Jack. She somehow managed to look younger than fifty-two.

Linda had helped her dress in her wedding gown, while a photographer hovered around taking candid shots. Dee had hoped her father would have changed his mind and come to see his daughter getting married, but there was no sign of him. Not even a phone call to wish her good luck on her big day.

Dee sighed for about the tenth time that morning. Linda paused, her hand on the gown's shoulder piece. Dee had chosen a dress with cap sleeves, thinking it would hide any remaining flab in her arms. Along with her still-soft abdomen, she had trouble shifting the fat from her arms. A friend, Meg, who had also been trying to lose weight, often called them her 'bye-bye' arms.

"Why?" Dee had asked her.

Meg had held her arms out wide and flapped them up and down with a grin. "Because the fat flaps when I do this. It's like they're waving bye-bye."

Dee groaned. "You're weird," she told her friend.

"I know you are, but what am I?" Meg returned in a childish voice before they both began giggling madly.

They had been friends since the beginning of high school, despite her father's efforts to isolate Dee from any friendships. One time, when Dee had been planning to go out with her friend, he tried to prevent her by telling her to "stay home and not spend any money." Yet he was always down at the local pub.

Dee sighed again. Meg hadn't been able to make it to the wedding. She was a television reporter and had been given an amazing opportunity to work in Europe for six months as a foreign correspondent. Dee had been happy for her friend, telling her to take the opportunity. Even if part of her wished Meg could still be there.

"Stop sighing," Linda told her, returning to adjust the sleeve.

"I'm sorry."

"I know you wanted your dad to be here, but …"

"I know," she said. "He hates Richard."

"Well, it's his loss," her mother replied. "If he chose not to support you, then that's his problem. Sweetie, I realised a long time ago that your father was never going to change. That's why I left him."

Dee nodded. She had initially felt hurt when her mother left and hadn't understood the reason why she had done it. Especially when Dee had been left alone with her father. Linda had told her why, but it still didn't make her feel the loss any less.

"Oh, honey, you know I didn't want to leave you, but you were doing so well in school. I thought your father would at least see that and let you live your own life. If I'd known what he was doing, I would have come back and let him have it. With both barrels," she added.

"I just don't understand him. I mean, the whole time I was going out with Richard, he did nothing but criticise. Telling me I was getting a bit full of myself and that I wasn't good enough for someone like Richard."

"I wish I had all the answers for you. I just know your grandparents were just as hard on your father as he is on you."

"What do you mean?"

Linda glanced at the clock before sitting down on the sofa. Dee sat beside her.

"Your grandfather was a hard man. He always treated your dad like he wasn't good enough. In some ways, losing Tessie broke him. He blamed Jack for it, even though your dad couldn't have known what was going to happen."

Dee sighed. That explained one thing but not everything else.

"So, why does Dad hold on so tight?"

"Well, when you were born … I remember he was holding you in his arms and he said he was never going to let anything happen to you. That he would protect you with everything he had. I think in some ways he went overboard. Maybe he thinks that by controlling you, he can prevent you from getting hurt."

"But I have to learn to make my own mistakes. I can't just live my life for him."

"Oh, I know that sweetie, but I think he's just afraid that if he lets go, something bad will happen to you like it did with his sister. Instead, it just ends up pushing you away."

"Like it did with you?" Dee asked.

Linda nodded. "I had to get away before he destroyed whatever was left of my self-esteem. Sometimes, toxic people don't realise they're toxic." She put a hand on Dee's knee. "I'm proud of you for walking away. It was way overdue."

Dee hugged her mother. "Thanks, Mum. I really needed that."

Linda smiled and stood up. "Let's get this show on the road, kiddo."

Dee was surprised when she saw Julia had turned up to the wedding. Richard's stepfather smiled and winked as she walked with her mother up the aisle to her husband-to-be. His mother was also smiling but the look in her eyes could refreeze the polar ice caps, Dee thought.

*****

Her mind once more returning to the present, she sighed. Dee hadn't even spoken to her mother-in-law or even seen her since the wedding. As she prepared for bed, Dee couldn't help remembering what Carol had said at the dinner that evening. Julia was certainly a force to be reckoned with. It seemed as if she was the kind of woman who would lie to save face, telling those in her social circle that she was thrilled her son had found someone like Dee but, in her eyes, Dee would never measure up to her expectations. Carol had made it clear she knew exactly what kind of woman Julia Carter was.

Chapter Six

Richard had a business meeting the next day, so Dee was left on her own to wander the capital city. She decided to visit the museum and the local art gallery. Despite having lived so close to the city, she could only remember visiting the national museum once in her life. It had been a school trip when she was still in primary school.

Back then, the museum had a life-sized model of a room where people could feel what an earthquake felt like. Since it was small, only a few children could go in at a time. Dee had gone in with a friend, holding hands with her. They had held onto the rail but, once the simulation had begun, her friend had started to cry.

The teacher had taken her out, but she continued to cry, disturbing some of the other children waiting their turn, which then set others off. The only thing Dee could hear of her friend's frightened ramblings was that she had almost been hurt when something fell beside her in an earthquake.

Just a few years earlier, Dee had been at work when there had been a major earthquake. The area she lived in was prone to lots of tremors but this one had been vastly different. The sound had come first, a kind of roar that most would have mistaken for a train. Then the shaking had started, and everyone had dived for cover.

It had been much worse several hundred kilometres away, in the South Island. Many people had died that day. Richard had even related a story of his own experience. He had been in Christchurch on that awful day, trying to convince a local company to sell to him. The earthquake had brought negotiations literally to a shuddering halt.

He'd been annoyed that he had lost money he had invested in researching the company. Yet the company itself had lost far more as the building had been so badly damaged there was no way they could continue to work there, let alone conduct any kind of business. A few months later, or so Richard had told her, the company had to close its doors for good.

As she wandered the museum, she could no longer see the exhibition which had so frightened her friend as a child. Maybe it had been moved to another part of the building, she thought, continuing to look around at the exhibits.

"Hello."

She looked around and smiled at Carol.

"Oh, hello," she said. "It's nice to see you again."

"You too. On your own?"

Dee nodded. "Yeah. He had some business meeting to attend to. What about you?"

"Yep. Same." She made a face. "That man spends more time in business meetings than he does anything else. Even last night he spent half of his time trying to broker business deals than actually enjoying himself."

"That's what Richard keeps telling me. That those events are really about trying to make business contacts."

Carol snorted. "Men. I tell ya. Fancy a coffee?"

"That would be lovely," she said, following the older woman to the café on the first level. She started to get her purse out of her bag, but the brunette waved her hand.

"It's on me," she quickly remarked, lining up behind a large woman with two children in tow. The children were making nuisances of themselves, chasing each other around their mother. At least, Dee assumed the woman was their mother. She hadn't seen the woman's face.

The boy, who couldn't have been more than eight or nine, was just tall enough to reach the baskets of cutlery off to the side of the counter. He pulled at two of the baskets, spilling the silverware all over the floor.

Carol tapped the woman on the shoulder. "Excuse me. Is that your son?"

The woman sniffed haughtily and turned away, ignoring Carol's question. However, the older woman wasn't to be ignored.

"Lady, if that's your kid, then you better discipline him before I do because, not only has he inconvenienced other customers, he has made one heck of a mess for the workers to clean up. The least you could do is help them."

"Don't tell me what to do with my kid, lady."

"Well, obviously someone has to, or else you're going to have one big problem when he becomes a teenager."

The woman again sniffed and thrust her bank card at the girl on the counter, who looked upset at the mess the little boy had caused. Carol sighed and shook her head before turning back to Dee.

"Some people just shouldn't have kids," she remarked. "Now, what would you like, love?"

"Um, a cappuccino would be great. Thank you."

Carol turned back to the counter and began to order the drinks. Another worker came out to pick up the cutlery from the floor. Dee bent down to help her, picking up the pieces that had fallen under the display units. The girl, who was only about eighteen, smiled at her.

"Thank you, ma'am, but you didn't need to."

Dee shrugged. It had been the right thing to do. It was a pity other people hadn't done the same.

She had gone out to dinner once with Richard and he had been rather difficult, demanding food that wasn't on the menu and getting more and more obnoxious with each denial. There had been times when, after witnessing this behaviour, she had wondered why she was even going out with him. Yet there were other times when he had been courteous to a fault.

The man's behaviour was so contradictory at times that she had no idea who she was going to be dealing with next.

Her father had his faults, but at least he had taught her some manners, she thought.

Carol led her to a table in the back of the café, putting her purse down on the top. She frowned.

"Oh, goodness, I'm sorry. I didn't ask if you wanted something to eat."

"It's all right. I'm still on a diet."

The other woman scowled. "Why would you need to be on a diet? You don't need to lose weight."

"Richard says I do."

"Well, that man needs a good clip across the ears. It might knock some sense into him. If you lost any more weight, you'd be skin and bone, my darling."

Dee shrugged. "I still have a bit of a belly."

"Well, honey, if you didn't, there'd be something wrong. If Richard wants perfection, then he should have built a robot. No man in his right mind, if he has any sense, that is, wants a Barbie doll for a wife." She waved her hands over her own figure. Carol wasn't exactly skinny, but she wasn't fat either. "You think Stewart would be with me if he wanted a Barbie doll?"

"No, I guess not."

"Don't listen to a single word that man says," Carol advised. "He's an idiot. Most men are."

Dee couldn't help giggling as the other woman rolled her eyes before grinning.

"But not Stewart?" Dee put in.

"Are you kidding? He's the worst one of all. But I do adore him. God help me." She gave a little sigh.

The server came over with their coffees, taking away the little plastic number tag. Dee stirred her coffee absently. She always had sugar with her coffee, but Richard had put a stop to that.

"So," Carol said. "Tell me all about you."

"I would have thought you'd know already."

"Your husband has been suspiciously quiet on the matter. His mother … well, we both know she says one thing to one person and something completely different to someone else. I've heard her version. I want the truth."

Dee found herself telling the older woman all about how she had got the job at Carter Tech, meeting Richard, and her father's reaction to her dating.

"Well, he's a peach, isn't he?" Carol commented.

"I guess he was trying to protect me," Dee said, even knowing that he didn't deserve her defending him.

"Honey, there's being over-protective and then there's pushing someone down so hard they don't want to get up again. Maybe your father had his reasons, but he's still wrong."

Dee nodded. "I'm beginning to see that." She sipped her drink. "So, um, how long have you and Stewart been together?"

The older woman looked thoughtful. "Hmm, about … five years, I guess. His first wife divorced him about fifteen years ago. Walked out on him and took the kids with her. It was rather a wake-up call for him."

"What do you mean?" Dee asked curiously.

"Well, even he admits he was a bit of a jerk to his ex. Not that he ever hit her or anything like that, but he put more of his energy into his work than his family."

She listened as the older woman told her story. She discovered that Carol, who looked in her 40s, was actually in her 50s. Her new friend was one of the lucky ones who was blessed with what she called the 'good genes,' which allowed her to look at least ten years younger than she was. Her partner was about five years younger than her, not that it mattered to the couple.

Carol had let herself get talked into joining an online dating site. A friend had paid for a subscription for her for a year and so Carol had gone out on a few dates with men of varying ages … until she met Stewart. The couple hadn't clicked straight away. Carol was someone who believed the way a person behaved toward others was a good indicator of the kind of person they were. She told Dee that Stewart had confessed he'd 'messed up' the night they had gone out on their first date. He had been nervous and rather terse with the waitress in the restaurant. He'd been trying to make a good impression by acting as if he knew what he was doing. Despite being fairly well-off, he didn't go out much.

After the disastrous first date, Carol had tried matching up with other men on the site. Then one of her dates had been at a charity function for the organisation Stewart's daughter, Helen, now ran. Carol had begun chatting to Helen, who then introduced her to her father, who turned out to be Stewart.

"The rest is history," Carol said with a grin. "We ended up chatting the entire night and that was when he told me he blew it with me. He phoned me the next day and asked if I'd like to have lunch with him. And now, here we are, five years later."

Dee laughed. "That's a great story. And I'm sure Helen thinks she can take all the credit for match-making you two."

"Oh, don't you worry. She tells everyone she meets about her successful matchmaking. I told her if she was so sure it was all her doing, then maybe she should look at running her own agency. Quick as a flash she told me: 'I do'." Carol laughed.

"It sounds like you two have a great relationship."

"We do. I make her dad happy, and give him a good clip across the ears when he gets out of line. She likes that."

"Really?" Dee asked, wondering if the woman was serious.

"No, darling, of course not," Carol replied, laughing. "But I do pull him up and tell him off when he does something he knows he shouldn't."

After sharing their coffees, Carol decided to show her around the city. The older woman had lived there in her student days. Dee learnt her companion had studied fine arts and taught art at a private Catholic secondary school. Teaching, Carol lamented, was less about students learning and more about just doing enough so the kids could pass their requirements.

A few years earlier, she'd had a battle with her school board because the members had decided art should be sacrificed in place of 'other pursuits.' After all, art didn't bring in the money. While tuition was paid by the parents, some of them felt the school's funds were better spent on sports. The school boasted a long history of students who had gone on to become famous athletes. Until Carol had reminded them that a famous artist had also been educated at the school and that it still had the finest arts program in the country. At least at secondary school level.

"A couple of my students have gone on to do very well for themselves at Elam," Carol said, mentioning the Auckland Art School connected to Auckland University.

Dee nodded. "That sounds great. I kind of wish I had you as my art teacher at high school."

*****

They were sitting at one of the tables at a café overlooking the port. Dee could see one of the ferries coming in. After they'd wandered around the waterfront for an hour or so, Carol had suggested sitting down for a bit, saying her feet were aching. They had ordered a glass of wine each.

"You didn't have a good teacher?"

"It wasn't that," Dee replied, sipping her wine. "I mean, he was a good teacher. I really wanted to get into photography, but my dad didn't think it was a good career choice. Anyway, he went along to the parent-teacher night and told off the art teacher for encouraging me to follow some 'frivolous' pursuit. The teacher didn't even try to explain or stand up for me."

Carol huffed. "If I'd been your teacher, I would have given your father a piece of my mind. I'll give him "frivolous pursuit!" She snorted, making it clear she didn't think much of Jack Hargreaves.

"I don't know." Dee sighed. "I guess he just didn't want me to get my hopes up and pursue something that wouldn't make any money."

"You give him far too much credit, my darling. No one has the right to tell you what you should do with your life."

"He didn't want me marrying Richard. I guess he thought I was out of his league, or something."

Carol looked thoughtful. "Hmm, don't try to tell me there's no class system in New Zealand because I'm sure there is."

Dee's phone beeped and she took it out of her purse to look at the screen.

"Richard," she said. He had sent a text message asking where she was. "I guess his meeting's finished."

"Then I suppose we should head back to the hotel," Carol told her.

They managed to find a taxi to take them back. Richard was pacing the lobby when they returned.

"Where the hell have you been?" he demanded.

"I'm sorry, Richard. It was my fault," Carol told him. "We bumped into each other at the museum and I suggested we see some of the sights. We didn't think you'd be finished with your meeting yet. I know how those things can go on ..."

He didn't let her finish, glaring at the older woman.

"I was asking my wife, not you!"

Carol looked taken aback, but just huffed, apparently deciding not to say anything to aggravate the situation further. Stewart, who had obviously been at the same meeting, turned to Richard.

"Why don't you and your lovely wife join us for dinner?" he suggested.

Dee looked at her husband, wondering if he would consider the idea. He looked even more annoyed.

"Thanks," he said tersely. "But we have to get going. Traffic's bad enough at this time of day and it'll take three hours at least." As the older man opened his mouth to say something else, Richard seemed to think better of his attitude. "I have an early start in the morning," he said, sounding a little less belligerent. Stewart nodded.

"Of course. Yes, traffic in this city is horrible. The sooner they get that highway finished, the better."

Dee nodded in agreement. Contractors had been working on a four-lane highway which would supposedly cut down on some of the traffic congestion between Wellington and some of the towns further north. It would also cut down some of the travel time.

When she had been driving down, she had been unsure of all the road works. Since she hadn't been driving all that long, she was worried about what damage the construction would do to the car. Especially when there had been signs telling her to wash her car in case it was splashed with whatever materials they were using. The way the lanes had appeared to be haphazardly blocked off in certain areas would have been confusing if she hadn't been following another vehicle in front.

“We should get going then,” she said. “What about my bag?” she asked.

“It’s already packed and put in the car,” her husband replied. He handed her the car key. “I’ll just go pay the bill.” He smiled but it seemed false.

Dee said goodbye to the older couple, thanking Carol for the pleasant afternoon. The other woman hugged her.

“You know how to reach me if you ever need a friend,” she said.

Dee made her way downstairs to the underground parking and drove the car to the hotel offloading area. She was a little uneasy about driving. While she had her driver’s licence, it was still provisional, and she wasn’t supposed to have drunk any alcohol. Not that she’d had more than a sip or two of her wine.

She was relieved when Richard gestured for her to get out of the driver’s seat so he could drive. He sped out of the driveway and down the street as if a swarm of bees were after them.

Dee remained quiet in the passenger seat as he merged in with traffic leaving the city.

“You and Carol seemed to get along very well,” he said. “I hope you didn’t say too much about me.”

“Like what?” she asked with a frown. “I mean, I didn’t know our relationship was such a big secret.”

“Carol is a perennial gossip,” he told her.

“She seemed nice.”

He glanced at her before complaining about a driver who kept switching lanes in front of him. “What the hell do you think you’re doing?” he muttered. “Bloody foreign drivers!”

Dee frowned, wondering how he knew the driver in front was foreign, then saw that the vehicle ahead of them was a rental from the sticker proclaiming it was owned by a national rental company. Once he had managed to jockey for a good position on the highway, Richard turned back to her.

"I'm just saying be careful what you say to someone like Carol. People like that may seem nice on the outside, but they can just as easily stab you in the back."

Dee wasn't naïve, but she didn't think Carol was the kind of person who would do such a thing. Her husband's manner and tone sounded as if he were only telling her

because he worried about her, but she couldn't help thinking there was more to it.

Chapter Seven

As the weeks went on, Dee found married life wasn't as exciting as she had thought it was going to be. Richard was spending a lot of time at the office, which wasn't a problem, but Dee was bored. Since it was the middle of winter, she couldn't spend time in the garden. Not that she knew anything about gardening. She had tried reading, but the books in Richard's library hadn't interested her either.

Her husband wasn't full of suggestions either. He would come home late from work, gulp down the dinner that had been left to warm and shut himself up in his home office for another couple of hours before coming to bed. Pillow talk was not something he appeared to enjoy either. He never asked her about her day and didn't talk about work.

They went out almost every weekend in what seemed to be an endless round of social functions. If they weren't driving to Wellington, they were flying to Auckland or Christchurch to attend something there. Dee was already tired of it after three months.

She was relieved when Carol dropped by late one morning. She had decided to drive down to the city for the day.

"Drop whatever you're doing. I've come to drag you out for coffee," she announced.

Dee broke out in a grin and held her arms wide.

"I'm all yours," she replied, grabbing her coat, keys and bag without hesitation.

They opted to have lunch at a café in the local shopping mall. The Plaza, as it was named, was a complex with more than 100 stores, including a supermarket. It was located in the centre of the city and catered for a wide range of tastes and incomes.

The café they chose was next to the food court but was a little more upmarket with sandwiches, savouries, and sweet pastries. They also had a small lunch menu which offered a range of dishes from toasted sandwiches and fries to Eggs Benedict.

They sat down at a table in the corner after ordering. Carol beamed at her.

"So, how are you doing, sweetie?"

Dee shrugged. Despite her husband's warnings about Carol's predilection for gossip, she had connected with the older woman on social media and they had sent several messages back and forth. She had already complained that she was bored.

"I don't know," she said with a sigh. "I mean, there's only so much I can do around the house. I don't cook, I don't clean. I left all my books at my dad's, so I don't have anything that I like to read."

"What about Richard's books?"

"Ugh, I doubt even he's read them. He hates reading."

"So, what you're saying is, he has them there for show."

"Pretty much."

"Oh, baby, you need a hobby."

"Yeah, but what? I mean, I've never really been into embroidery or anything artistic, other than photography."

"What about that, then?"

She had mentioned to her husband that she was thinking of trying a couple of classes, but Richard had told her not to waste her time or money. Again, it was contradictory since they'd talked about it a few times when they'd been going out and he'd appeared interested. Now she wasn't so sure. He seemed so cynical about it, saying that with all the cameras in phones these days, anyone could take a photo and call themselves a photographer.

Dee felt there was a huge difference between someone taking selfies, or shots with a mobile phone and someone taking the time to learn how to use light and angles to produce a work of art.

"What about an online course?" Carol asked.

Dee grimaced. "I'm not so good with computers. Good enough to do my job - when I had it, that is, but …"

"There's not that much to learn. I took this course in English Literature and it was fun. I even got to join in some forums to discuss the books."

"Would it cost anything?" Dee asked, getting a little excited despite her doubts.

"Not the one I did. Tel**l you what, how about I show you when we get back to your place. I think you could try the same course I did. You love books and reading. I think you'd enjoy it."

Carol was right. Once Dee had managed to navigate her way around the website and create a profile for the course, she signed on for literature. The first book they had to read and discuss was Wuthering Heights, which she had read as a teenager. The course explored the various themes of the novel and other subjects like character motivation.

As she became more involved in the discussions, she found herself relating to many of the others also doing the course online. Having something to occupy her time made her feel a bit brighter. It soon became noticeable to her husband.

They were sitting in the small family room after dinner one evening a few weeks later. Richard liked to occasionally watch the news. It was on at six o'clock in the evening, but the networks also had a channel where they screened every programme an hour later. Her husband wasn't usually home in time for dinner at six-thirty, but there were exceptions.

Dee had curled up in the armchair to read while he watched the broadcast. She looked up as the sound muted. Richard was watching her curiously.

"What are you reading?" he asked.

"Pride and Prejudice," she replied.

"Isn't that rather an old book?"

"Your point being?" she returned absently, her head still in the book, then realised that sounded a little abrupt. "Sorry. It's a classic."

"Not my cup of tea," he said with a sigh.

"You don't like to read full-stop," she told him smartly, continuing to hold the book in her hands. "Even your company's annual report puts you to sleep. You said so yourself."

"Are you mocking me, darling?" he asked. She lifted her head and studied him. His tone sounded amused and he looked like he was laughing but his body was full of tension.

She put the book down next to her curled legs.

"Why would I mock you? Not everyone likes to read, dear. There's nothing wrong with that."

He eyed her curiously. "I suppose you're right. You've been reading a lot of these old books lately. What's the reason for this sudden desire?

"It's nothing. I've just joined this online course where we discuss books. Things like thematic relationships and so on. It's actually quite interesting."

"Hmm. I've noticed you've seemed a little happier these days."

She bit her lip. "It's not that I've been unhappy," she told him. "It's just that I have nothing to do during the day while you're at work. I mean, I suppose I could go volunteer at the charity shops or the museum …"

"No wife of mine should ever have to volunteer for anything," he said with an edge to his voice.

She took in a deep breath before responding. "Maybe not, but I have to do something. I'm not the type to do crafty things like … I don't know … painting or embroidery."

"I thought you wanted to do photography?" he asked.

There he went again, contradicting himself. He had already dismissed it which suggested he didn't think of photography as an art form.

"I do, but I don't have a good camera."

"You have a phone."

"An I-phone," she said with a sigh. "It's not the same. There are techniques to do with light and shade. I mean a phone camera is good, but I want to learn how to do real photography, not just something people put on social media. I mean, it's a little like … I don't know, like using one of those painting games that Robin's wife is always playing and calling that art."

He scowled. "There's a big difference between a game and taking a snapshot."

"One of those paint-by-number things, then," she suggested, meaning a kit which included the paints and the picture already sketched. "It still takes a bit of work, yes, but you're still told what colours to use and where. All the actual drawing is done for you."

He nodded, appearing to understand the analogy. "I see." He turned back to watch the television for a while, leaving her to return to her book. She began to lose herself in the story once again.

A few minutes later, he switched off the television. She looked up again as he made a noise low in his throat as if trying to catch her attention.

"So, this online course ..." he began.

"It's free."

"That wasn't what I was going to ask, but I'm curious. Who is offering such a thing?"

"It's some website. They don't ask for personal information or anything if that's what you're worried about."

She explained that while she did have to create a profile, she didn't have to provide much more information than her name and email address. The registration details hadn't asked for any financial information.

"This is a university?" he asked.

"I guess so."

He didn't look happy. "Well, that doesn't seem like good business. If I had started with Carter Tech providing free services, I would have gone broke a long time ago."

She suppressed the urge to snort derisively at her husband. Considering the man had been born with practically a silver spoon in his mouth, she found that hard to believe. He had built the company from the ground up, but it had been the money he had inherited from his father that had provided the initial investment. Probably knowing his wife's fondness for money, Alan Carter had left a sizeable amount of money in a trust fund for his only son, which Richard had received when he was eighteen.

"I don't question it," she told him. "I'm just enjoying the journey."

"Who ... uh, who put you onto this course?"

She bit her lip. She hadn't mentioned that Carol often called her just to chat and had stopped by for coffee a few times. She was well aware of Richard's attitude toward the older woman.

"Carol," she said, unable to bear the scrutiny.

"Foster?" he asked, sounding displeased. "I told you not to have anything to do with her."

"No, you just said to be careful around her. She's my friend and I don't appreciate what you're insinuating!"

She wasn't expecting the fit of temper as he began to shout at her.

"I told you she's a gossip. I don't want you talking to this woman! What happens between us is none of her business!"

"I don't go around talking about us to all and sundry," she retorted. "I needed someone to talk to, that's all."

"You've got me."

"You're at work all day. If I had to just sit here staring at the walls, I'd go completely nuts."

"I have a job," he said. "I'm the one who puts food on the table for us."

"I had a job. You made me quit."

"It didn't make sense for you to travel for two hours every day!"

"That's not the point!"

"You don't need to work."

"I need to do something! I'm bored sitting around here all day."

"Then go shopping," he told her.

"Shopping? Is that what you think women do all day? Is that what Miranda did?"

"Don't bring her into this. You know nothing about my wife."

"Ex-wife!" she hissed. "Obviously, you two had such a perfect marriage if you're defending her."

He stared at her, his brow creasing in a frown. "What the hell are you talking about?"

"The fact that she cheated on you."

"One thing has nothing to do with the other."

"So, what you're saying is, Miranda was happy being the social butterfly, organising parties and making you look good. She fit so well in your life she didn't need anything else." She glared at him. "Well, maybe you should have stayed married to her! I'm sorry that I need something else to fill my days. God forbid I should ever have friends or want to think for myself!"

She got up abruptly, dropping the book in the armchair and left the room. It was still early and wasn't time to go to bed, but she was too angry and hurt by the argument that she didn't want to face him again.

She showered and changed into her nightdress, getting into bed. For a while, she tossed and turned, too wound-up to sleep. Eventually, she dropped into a light doze, waking only when he came to bed. She had no idea what time it was, only that the house was in pitch darkness.

She could smell the cigar he had smoked and the brandy he'd drunk. Dee lay with her back to him, refusing to move. He sighed; clearly aware she was awake. She felt his hand on her arm, but she remained where she was.

He got up again and went into the ensuite bathroom. Dee shifted in the bed, trying to get a little more comfortable, hoping it would help her relax.

A few minutes later, he returned to the bed, getting in beside her.

"I'm sorry," he said. "You're not Miranda. I ... I didn't mean to make you feel like I was comparing you to her. As for what happened between her and me... that's something I'd rather not talk about. I'm sorry if I said anything to offend you." She kept silent. "Deanna?" He sounded almost plaintive. She had to roll over to look at him.

"You're wrong about Carol," she said.

"I've heard otherwise," he replied but acknowledged that she saw things differently. "I do want you to have friends. But ... I was thinking ... what if we were to ... I don't know. Have a baby?"

She frowned at him. Children was a subject they had never really discussed before they had got married. She wasn't even sure she wanted a child. Not so soon after they'd got married.

"You want children?" she asked.

"Don't you?"

"Yes, but we've never really talked about it." She knew it was a lie but she wasn't ready to tell him that she just hadn't given it any thought.

"We're talking about it now, aren't we? Deanna, I want us to work. I do love you and I want to have a family with you."

Chapter Eight

The plane was delayed. Only by about ten minutes or so, but long enough to make Dee feel a little antsy as she waited in the terminal for the plane to arrive. A few people were sitting in the rows of hard plastic seats watching the runway, but there hadn't been any flights arriving for a while and it was at least half an hour or more before the next departure.

The airport was small compared to the metropolitan ones she'd been in but, since it was only a regional airport, it didn't require too many facilities. Most of the domestic flights coming in were usually only stopping long enough to let off local passengers but the rest were often flying to either Auckland or Christchurch.

Dee had heard that some years ago there had been an independent company which sold flights to Australia, departing locally, but the company had gone bankrupt after only a couple of years in operation. She wasn't sure if the city council had ever considered proposals to extend the runway to allow jetliners to land and take-off there, but considering the airport was a short distance away from many suburban homes, it probably wasn't an option anymore.

There had been a lot of work done on the parking at the terminal in the last two years. There was more parking for those needing them long-term. She guessed many of those who parked there often travelled for work. Richard had told her that many people who worked in the bigger cities were buying properties in the smaller regional centres as the housing was cheaper. It often meant a two-hour commute, or longer in peak hour traffic if they were driving. He talked about it as some kind of trade-off. He was almost smug about the fact that he had chosen to build his company in the city instead of in Wellington long before property values had risen so high to make them unaffordable for anyone on the average income.

There was a slight burst of static from the public address system before the announcement that the flight from Auckland had just landed and was currently taxiing on the runway. Dee lifted her head and watched the plane slowly coming in. She could see workers on the tarmac, getting ready to pick up luggage from the plane's hold. Other flight crews were busy guiding the plane in.

It took a few minutes before passengers began disembarking. Dee kept watching as they each descended on the steps before stepping onto the tarmac. She counted at least thirty passengers before she saw who she had come to meet.

She fidgeted, her body almost tingling with excitement as a redhead followed the path in through the automatic door and continued through into the terminal. A few people turned their heads to stare at her, obviously having recognised her face, despite the lack of makeup and the sunglasses.

Meg squealed and dashed forward, her arms out to embrace Dee.

"Oh my god, it's been ages!" She stepped back out of the hug to look her up and down. "My god, girl, look at you. You've lost so much weight! Has it really been that long?"

As usual, when Dee met her best friend, she could barely get a word in edgewise. Not that she minded.

"I missed you, babe," she said.

"Me too. Ooh, let's get my bags and get the feck out of here. I'm shattered! I've spent about two days in the air."

Meg continued to chatter, telling Dee she had travelled from London to Singapore, then Sydney, Auckland and then Palmy. She'd had a six-hour layover in Singapore but, because of security concerns, she hadn't been able to leave the airport. Then there had been a delay landing in Sydney and the plane had to circle the airport for an hour.

Dee helped her get her bags and guided her to the parking area. She left her friend to get settled in the car while she went to pay her parking fee.

Meg was busy admiring the car's interior and, when Dee returned, she was stroking the leather seats.

"This is a nice car, mate."

Richard had presented her with the keys to a brand-new BMW electric hybrid not long before the wedding. Dee could be cynical and think the only reason he had bought a hybrid was for the good PR, suggesting his company was trying to be environmentally friendly. That and there was a certain prestige in owning such a vehicle.

"Richard bought it for me before the wedding. I've kind of got used to driving it now."

Meg sighed happily. "I can't believe your dad wouldn't even let you get your driver's licence." She added that she was pleased Dee had finally done it.

She had initially been a little worried when her husband-to-be had insisted she learned to drive, but it made her feel a little more independent. It also helped when Richard wanted to drink at whatever social event they went to, knowing she didn't like to drink too much. Even if he did criticise her driving.

She mentioned this point to Meg, who scoffed.

"God, what does the man expect if you've only had your licence a few months. We can't all be perfect right off the bat."

Meg hadn't been impressed when Dee had told her Richard had signed her up with a personal trainer. While she agreed that Dee needed to lose weight, she thought the man had gone the wrong way about it. Meg formerly had her weight issues but the six months in Europe had been good for her. She looked stunning, even with dark circles under her eyes.

*****

They sat down with coffees at the house. Dee had suggested perhaps her friend needed to rest and get rid of the jet lag, but Meg explained that she needed to reacclimate herself to the time zone and having a nap wouldn't fix that.

Her friend was staying overnight but would be taking the bus to Wellington in the morning. Dee was a little relieved that Richard had gone to Wellington himself for a meeting with a big client and wouldn't be back until late the next afternoon. It gave them plenty of time to catch up without interruptions.

"So, how was Europe?" she asked.

"It was amazing! I mean, yeah, I was there to work, but I got to travel a little bit. I went on the Chunnel over to France."

"The Chunnel?" Dee asked, confused by the term.

"It's what the locals call the Channel Tunnel," her friend explained, adding that it was a tunnel under the English Channel between France and England.

Dee listened as Meg began telling her about the sights she had seen on her travels. The stories made her feel a little like a country bumpkin. Having never gone anywhere in her life, she felt unworldly and naïve. The more she heard, the more she wanted to experience it for herself.

She sighed, knowing her envy was showing through.

"It sounds so awesome," she said. "I wish I could do that."

"Well, I bet Richard would take you."

Would he really … she wondered, given that he was more interested in working than in doing anything he considered so plebeian. Tourism was something people did when they had retired or were students on an overseas experience. The only other reason for travelling was for business and there wasn't time for checking out local attractions.

There was also his desire for them to have a baby. It had been a few weeks since the night they had argued and the subject had never come up again. She hadn't asked him about it and wondered if perhaps he had only said something to placate her. Having a baby would put the kibosh on any thoughts she had of travelling. At least for a while.

Parenthood just didn't fit with the image she had of her husband. He didn't appear to like children very much. The few times he had gone shopping with her, he had been critical of the young children being taken around the store by their mothers. Even the well-behaved ones.

She sat curled up in the armchair, running her thumb up and down the now empty mug.

"What is it?" her friend asked.

"Richard wants me to have a baby."

Meg looked as if she was trying to come up with the right words.

"And you don't?" she asked slowly.

"I don't know. That's the problem." She told Meg about the argument and what Richard had said when he had finally come to bed. Her friend scowled.

"Bloody hell, Dee. He had no right to say that at all about Carol. I mean, to me she sounds like an amazing person and it's not like you're telling her all the family secrets, is it? Damn, I'd love to give that man a piece of my mind."

"You don't think I'm off base?" she asked.

"Hell no. Look, you're my best friend, Dee, and I have to say that when you told me you were getting married, I did think you might be rushing into things. But now I see it wasn't you rushing into it. He's kind of pushy."

"He says he loves me."

"Right. He says that but how much of it is true." Meg reached out and gently squeezed her arm. "Oh, sweetie, I'm not saying you're not worth loving …"

"No, I know," Dee assured her.

"It's just that, he sounds like the kind of guy who will say things like that to get his own way. It's a little like the things your dad used to say to you."

"What do you mean?"

"Remember that time you got an almost perfect score on your school report and took it home? Your dad just looked at it and pointed to the one subject where you didn't get an A and told you that you should have tried harder? I mean, for feck's sake, it was bloody P.E! Which you hated! Any kind of organised sport was never your thing and he knew that. Hell, he was always telling my mum you were more a brainbox than you were an athlete!"

Dee remembered that. Her father had always criticised her to her face, making her doubt her abilities, yet he would praise her behind her back to other people.

"You know what your dad did to you is gaslighting, right?" Meg told her. "He made you doubt yourself so you would just do what he wanted you to do."

"He didn't want me marrying Richard," she said.

"Because he wanted to control you."

She wondered if Meg thought the same thing about her husband. Dee couldn't help thinking back to the incident the night before they had gone to meet his mother and the bartender at the hotel. Was Richard trying to be just as controlling?

She couldn't help but think about the first time they had gone out when he had refused to take no for an answer. All the other times he'd taken her out but she never had a choice of where they had gone or what they did.

They talked until Meg's exhaustion began to show, her yawns becoming more frequent. She went to bed after an early dinner. Dee curled up in the chair, reading the latest prescribed novel for her course.

Right before she decided to go to bed herself, the phone rang. Dee picked it up. She could hear loud music in the background.

"Hello?"

"It's just me," Richard replied. "I just thought I'd check in. Is your friend there?"

"Yes. She got in this afternoon. She's gone to bed already. Where are you? It's really loud."

"I'm at the hotel. Just having a late dinner and a couple of drinks."

"Oh. How did the meeting go?"

"Good. It went very well. But you don't need to hear all the gory details."

A woman began speaking in the background. Richard's voice became muffled and she guessed he had covered the microphone with his hand. She frowned, wondering why he would do such a thing. After a minute or so, he spoke clearly into the phone.

"I should go. Everything all right there? Are you missing me?"

She laughed. Even to her, it rang false. "Of course, I'm missing you," she replied. "But it's only one night. I'll see you when you get home tomorrow."

"All right. See you tomorrow … darling." She heard the woman laughing in the background. It sounded awfully close to the phone as if the person were standing right next to Richard.

She hung up the phone but continued to frown at the handset, wondering why something about the call felt off. It was nothing she could identify but it felt as if he were hiding something.

She didn't sleep well that night, going over the conversation in her head. When she told Meg about it at breakfast, her friend had no idea either.

"I don't know him that well, so I can't say if something was off, but if you think there was, then there has to be."

"I don't know. Maybe I'm imagining things."

Meg shook her head. "No, sweetie. You're not like that. Can I ask you something?"

"You can ask me anything. You know that."

"Why did you marry him if you had so many doubts about him?"

"I … I don't know," she murmured with a sigh.

After Meg left, she thought it over. If she was honest with herself, she hadn't married him for love. In many ways, she felt as if she had been pushed into it. Part of it, she knew, was the fact that she had wanted to get away from her father. Maybe she had convinced herself that she could learn to love her husband. That him loving her would be enough.

Her mother had loved her father deeply, but Linda had confessed to her, long after the divorce, that the love between them wasn't enough for her to be able to see past all the things that were wrong in the marriage. Jack's need to control everything in their lives had been too emotionally draining.

Dee wasn't sure what to tell Richard if he brought up the subject of having a baby. Bringing a child into a marriage she wasn't completely happy in wasn't the best option. While it might solve the problem of her feelings of isolation, it certainly couldn't be a healthy environment for a child. She remembered how bad things had been before her mother had left for good.

Her parents had been fighting a lot. There had been one night when they had been screaming at each other and she had gone to her room, her hands over her ears as if that could drown out the sounds.

*****

By the time Richard came in the door, she had almost made up her mind to tell him she had made a huge mistake. He had a huge grin on his face and was holding a bouquet of her favourite flowers in one hand and a bottle of champagne in the other.

"I take it the meeting was a success," she said.

He put the bottle on the table and dropped the flowers beside it before walking over to her and sweeping her up into his arms to give her a passionate kiss. She was breathless when he finally let her go.

"We're going to Melbourne," he exclaimed!

She stared at him. "Melbourne? What? When? Why?"

"Next month," he said. "For the Melbourne Cup. I just joined a syndicate."

She shook her head, still trying to make sense of what he was saying. "What's the Melbourne Cup?"

"It's a horse race," he told her. "One of the biggest events on the racing calendar every year." He seemed so excited about it that she didn't have the heart to tell him what she had been thinking.

"So, what do you mean you joined a syndicate?"

"These friends of mine own a racehorse. One of their syndicate members had to drop out and they invited me to join. I've always wanted to own a racehorse." He sounded almost like a giddy schoolboy and she couldn't help smiling at his mood.

"So, what do we have to do?"

She listened as he told her she would have to buy a dress to wear for race day, which included a fascinator. She had no idea what that was, and he showed her images on the internet.

He continued to talk excitedly about the trip through dinner and even as they prepared for bed.

"We could go for a whole week and I can show you around Melbourne. It's a lot like here, actually. I think you'd really like the city."

"Honey, I don't even have a passport," she called as she pulled back the covers and fluffed up the pillows.

He came out of the bathroom, still brushing his teeth. She chuckled at the way he looked with the toothbrush sticking out of his mouth and toothpaste foam dripping down his chin.

He tried to say something to her, but it came out garbled. She rolled her eyes and laughed at him.

"Take the toothbrush out of your mouth while you talk."

He grinned sheepishly. "We can get the passport sorted," he said. "We've got a couple of weeks." He returned to the bathroom to rinse his mouth out. A minute later he came back out and stood in the doorway. "So? What do you think? It'll be like a second honeymoon."

"We never even had a first honeymoon!" she retorted. He had promised one, but something had come up at work.

He stared at her for a long moment, then with a low growl, made a dash for her, tackling her to the bed. She squealed with laughter as he tickled her.

"Say yes," he told her. "Say it, or I'll have to tickle you into submission."

She laughed and tried to squirm away from him. "All right, all right," she said finally. "We can go."

He kissed her passionately. "You know why I married you, lady?"

"So, you can make me do anything you want?" she returned.

He gave a low growl. "You are trouble, missy."

He kissed her again before stripping off her nightgown. For the first time in their entire relationship, Dee felt his passion in his lovemaking. For the first time since the wedding, Dee felt she could possibly make this marriage work.

Chapter Nine

"And here we have Australia's most famous racehorse, Phar Lap." Dee strained to listen to the tour guide as she began telling those gathered about the horse exhibit. She wrinkled her nose a little. She had never really liked horses that much and couldn't understand the attraction. The guide continued with her spiel, telling them that when the animal had died, its skeleton had been sent to New Zealand while the hide had been removed and mounted. It was an odd thing for people to worship, she thought.

"I don't get it," she said.

Several others in the large group shot her glares while her husband squeezed her hand. "What don't you get?" Richard asked.

"It's just a horse."

He looked almost outraged at her words, as did a few others.

"*Just* a horse?" he asked in indignation. "***Just*** a horse?"

"Well, I'm sorry if I'm not as well-versed on horses as you," she replied. "I just don't see what the big deal is."

"It's not just that he was a famous racehorse," a voice spoke up behind them. "It's the romance of the story. The awkward, gangly creature that grows up to become a living legend in his own time, only for his life to be tragically cut short."

Dee stared at the newcomer. Phillip Mason. It was hard to believe he would ever even use the word romance, considering how cynical he had been the last time they'd met.

Richard snorted, looking around at the other man. "Mason. What are you doing here?"

"Same as you, by the looks of it. Hello, Dee, you're looking very well."

She suppressed the urge to giggle as he took her hand and lifted it, placing a soft kiss on her knuckles. At the same time, Richard's grip on her hand tightened.

Phillip Mason turned and looked over the exhibit. "So, how's our boy?"

Dee cocked an eyebrow. "Sorry?"

"Well, he didn't just belong to the Aussies now, did he? He was born and bred in New Zealand. Timaru, actually." He went on, telling her that his family had a farm in the area but had left it decades before Phillip was born. He spoke fondly of the town, telling her a little more of the history of the famous horse.

"I didn't know that," she said.

"Not surprising," the other man said. "My old man used to tell me horse-racing is a mug's game."

"So, why are you here, then?" Richard asked, his tone implying he wasn't at all happy at the man's intrusion. He nudged Dee to catch up with the rest of the tour. Phillip trailed along behind them.

"Well, this mug decided to check out the Melbourne Cup. See what the fuss is all about."

"Richard joined a syndicate," Dee told him, still not quite sure what it all meant. "We're going to … where is it?" she asked.

"Flemington," Richard told her. "You didn't have to tell him that."

She shrugged. It wasn't as if it was a huge secret, she thought.

"Ooh, which syndicate?" Phillip asked. "I might know them."

"Robinson," Richard replied. "And I sincerely doubt you know them."

Phillip frowned. "Robinson. Robinson. Weren't they involved in some scandal recently?"

Richard's temper flared. Dee frowned at her husband, wondering why he was suddenly so angry. He had told her that someone had to drop out of the syndicate but hadn't gone into any details. She wondered if the person who had dropped out had been forced to, due to whatever scandal Phillip was talking about.

"Yeah, it was to do with some doping thing, wasn't it?"

"Drop it, Mason!" Richard hissed, clearly not wanting to discuss the subject. "This is none of your business, anyway."

"Fine. Well, I'm sure we will run into each other at the Cup on Tuesday." He smiled down at her. "It was good to see you again, Dee. Don't let this guy keep bossing you around."

They continued with the tour, but Richard kept a tight grip on her, making her feel like he was afraid to let her out of his sight. Once the tour was over, they left the museum, getting on a tram to return to their hotel. She kept a wary eye on her husband. Before Phillip had turned up, Richard had been almost jovial, telling her stories he had heard about the history of Melbourne.

*****

Once they were in the hotel, he turned on her. "What the hell was that?" he asked.

"What?"

"You and Mason."

She looked at him, confused. "What do you mean?"

"What the hell did you tell him about the syndicate for?"

"I didn't think it was some big state secret, Richard."

"I don't like him around you."

She glared at him. "You don't own me, Richard. I can talk to other people if I want to. And that's all it is. Just talking!"

"I don't mind you talking to other people. Just not him!"

That was rich since he didn't like her talking to Carol either. She had talked to the other woman a couple of times since the night he'd told her about the trip and her friend had been somewhat nonplussed at the way Richard had seemed so excited about coming to Australia. Carol had implied it had been way out of character for him.

Dee wondered what her friends knew about her husband, but part of her wasn't willing to find out.

"Why? What did he ever do to you?"

He ran a hand through his dark blond hair. "Nothing. It doesn't matter. Just stay away from him."

"No, you can't tell me not to talk to him without giving me a good reason."

"I thought I made it clear last time. I don't like him flirting with you."

"If that's what you call flirting, then I don't know what to say, Richard. I wasn't flirting."

"I never said you were!" he said, raising his voice.

She scowled at him. "Don't shout at me, please. And tell me why you hate him so much."

"It's nothing to do with you."

"Then why were you so angry with me the night of the charity auction? And, by the way, I was not flirting with him then either."

"I know. Stewart Boylston set me straight on that. He said that when you came in, you looked uncomfortable and Mason was just talking to you to put you at ease. I still didn't like it, but ..."

"Well, if you'd been there to meet me, there would have been no need for Mr Mason to talk to me, would there?"

He gazed at her; his expression was unreadable. She had the vaguest feeling he wasn't happy about the way she was talking back to him. He never liked it when she asserted herself. For all his talk about the way her father used to control her, he could be just as controlling when he wanted to be. As if he expected her to just be the obedient wife and not have her own ideas. Well, they lived in the twenty-first century, not the Middle Ages, and she was damned if she was going to let him order her around like she was a piece of property.

She glared back at him, daring him to say something. He visibly relaxed.

"You're right. I'm sorry. Can we please just drop the subject?" he asked. "I'd really like to take you to this restaurant I dined in last time I was here."

"All right," she relented. He grinned at her, apparently placated. "Why don't you wear that red dress I got you last month? It looks very sexy on you." As if to demonstrate how sexy he found her, he pulled her close and ran his hands up and down her body.

"Richard!" she exclaimed, feeling her face grow warm. As much as he was clearly trying to make it sensual, she felt more like he was asserting ownership. He'd picked out the dress himself, even though it wasn't her style. She preferred conservative clothing, rather than anything that showed off her figure. No matter how good it now looked.

He shrugged. "What? Can't I tell my wife I think she's sexy?" She blushed even more. 'Sexy' was never a word that sat comfortably with her. What made it worse was that she was never sure he meant it. Richard wasn't the type of man to give compliments. Sincere ones, at least.

"I'm glad you listened to me and lost all that weight," he murmured against her hair. "Too much weight on a woman just doesn't look good." He made a disgusted kind of sound.

Dee couldn't help but think of the times he had taken her out, only to make some caustic remark about another woman nearby. One would be wearing too much makeup, making her look like a 'drag queen.' Another would be 'trying too hard.' But the worst incident happened when they had gone to a restaurant and they saw a man dining with a woman not much older than Dee. She was obese, but not morbidly so. Richard began making jokes about the woman's size, comparing her to a hippo, and claiming she was just shovelling her food in her mouth like a bulldozer.'

Dee had almost walked out of the restaurant, feeling so disgusted with his behaviour.

After that incident, he had apparently learnt his lesson and hadn't made such remarks again; At least, not in her presence. She often wondered if he hated women with a bit of weight on them so much, how would he handle it if she did get pregnant?

*****

He pushed her in the direction of the bathroom, telling her to shower and change into the dress. To please him, she also put on some slightly heavier makeup. Dee hadn't had much practice at applying makeup before she had married him, so she had asked Meg to help her with it. Meg had given her Susan's contact number, a friend from university who had become a talented makeup artist. Sue had taught her how to use cosmetics to enhance her best features.

By the time Dee was ready, she could hear Richard outside the bathroom door because he had already showered and changed. Then he sat out on the hotel terrace smoking a cigar while he waited for her, but was now pacing and sighing impatiently.

"Are you ready yet?" he called almost plaintively. He was still talking as she opened the door. "You know I don't why you women have to take so long ..." He trailed off, staring at her, then gave a low whistle. "Wow! I take it back. If that's what it takes to get you looking like that, take as much time as you need, darling."

*****

The restaurant he had chosen to take her to was about twenty minutes from central Melbourne. It had a view of the Marina where Dee could see several boats docked. Inside the restaurant, it was spacious and well-lit - the décor giving it a bright, airy tone. The huge plate-glass windows helped to create the tone.

They were led upstairs to a table that was close to the balcony. It was a little cool that evening, so Richard had opted for them to dine inside.

"This is beautiful," she commented to the host.

"Thank you, ma'am," he replied, while Richard smiled at her comment.

"Would you care for something to drink?" the host asked. He was only about a year or so younger than Dee, with a strong accent that indicated he hadn't been born in Australia. He had an olive complexion with dark, wavy hair.

"How about a bottle of your finest wine?" Richard suggested.

"We have a 2006 Dom Pérignon Vintage Chardonnay Pinot Noir. It's an excellent wine, sir. Full-bodied, with the aroma of fresh fruits."

"Hmm, that sounds good. We'll have that."

"Of course, sir." The man handed them each a menu. "I will have the server bring your wine. In the meantime, please let us know if there's anything else you and your lovely wife require." Dee smiled and blushed at the compliment. The host turned and left.

She looked at her husband. "He seemed nice."

"He comes from South America. Argentina, if memory serves."

"So, you've been here before?" she queried, forgetting what he had said to her earlier.

"It's been a few months. Remember that business trip I took not long after we got married?"

She frowned, trying to remember. He was often away on business trips and it was hard to keep track. He shook his head.

"It doesn't matter. I came here with a few people from the company I was involved in the business deal with."

"Oh, I see."

"They do a lot of functions here. Weddings, corporate functions. I liked the atmosphere and I decided I'd bring you here once the opportunity presented itself. I know you're not used to such luxury, darling, but I think you'd enjoy yourself if you just learnt to relax a little."

She gazed at him for a long moment. "Are you suggesting I'm uptight?" she asked cautiously.

"If I'm allowed to be honest, yes. I'm not trying to hurt your feelings, darling. I just want you to forget about everything but the experience."

She still couldn't help feeling like other guests in the restaurant were judging her, thinking she was out of her league. Maybe the way she was dressed helped disguise the fact that she hadn't grown up rich, but she still felt out of place.

Another couple came in and were seated nearby. They were an attractive couple, aged in their mid-forties, from what she could tell. Both were wearing clothing that had been bought in an upscale boutique. She didn't know very much about fashion but knew enough to recognise the styles and fabrics were not created in some factory where the workers were paid less than minimum wage.

They both appeared completely comfortable in their surroundings, chatting amiably with the host as if they were old friends. The man was blond with fair skin. His wife's hair was dark with flecks of grey.

"See that couple?" Richard asked in a low voice. "Do you know who they are?"

"No," she said. The man looked vaguely familiar, but she couldn't place his name.

"That's Kieran Stern and his wife. Kieran used to be on a television show a few years ago back home. He's been here for about fifteen years. I heard he moved here because there weren't enough opportunities to secure decent roles. He's been acting on a soap for a few years now."

"How do you know?" she asked quietly.

The conversation was interrupted by the server, who greeted them with a friendly smile and poured them each a glass of wine. She asked if they were ready to order.

"Not yet," Richard told her.

"Could we have a few more minutes, please?" Dee asked quietly.

"Of course," the woman replied. "I'll be back in about five minutes."

"Thank you." Dee waited until she had left before turning back to her husband, repeating the question.

"My executive assistant," he said. "She's always gossiping about developments on the show."

She huffed and snickered. "Are you telling me you eavesdrop on a private conversation?"

"How is it eavesdropping when she's on her phone, at her desk, and I'm trying to get her to type up some papers for me?"

"All right. Point taken. So, what about them?"

"Kieran, if the women's magazines are right, grew up dirt poor in South Auckland."

Dee snickered again at the thought of her husband reading any kind of magazine, let alone one targeted at women. He rolled his eyes at her.

"My point, darling, is that he didn't grow up in the lap of luxury either. However, he's here in a fine dining restaurant. The only one judging you as not belonging in such a place is you."

"So, you're saying, no one cares?" she asked.

"If you act like you expect everyone to look at you as some kind of gold-digger, then that's how they'll treat you."

He did make a good point, she thought. She sipped the champagne, determined to at least try to relax and not look as if she wasn't enjoying herself.

She deliberately ignored the prices on the menu. She had read somewhere that most retail assistants could tell if someone was rich not by the clothing they wore, but how they behaved in the store. Rich clientele didn't even look at prices.

She decided to just relax and enjoy the experience.

Chapter Ten

She tried not to feel self-conscious in the dress she was wearing. It was black with white strips crisscrossed all down the sides and very figure-hugging. Dee thought it had looked more like a cocktail dress than something one would wear to what she was soon learning was a world-famous event, but the woman in the department store had assured her it was a style lots of women would be wearing.

Richard certainly seemed to appreciate the dress when she had emerged from the bathroom, all dressed up and ready to go.

"How do I look?" she'd asked him.

"Like the wife of a Melbourne Cup winner," he told her. "Turn around."

She'd spun in place as he'd ordered, letting him get a good look at the dress. He'd proclaimed it 'very nice,' although with a much cooler tone than he'd used the other night when she'd worn the red dress to please him.

The saleslady had also suggested a fascinator, which Dee realised was a headpiece, rather than a hat, worn on one side of the head and decorated with either flowers or feathers. The woman had shown her a couple and Dee had chosen one that was black with a silk rose in white. It also had a small net which was fitted to the edge and partially covered her eyes.

According to the saleslady, it was supposed to add some kind of allure or mystery.

As a member of a syndicate, Richard had tickets to the social event which began a few hours before the main race, although there were other races during the day. Dee was left to wander around on her own while her husband chatted with men she assumed were either other racehorse owners or members of his syndicate.

She was already bored, having absolutely nothing in common with any of the people attending. She still knew nothing about horse racing and wasn't eager to learn.

"Hello."

Startled, she turned and stared at Phillip. The dark-haired man smiled at her.

"Wow! I spotted you earlier and thought you looked amazing but now I see you up close and you look stunning!"

She blushed. "Thank you."

"Has he left you alone again?" Phillip asked.

"It looks like it," she said with a sigh.

"Well, that's not good. That's not good at all. He really should keep a better eye on you. I mean, if you were my wife, I would be afraid some other guy would come along and chat you up. I wouldn't let you out of my sight."

"That's kind of sexist, isn't it?" Dee asked.

He grinned. "Yeah, but at least I'm honest about it."

She laughed. "You're incorrigible."

"That's me. My mum always said my middle name was Trouble."

"Oh, I can believe it," she returned.

He looked over toward one of the grandstands. It was already full of people who had come along to watch the race.

"You know, it's a public holiday here."

"What? For the whole country?" she asked.

"Technically, no, it's just the state of Victoria. But the whole country practically comes to a standstill."

"I still don't get what's so fascinating about horse-racing."

He canted his head. His expression was one of amusement, but what amused him she had no idea.

"You know, me either. So, we never got a chance to talk the other day. What have you been doing with yourself?"

She began telling him about the literature course she had been studying. He frowned at her.

"You read classic novels?"

"And we discuss them on forums," she said. "It's a lot of fun." She laughed. "I got into this debate about Little Women and whether Jo should have got married. There was this woman ... I think it was a woman ... who kept arguing about some feminist interpretations of the book and how the author sold herself out in the end." She rolled her eyes and laughed. "I mean, come on. Feminism wasn't even thought of when that book was written."

"I've never read it," Phillip told her.

"Never?"

"I'm not much of a reader," he confessed.

She huffed. "Yeah, Richard hates reading too. You and he have a lot in common."

"We used to be friends. A long time ago."

She stared at him, surprised by the revelation. "Friends? Really? What happened?"

"It's a long story and I don't want to bore you."

"No, please, tell me."

He sighed, looking reluctant. "Let's just say that we both went out with the same woman." He appeared to be staring at something behind her and his whole demeanour suddenly shifted. "Uh, anyway, I should go, um, mingle. It was good to see you again, Dee."

Confused, she watched him walk away, wondering why it looked like he had suddenly felt the need to run a mile in the opposite direction. She turned around to see if she could figure it out but didn't see anything that would explain his behaviour.

A tall woman in a white dress was watching her. She had an attractive face framed with rich brown hair and blonde highlights. Disconcerted, Dee turned away.

She wandered over to the fence to watch whatever was happening on the track. According to the announcements over the public address system, the main race was at least another half an hour away.

"Deanna?"

She turned to look at the woman who had spoken. It was the woman in the white dress.

"Yes?"

The woman nodded. "I thought that was you. I saw your photo in the paper a few months ago. I've been meaning to contact you."

"I'm sorry. Who are you?"

"I'm Miranda. Richard's ex."

Dee stared at her. Richard had got rid of all the photos of his ex-wife and she hadn't bothered to look up anything on the woman, thinking it was all ancient history and not any of her business. Her husband barely spoke of her.

Miranda looked a little disconcerted herself. "I'm sorry. You're probably wondering what I'm doing here."

"It did occur to me."

The other woman told her she had remarried about three years earlier and that her husband also owned a racehorse, as well as a stud farm in the Waikato.

"I see."

"It's hard work, but we like it."

Dee frowned. The little she knew about Richard's ex-wife was that she had been a socialite. Yet, as she talked about working on the farm, she seemed to be incredibly happy with her lot.

"Look, I know this is out of the blue, but I wanted to meet you. When I heard Richard got married again, I admit I was a little concerned."

"About Richard?" she asked.

"No," Miranda said. Her gaze appeared distracted. "I should go find my husband, but I'd really like to talk with you some more. Maybe when you're back in New Zealand. I'll give you a ring, all right?"

"Um, sure."

She watched the woman walk away, wondering what Richard's ex-wife was concerned about. She was confused. Wasn't this the woman who had cheated on Richard? Maybe he hadn't said anything to make her out like a bad person, but he had not been exactly full of compliments either. Yet Miranda had seemed nice. Even down-to-earth. Not at all as Dee had pictured.

Still stunned by the meeting, she remained where she was, listening to the announcements over the p.a.

"There you are. I've been looking all over for you." She suppressed a snort. Richard had been so busy talking business with his 'friends,' he had probably forgotten all about her. "Come on. The race is about to start."

She joined her husband, quietly laughing at the way he began shouting at the horses, like almost everyone else watching the race. She spotted Phillip with another group and snickered as he rolled his eyes. Richard wouldn't approve, but she liked the other man. He seemed fun. He was attractive, of course, but more than that, he made her laugh. Richard didn't seem to share the same sense of humour. She could barely recall many moments where she had shared a laugh with the man she had married. What did that say about her, she wondered, that she was thinking about another man while she was standing beside her husband?

The atmosphere at the track amped up even more and everyone began screaming. Dee tried to ignore the shouts, but she wanted to cover her ears. Even some of the women were screaming. She watched the race but had no idea which horse belonged to whom and still couldn't see what was so great about riders on the back beating their mounts and making them run around a track a couple of times.

She couldn't help thinking back to a couple of days after her husband had announced the trip. Richard had been so condescending when he had explained about the race.

Not only was it worth millions of dollars in prize money to the owners of each racehorse, but many people bet on the race hoping to make a lot of money out of it. Then he went on about some horses being 'hot favourites' to win and how the betting system worked, and she was thoroughly bored by the end of it.

As the race ended, Richard looked angry. He stomped away like a five-year-old having a tantrum. From his behaviour, she guessed his horse had lost.

She approached him gingerly. "I'm sorry," she said.

He looked down at her. "What did you do?" he asked, his tone almost insulting.

"Your horse lost, I guess?"

"Yeah, it came second."

"Well, that's good, isn't it?"

"It should have come first!"

He walked away, ranting something about the horse being useless and the trainer should be fired. Dee sighed. While everyone else appeared to be celebrating the winner, Richard's face looked like a thundercloud. Even the brightness of the day seemed to have dimmed.

Since the rest of the syndicate members were going out to dinner once the festivities were over, she was forced to stay by Richard's side for the rest of the afternoon. She could see his mood getting darker and darker.

It was one of the many things she had noticed that were unlikeable about him. When things didn't go his way, he tended to act immature and childish. There had been a few times when she had refused to do something he wanted, and he'd sulked. It had been the same the night of the charity fundraiser, not long after they'd got married. He had sulked then when he'd thought she had been flirting with Phillip.

The dinner was at a nearby restaurant. Bookings were months in advance. Fortunately, the syndicate had made its reservation months earlier, so they were able to get a table. There appeared to be many other racehorse owners there, and some of the members of their party would chat back and forth with other tables as if they hadn't already spent several hours socialising.

Richard was still sulking. He refused to participate in the chatter and drank more than half a bottle of champagne during the dinner. He was rude to the servers, ordering them about as if they were beneath him. Dee didn't dare tell him off for his behaviour, although it was obvious some of the others could see what was happening and tried to talk him out of it or cheer him up by telling jokes. They sent her pitying looks.

It was later still by the time they got back to the hotel. He hadn't said a word to her the entire evening. She went to change her clothes and take off her makeup, but he grabbed her wrist in almost a bruising grip. He glared hard at her.

"Did you enjoy yourself today?" he asked. It wasn't so much an enquiry as an accusation.

"It was fine," she said.

"Really? So, someone didn't see you talking to Mason?"

His grip tightened even more on her wrist, twisting the flesh, and causing a burning sensation.

"Richard, stop it. You're hurting me!"

"Why were you talking to him?" He had raised his voice, so it was not quite yelling. She wondered if he was deliberately keeping the volume low so no one in the room next door would hear.

"We were just talking," she said. "What else was I supposed to do while you were partying with your friends?"

He let go of her wrist but grabbed her arms with both hands, shaking her.

"Why were you even talking to him? You know I hate the man!"

"He told me you used to be friends," she tried saying but he wasn't listening, almost yelling in her ear,

saying she had no right to be talking to other men. That she was his and he wasn't going to stand for that kind of behaviour.

"You embarrassed me!" he growled.

"I embarrassed you when you were stamping your feet and acting like a five-year-old?" she responded.

It was obviously the wrong thing to say. She wasn't prepared for what came next. He slapped her hard across the face. Her cheek stung and her glasses were thrown clear across the room. She stared at him in shock. He'd hit her. He had actually hit her! She tried to pull away from him, but he wasn't done. She continued trying to fight him as he ripped at the neckline of her dress, tearing the front. He was not as well-built as some men, tending more on the side of slenderness, but he was strong enough to rip the fabric off her body. Afraid he would hit her again, she stopped fighting him as he pushed her to the bed.

Chapter Eleven

"Dee, there's a phone call for you."

Dee looked at Jenny. The housekeeper had become an invaluable help to her over the past few months and she looked on the older woman as a good friend. The day after they had returned from Melbourne, Jenny had quickly noticed something was wrong and tried to get Dee to open up.

While she wasn't usually one to confide in someone who worked for Richard, she sensed that Jenny was the kind of person who didn't share private conversations. It had still taken a little time for her to tell the housekeeper what had happened in Melbourne.

"You don't have to put up with that," Jenny had remarked as they shared morning tea a couple of days later. Richard, thankfully, was on yet another business trip and wouldn't be back for a day or two.

"I have nowhere else to go," Dee confided. "I don't know. I mean, what if I caused it?"

Jenny frowned. "What do you mean, you caused it? Sweetie, no one has the right to hit you, no matter what happened. And it sounds to me like you didn't do anything. So what if you were talking to that other man. Talking isn't cheating and if he tries to say it is, well, he's wrong. My partner, I mean, my ex-partner, smacked me around because I had male friends. As far as he was concerned, the only man I needed in my life was him."

Dee smiled as she sipped her coffee. "I bet that didn't go down too well," she replied.

In the months she had gotten to know Jenny, she had learnt that the older woman had been in an abusive relationship. She had two boys she loved dearly and tried not to say anything negative about their father, hoping they would see him for what he was.

Dee regarded her as quite a strong woman who wasn't the type to back down in a fight. She was slim and petite, but fierce with it. Dee often wondered whether women who were small in stature often developed strong personalities to make up for their lack of height so others would not under-estimate them.

"I don't know," she said with a sigh. "I mean, sometimes he can be ... sweet. Well, maybe sweet isn't the word, but ... When he wants to be, he's good to me."

"That's the operative word," Jenny replied. "When he wants to be. Word ... phrase." She twitched her nose. "You know what I mean."

"So, what are you saying?"

Jenny sipped her drink. She preferred herbal tea to coffee but had once admitted that she had been a sugar junkie for many years. She had suffered a major health problem that put her in the hospital so she decided to quit sweets for good.

She had started working as Richard's housekeeper about six months before Dee had met him.

"I have to confess something. I really don't like Richard. I mean, he's my boss, and your husband, but I think he's arrogant and manipulative and ..." The other woman's brown eyes studied her. "Do you love him?"

Did she? There were times when she wondered if she even liked him. She had found him attractive at the beginning, but she'd felt more overwhelmed by him. From the moment they had met, it felt as if he'd just taken control of her life.

She sighed deeply. "I … I don't know," she said.

"Well, there's your answer," Jenny replied.

"How do you mean?"

"If you don't know how you feel about him, you're not in love with him." Her friend looked her over. "Be honest, love. Why did you marry him?"

"I guess … I guess I wanted to escape my dad."

"Well, let's face it. Your dad wasn't exactly father-of-the-year." She had told Jenny a little bit about her upbringing and the way her father had tried to stop her leaving.

"I know." If she had to think about it, her reasons for marrying Richard had mostly to do with needing to get away from her father, but she still could have walked away from Jack at any time. Richard, or so she had thought, had offered her security.

"God, I'm such a fool," she said.

"No, you were just naïve. Hon, guys like Richard, and your dad, no matter what excuses they offer, it's all really about control. Richard thought you were an easy mark."

"Why? I mean, why did he pick me?"

"Don't take this the wrong way, sweetie, but I think he saw you as weak. You were still living with your dad. You took a job he wanted you to take rather than putting your foot down and going for what you wanted. You were scared."

"Of what?" she asked.

"If you walked away from your father as your mother did, you were afraid he wouldn't love you anymore. The thing is, what Jack did to you was never about love. He thought by controlling you he could keep you."

Dee slowly realised Jenny was right. She had been afraid. Her mother had walked away, and Dee had feared if she tried to assert her independence, tried to go against her father's wishes, he would walk away from her too. She was afraid of being abandoned. Jack Hargreaves had never taught her independence. That was something she had had to learn by herself.

*****

It had been a week since that conversation with Jenny and Dee felt completely trapped in her marriage. Richard hadn't even apologised for his actions that night and she constantly felt like she was walking on eggshells around him, not daring to say anything in case it upset him.

He appeared to be drinking and smoking more than usual. Dee wanted to sleep in another bedroom, repulsed by the odour of stale whiskey and cigars, but he refused to let her leave. The night before, he had been worse than usual and she had barely slept, only dropping off to sleep once he'd got up to go to work.

She got up late morning. Jenny had looked questioningly at her when she appeared shortly before eleven but had left her to read in the family room. Dee hadn't expected her friend to come in until around lunchtime.

Jenny held the phone out for her. Dee took it and Jenny went out again, obviously to give her privacy.

"Hello?"

"Deanna? It's Miranda. I hope I'm not catching you at a bad time."

"No. I'm … I'm fine."

"I'm in town. We're here for a race meeting tonight. I was wondering if you could meet me for coffee. In the Plaza?"

She bit her lip, again wondering why Richard's ex-wife was so keen to meet with her. At least the other woman seemed to be quite friendly.

"Sure. What time?"

They made arrangements to meet mid-afternoon at a café. The same café Carol had taken her to, the day they had had lunch together. As she hung up the phone, Jenny came back in. She told her friend about the brief but odd conversation she'd had with Miranda at the racecourse and her plans to meet up with her.

"I don't know anything about Richard's ex-wife," Jenny told her, "but if you want my two cents, I don't think it could hurt to hear her out. She might have some insight."

"I guess so."

"Do you feel like some lunch?" Jenny asked. "You still look a bit peaked."

"Um, I don't know. I'm just tired."

"All right. But make sure you eat something before you go and meet Miranda."

Dee smirked at her. "Yes, Mother."

Jenny flapped a hand at her, grinning as she left the room.

Dee decided to shower and dress in charcoal grey pants with a raspberry top, knowing she looked good in the outfit. She chose not to wear heavy makeup, just adding mascara to her lashes and a little lip gloss. She still appeared to have dark circles under her eyes but didn't want to make it worse by adding foundation, hoping the plastic rims of her glasses would cover it.

*****

Dee made it to the café a few minutes before the appointed time and saw Miranda was already there, sitting at one of the tables by the window. Miranda smiled and waved at her.

"Hi," she said, standing up to greet her as Dee entered. "I'm glad you could make it. Now, what would you like to drink? Have you eaten?"

"I can …" Dee began but the other woman shook her head.

"No, it's on me," she insisted. "I asked you here."

She decided to capitulate rather than argue. She watched as Miranda went up to the counter to order their drinks. She returned holding a small plate with a cake each.

"Oh," Dee said. "I didn't ... I'm on a diet."

Miranda frowned. "You're too thin as it is," she said.

"Well, Richard likes it."

"That man has his head so far up his backside he wouldn't know what a healthy weight is, and from what I can see, you're too thin. You must have lost at least ten kilos since you two got married."

Dee looked at her questioningly. Miranda just shook her head, her dark curls appearing to bounce. A loose tendril caught on her bottom lip and she casually brushed it away.

"There was a photo of you two in the society column in the Herald a few weeks after the wedding. I think you were at some charity auction."

Dee nodded, remembering there had been a photographer there.

"Anyway, the reason I ..." Miranda paused as the server placed their drinks on the table. She smiled at him. "Thank you."

"You're welcome." He was tall with dark blond hair cut in a spiky sort of style. As he began to turn away, Dee noticed he had a hoop earring in one ear and another one near the top of his ear. He offered her a friendly smile before walking off.

She stirred sweetener into her coffee. "You started to say something."

"I couldn't help noticing you talking to Phillip Mason at the Cup. You seemed very friendly."

She felt her stomach plummet a little. Maybe Richard had been right to be angry if that was the case. Miranda made some kind of gesture with her hand.

"No, no, please don't think I'm admonishing you. Phillip is very charming, and he really is a good man. In many ways, far better than Richard."

Dee frowned at her. "What do you mean?"

"Didn't Richard ever tell you why we split up?" the other woman asked with a frown.

"There was something about you cheating on him."

"I suppose he left out the fact that he was sleeping with his p.a.," Miranda replied. "And as far as the cheating was concerned, it may have looked like I left him for another man. I did leave with Phillip."

Dee stared at her, wide-eyed. "Is that why …?" she began.

Miranda went on to explain that the two men had once been good friends, but when she had left with Phillip, it had ended the friendship.

"The thing about Phillip is, I did love him, but I was never in love with him. I loved Richard, but I couldn't live with him. Not after …" She paused, dropping her gaze.

"What happened?" Dee asked. There had obviously been more to it than cheating.

"Richard is what some people would call a control freak. He's very old-school in that he thinks the women in his life should stay home and have babies. He's like that with all women, but he wouldn't dare say it to anyone who works for him because he knows he'll be slapped with a discrimination suit faster than he could blink."

Miranda continued by telling Dee that, when they had begun dating, he had controlled everything, from where they went, to what they did. Her own experience hadn't been that different, except for the dates when he'd taken her to places he thought she'd like. Looking back, however, it felt as if she had been manipulated there as well.

She listened with growing horror as she realised that once they had been married, Miranda had felt just as trapped in her marriage as Dee did.

"Then I got to know Phillip and he convinced me to leave Richard."

"Did you actually cheat on Richard?"

Miranda snorted. "That's the story he keeps telling, but I never slept with Phillip. In many ways, he was like the brother I never had. I met my husband through him and now, I couldn't be happier."

She leaned forward. "I want to tell you something. I haven't even told John yet." She lowered her voice to just above a whisper. "I'm pregnant. I found out a couple of days ago. I'm so excited! We've been trying for a baby forever!"

"Oh, wow. Congratulations," Dee told her, genuinely happy for the other woman.

The brunette beamed, her face practically glowing with happiness. "I can't wait to be a mum," she said. "Promise you won't say anything?"

"I won't," Dee promised.

It was rather odd that the woman, who had supposedly been happy organising parties and being a socialite while married to Richard, had found happiness in the most basic of things. Yet when she thought about her own life, having a child was something she had never really wanted for herself. When she had been talking with one of her former colleagues, just before the wedding, the woman had asked her about having children and she had told her she wasn't sure she wanted to be a mother.

"You'll change your mind," the other woman had said. She had meant it kindly, but the idea rankled a little. As if being a wife and mother were the only things that mattered in a woman's life.

"Richard wants me to have a baby," she said.

Miranda nodded. "If you want my advice, don't bring a child into this mess. You need to get out before that happens."

"I ... I don't know what to do. I don't have anywhere to go."

"Yes, you do," the other woman told her. "You can come and stay with us. In Cambridge."

Miranda sighed. "I'm worried he's going to do something. Richard never hit me, but then I left him before ..." Her eyes widened as Dee felt herself going red. She lifted her hand to her mouth in horror. "Oh no! He didn't!"

"It was in Melbourne," Dee said softly. "He said someone saw me talking to Phillip...and I..."

"No, don't you dare say this is your fault. I saw his little tantrum after the race. And let me tell you, it's not the first time he's done something like that. I can imagine what he was like as a little boy. His mother probably spoiled him rotten and never disciplined him."

"His mother hates me," Dee told her. "She called me a gold-digger."

"Oh, don't worry. She's called me much worse." Miranda put a hand over hers. "Dee, I can't tell you what to do, but I would hate myself if he hurt you and I just stood by and did nothing. Please, at least think about what I've said today."

Dee nodded. She found herself liking Richard's ex-wife, who was clearly happier than she had ever been in her first marriage.

*****

She returned home a couple of hours later knowing she had a lot to think about. Jenny had gone home for the day, but she had left a note on the kitchen counter. Meg had called saying she was in town for a couple of days and wanted to know if she and Richard were free for dinner the next evening. She was hesitant about asking her husband, given the tension that had been between them the past couple of weeks, but decided to wait and see what kind of mood he was in.

When he came home, she was surprised to see he had a bouquet of her favourite flowers in one hand. He pulled her into an enthusiastic hug before handing her the flowers.

"Darling, I know things have been rather tense the past couple of weeks and I just wanted to say I'm sorry. I've been acting like an arsehole lately. I was hoping I could make it up to you."

She bit her lip, then nodded. "We can talk about it over dinner."

"I was going to take you to your favourite restaurant," he replied with a smile.

"Jenny's already made dinner," she said, watching him closely. His smile faded a little as if he didn't like her answer. "You don't want it going to waste, do you?" she added with a smile.

His laugh sounded false. "No, you're right. Let's not waste it."

"We could go out tomorrow night," she said, moving to pour him a glass of wine. "Meg called and asked if we were free for dinner." Her friend had explained she and her boyfriend were in town to visit his parents for a couple of days and thought it was a good opportunity for a double date.

"I never did get a chance to meet this friend of yours," he said. "All right. Dinner tomorrow night it is."

She remained wary over dinner, even afterwards as Richard offered to watch a movie with her on one of the online streaming sites. He seemed to be in a good mood, asking about her day and what she was reading for her course, even appearing to be interested in the classic novel she was discussing in the forums.

She lay awake that night thinking about the evening. Despite everything Miranda had told her that afternoon, she was wondering if she was wrong about her husband. He seemed to be genuinely apologetic about his attitude and wanting to make it up to her. Yet, certain things niggled at her. The way his mask would drop a little when he couldn't get his own way. It felt too much like he was trying too hard to please her, making her wonder if he was just preparing to manipulate her once again. Like he was 'buttering her up.'

They slept late the next morning. Richard normally went off to work, even on weekends, but that particular day he seemed to be continuing his efforts to make it up to her, taking her shopping and not even complaining when she wanted to try on a dress she had seen in a shop window.

He took her to lunch at a café near the lagoon and they sat watching the ducks as they ate. Richard kept up a charming front, avoiding the subject of the night he had hit her.

Dee couldn't help noticing a tall dark-haired woman sitting at another table in the café. The woman kept looking over at them but averted her gaze when she realised Dee had seen her.

Dee got up from the table. Richard smiled up at her. "Everything okay, darling?" he asked.

"Yeah, I just need to go to the bathroom. I'll be back."

When she returned to the table, the woman was sitting beside Richard and the pair were chatting like old friends. It almost seemed like they had been flirting during the few minutes she had been gone. The other woman laughed at something Richard said, and it sounded so familiar, Dee couldn't help wondering where she had heard it before.

"Deanna, this is Kylie. She works with me at head office."

As she sat down, she noticed Kylie was wearing an extraordinarily strong perfume. She tried not to show her distaste. She normally wore light scents and it was far too strong for her. Dee tried to be friendly as Kylie chatted with them some more, but didn't like the way the woman sat so close to her husband, or the implied intimacy between them.

It wasn't until they were in the car returning to the house that she realised where she had heard the woman's laugh. It was when Richard had called her from his business trip. He had covered the mouthpiece of the phone to talk to someone. That someone had been Kylie. She was sure of it.

*****

Meg was supposed to arrive around six. Dee had already arranged for pre-dinner nibbles for them to enjoy with a few glasses of wine and was setting them out in the den when Richard came up behind her. He wrapped his arms around her waist and kissed her neck.

"You're turning into quite the hostess, my dear," he said.

She had no idea how to respond to that and just thanked him. He continued holding her. She laughed as if she was amused by his actions and pulled away.

"Honey, I need to finish this. Meg will be here with Andy in a few minutes."

He frowned. "Andy? Who's Andy?"

"Her boyfriend. I thought I told you about him. They've known each other for years but only started dating about two months before she went to Europe."

Andy was a sweet guy who liked to spoil Meg rotten. Because he worked as a freelance editor, he'd been able to visit her in Europe.

"So, you know this guy?"

"Only through Meg," she explained.

"But I thought you two went to high school together."

"We did. Andy's a couple of years younger than Meg. They met when she started her degree at university."

He tried to look sheepish. "Oh, sorry. Guess that makes me sound like a jealous husband, huh?"

She went to him and kissed him, hoping that would placate him. The doorbell rang and she quickly pulled away.

"That's them. I'll get the door."

"Why don't I get it?" he suggested. "You've done everything else." He turned away to go to the door. She frowned. He was never this accommodating. He had always claimed it was the hostess's job to greet guests if the housekeeper wasn't around.

She heard her friend greeting Richard enthusiastically and making the introductions, but she caught a note of surprise in her friend's tone. Meg came in, followed by a tall man with spiky blond hair and a dimpled smile.

Dee greeted Meg with a hug and let Andy kiss her on the cheek.

"You're looking well, Dee," Andy said.

Meg shot Richard a look. "Hope you're looking after my girl," she told him.

"Always," he quickly replied.

They sat down to chat. Andy and Richard soon began talking about the latest developments in technology. It was obvious Andy knew who Richard was, as it prompted a little debate between the two men over some business deal that he had never thought to tell her about.

Meg sipped her wine and raised her eyebrow at Dee, smirking as Andy seemed to win the debate. Instead of looking put-out, Richard appeared impressed with the other man's knowledge.

By the time they left for the restaurant, the two men looked to be getting along very well. They continued to chat all through dinner. Meg just looked amused.

It was late by the time the other couple dropped them back at the house. Dee immediately went to prepare for bed. Richard followed her, pulling at the knot in his tie.

"Andy seems to know a lot about technology companies."

Dee nodded. "I think he writes a column for a tech magazine when he's not busy with his editing projects. Meg says he has all the latest gadgets."

"Well, I would have expected nothing less from someone like him. Perhaps he'd like to write a column on Carter Tech."

She frowned. "I thought the lady from that business magazine was doing an article?" she asked.

Her husband smirked. "Well, I doubt she'd be able to do justice to the tech side of things. I mean, let's face it. Women don't know much about technology."

"I beg your pardon?" she said.

He hastily backtracked. "What I meant is, not many women have a lot of technical know-how."

"Just because I don't have the latest gadgets or am not confident on the interweb thingy, doesn't mean you can lump all women in the same category. I'm sure there are plenty of women who work in I.T and do very well at it."

He snorted. 'Interweb thingy?' He laughed.

Dee rolled her eyes at him and went to brush her teeth. She had said it that way on purpose, thinking if he was busy being amused at what she'd said, it might defuse any potential blow-up. She didn't want a repeat of what had happened over two weeks ago.

He came into the bathroom and leaned on the doorframe, watching her.

"You're right. I'm sorry. I'm sure there are plenty of women out there who are far better at working with technology than you."

Again, she rolled her eyes at him, spitting the toothpaste foam into the basin before rinsing her mouth out. She turned to leave the bathroom and he caught her arm.

"I had a good time tonight," he said. "I liked your friend. And her partner. They looked like a nice couple."

She reached up, practically standing on the balls of her feet to kiss him on the mouth.

"Thank you. For today and this evening. I enjoyed it too."

Chapter Twelve

The weeks passed and Christmas came and went. Richard's mother called a few days before the holiday, asking if they were coming down to Nelson again, but he refused, saying he had too much work on to take any time off. Dee had heard enough to know he had been working on some business deal, but it wasn't going well.

He had been great for a couple of days, giving her compliments, asking for her input on activities they should do together, and it had been nice not to have to walk on eggshells. Once things began to go badly at work, however, he reverted to his normal behaviour. Even the smallest slight and he was snapping at her. Dee resorted to only speaking when he addressed her directly. Jenny would shoot her concerned looks and she knew her friend was more worried than ever.

Miranda called now and again just to see how she was. Nothing was ever mentioned about her leaving Richard and going to stay with the other couple. As much as she liked the other woman, and valued the growing friendship, she didn't want to impose on them. She had a small amount of savings in her bank account from her old job, but it wouldn't be enough to support her for more than a couple of months.

One hot midsummer morning, Dee had woken with a headache and decided to lay in bed for a little while, hoping the pain would go away. She tried to go back to sleep but ended up kicking the cover off. The phone beside her bed rang shrilly, causing the pain in her head to go from a mild ache to feeling like someone was using a jackhammer on her brain.

She reached for the phone and felt for the button to answer the call.

"Hello?" she said listlessly.

"It's me. I'm sorry. I'm going to be working late."

She frowned. "Again? Richard, that's every night for the last week!"

"I know. It's just this new business plan." He paused. "Are you all right? You sound a bit off."

"Just a headache," she replied. "I'm fine. I've been lying in bed trying to sleep it off."

"Well, maybe you need to talk a walk. Get some fresh air."

"You're probably right. I'll see you tonight then."

She decided to get up and put on a pair of shorts and a loose top. She picked up her nightdress and went into the bathroom to put it into the laundry hamper. There were a few clothes in the hamper, and she picked them up, thinking Jenny could put them in the wash. As she lifted them, her nose was assailed by a very strong scent. Frowning, she sorted the clothes, trying to find the source of it. When she picked up Richard's cotton shirt, it reeked, making her feel dizzy and nauseous. At the same time, it seemed so familiar.

Dee went out into the kitchen, looking for Jenny, who was making tea. She looked up as Dee entered.

"I was just about to come and find you," she said with a smile. The smile swiftly dropped as she saw Dee's expression. "What's wrong?"

Without a word, Dee held out the shirt. Her friend's nose wrinkled. "Ugh, what is that? Is that perfume?"

"I think so."

"Ugh, it reeks. You don't wear anything that strong." Her eyes widened as she realised the implications. "He wouldn't!"

"I don't know," Dee said quietly. "Maybe he thought I wouldn't notice."

"Hoped is more like it," Jenny replied.

She wanted to call Miranda and ask her about the cheating but had no idea how to broach the subject. She sat down with Jenny, sipping her tea and wondering what to do.

"I don't want to accuse him and be wrong."

"But what if you're right?"

Dee sighed. "I just don't know."

"I think right now you need something to distract you. How would you feel about going to the movies with me tonight? I mean if he's working late ... The boys are with their dad for the weekend, so I don't have to be home early either. We could make a night of it."

She nodded. It would provide a distraction from the problem, she thought.

"You know, you're right," she said, feeling better having at least talked things over. It didn't solve the immediate problem but some time away from the house would help clear her head a little.

*****

They chose to eat at a local bar and grill before going to the movies at the local cinema complex. The movie was a period drama, an adaptation of one of the books Dee had been studying. While it wasn't a completely faithful adaptation it did help her understand some of the nuances in the novel that she had missed. She enjoyed the film and the company. Jenny had been right about one thing. The night out had done some good.

As they were in the car on their way home, Jenny stopped at a set of traffic lights. Idly looking through the side window, Dee saw a couple walking out of a restaurant. They had their arms around each other and were kissing. She stared in shock as she recognised the woman.

"Oh, my God," she exclaimed. It was Kylie, the woman who had been flirting with Richard in the café. Not only that, the man kissing her was Richard!

"What's wrong?" Jenny asked.

The lights had turned green and she urged her friend to drive on before her husband could see her. Given the couple's preoccupation with each other, she doubted he would, but she figured it was better to be safe than sorry.

She could barely breathe. Her breaths were coming in short, shallow gasps and she felt dizzy and sick all at once. Jenny stopped the car and turned to her.

"Breathe, sweetie. Come on. Deep breaths. It's all right. It's an anxiety attack. Just breathe." She demonstrated by inhaling slowly and blowing out her breaths. "Come on. Do it with me."

Dee copied her friend and, within a few minutes, she felt calmer.

"You okay?"

"I saw Richard. With … her."

Jenny frowned. "Her? You mean, the one with the perfume?"

She nodded. "I thought I'd smelled it before. Her name's Kylie. I met her a couple of months ago. They work together." She quickly explained what had happened on that occasion.

"Well, if that was her perfume on his shirt, then it's a safe bet they're not just 'working together'," Jenny told her. "Sweetie, I don't want to say I told you so, but …"

"I know. I just don't know what I'm going to do."

"You have to do something soon. Guys like him, when they hit you, it's never a one-off. Don't let the mask fool you. That's what they do. They get mad at you, blame it on an argument, or the drink, or whatever, then they'll apologise, tell you they'll do anything to make it up to you. They behave for a while and then, bam! It starts all over again."

"I wonder when this happened," Dee mused. Jenny frowned at her.

"What do you mean?"

"The cheating. I mean, if it's the same woman I'm thinking of, he was with her three months ago. Why didn't I notice?"

"Maybe he just forgot to hide the evidence?"

"The perfume's pretty strong," Dee told her friend. "You'd think I'd have noticed something before now."

"I guess it is. I don't know, sweetie. I don't have the answer."

Jenny drove her home, parking in the driveway. Dee looked at her.

"What should I do? I can't confront him."

"What do you want to do?" Jenny asked.

That was the problem. She just didn't know. If she confronted him with what she suspected, he might do one of two things. Either tell her she was imagining things or get angry and hit her again.

The question was, how long had it been going on? Had he been cheating with that woman all along? Who exactly was she? Richard had said they 'worked together,' but what did that really mean?

She pretended to be asleep when her husband came home. Fortunately, he either didn't notice she was still awake or chose not to check on her. She didn't sleep at all that night.

She had thought again about calling Miranda and asking her about Richard's cheating, but felt it best not to disturb the other woman, thinking she had enough to deal with. When Jenny came to work, shortly after Richard had left for the office, Dee still had no idea what she was going to do.

Jenny seemed to have, if not a solution, at least an idea about what to do next.

"Look, I know you're not confident on the computer, but maybe we can do a little research on her."

"We can do that?" Dee asked. Jenny looked a little amused by the question.

"Of course, we can. I'll help you."

They decided to set up the laptop in the family room and Jenny began searching through Carter Tech's website. She clicked on a link for company executives. Kylie's name and an image popped up.

Jenny studied her. "Really?" she said. "This is the woman he's cheating on you with?"

"Yes. Well, that's the woman I met."

"Well, let me tell you, you're far better looking than her." She peered at the screen. "Hmm, well, she's CFO and it says here she's been with the company for about five years."

Dee frowned. Miranda had left Richard more than five years ago. It was probably a good thing she hadn't talked to the other woman as she guessed she wouldn't know Kylie. She felt sick.

"I wonder if he's been seeing her all that time," she mused.

"Don't torture yourself, sweetie."

"I'm just … imagining him with her. Seeing them together, talking about me. Laughing about me. God, I am such a fool."

"No, you aren't," Jenny told her. "He's just very good at what he does."

"But you said he picked me because I was weak."

"No, I said he thought you were. There's a difference."

"What do I do now?"

"You have to leave. I mean, do you really think you can be with him, sleep with him, knowing what you know? If you were to confront him, what then?"

"That's what scares me," she told her friend. "If I confront him, what are the chances he's going to hurt me even worse."

Jenny nodded. Before she had the chance to say any more, the phone rang. She picked it up.

"Carter residence. Yes, she's right here."

With a frown, Jenny handed the phone over. "It's Wellington hospital," she said.

Dee stared at her friend before taking the phone. "Yes?"

"Mrs Carter, I'm afraid your father's been brought into the hospital." Despite her problems with her father, it was clear he still had her name down as his next-of-kin. She knew it had to be bad if the hospital was calling her. She figured they wouldn't for something minor. "He's had a serious heart attack."

"Oh, god," she exclaimed. "Thank you. I'll come as quick as I can."

She hung up and looked at Jenny. "My dad's had a heart attack. It's serious."

"You need to go, then. Go pack. You might be down there a while."

She nodded. "Yeah. Yeah. Um … what about … this?" she asked, gesturing to the laptop.

"Don't worry," Jenny said. "I'll fix it. I'll delete your cookies and history, so he won't ever know what you've been looking at."

She frowned, not understanding anything her friend had said. Jenny just grinned at her. "Yeah, who'd've thunk I'd know more about computers than you?"

"Ha ha ha."

She went to pack an overnight bag, not sure exactly what she would need. Since they hadn't given her much in the way of details, she had no idea just how serious it was or how long her father was going to be in the hospital for.

She grabbed her car keys. She was nervous about driving to Wellington but didn't see that she had much of a choice. Jenny was busy wiping down the counters in the kitchen but looked up.

"All right?"

Dee clutched the keys in her hand, feeling uncertain.

"No, not really, but … What do I tell Richard?"

She had thought about calling his cell phone and leaving a message but he often left it switched off. Especially if he was going to be in meetings all day. She was reluctant to even talk to him, knowing if she did, she might accuse him of the affair.

"You don't have to tell him anything. Just call his assistant and get her to pass on the message."

She nodded. "You're right." She picked up the phone and dialled his office. The assistant answered after a few rings.

"Hello, um, it's Dee, I mean, uh …" She shook herself mentally and told herself not to act like such a wimp. "This is Richard's wife."

"He's in a meeting." The woman's tone was cool. Dee had met her once and had the feeling the woman didn't like her at all.

"That doesn't matter. Could you please give him a message for me? Tell him that my father is in Wellington Hospital and I'm going down there. I don't know when I'll be back."

"I see." She had the feeling the other woman didn't believe her. She knew there was no way she could convince the assistant and wasn't about to argue with her. She remained polite, resisting the urge to tell the other woman off.

"Just please give him the message."

"All right." The assistant hung up abruptly.

Knowing she had done her best to let Richard know what was going on, Dee put the phone down. Jenny came around and hugged her.

"It's going to be okay," she said.

"You don't know that."

"No, I don't, but you just have to keep positive. Drive safe and call me when you get there."

"I will," she said, telling her friend to take a few days off. She didn't want Jenny to be around Richard if he came home in a temper.

She left the house, unsure of what awaited her.

Chapter Thirteen

The hospital staff had been very nice when she got there. Her father was in Intensive Care. He had been at work and had complained of feeling unwell before collapsing from what turned out to be a massive heart attack. The nurse tending him had quietly told her that he had almost died while doctors were trying to stabilise him. The prognosis wasn't good.

As soon as she was able to get a room at the motel the hospital staff had suggested she stay in, Dee phoned her mother. Linda was shocked and upset. Despite all the problems in their marriage, she still cared about Jack.

"I don't know if I can get a flight, honey," Linda told her, adding that it would take a day or so for her to organise her travel and even then the chances of her getting a flight quickly were slim. The airport in Rome was extremely busy. She wondered if there was even any point in coming home if Jack's health was that bad.

Linda had been reading a bestselling book about a woman's journey of self-discovery and had decided, if not to copy the woman's journey, to go on her own. She had begun her journey in Italy so she could visit many of the country's cultural sites. She hadn't planned where she was going to go next. Just 'wherever the wind took her.'

"It's okay, Mum." It wasn't really, but Dee knew it wouldn't change things. Her mother had made her choice.

"I still love your dad, you know," her mother said.

"I know, Mum. And I know you want to be here, but I don't think he'll know anyway. He's under heavy sedation."

She heard her mother give a quiet sob. "I know we had our problems, but ..."

"I know." She knew she was repeating herself but Dee had no idea what to say to her mother without accusing her of lying about her feelings.

"Well, keep me informed, honey. Is Richard with you?"

"No," she said. "He couldn't get time off work," she lied.

"He's the boss. Surely ..."

Dee cringed. She had made the excuse for her husband but wondered if he even cared enough to be with her when she needed support. That was even if the assistant had passed on the message. She had called twice more and left a message on his cell phone explaining everything.

Sighing, she went to bed, deciding to watch television until she got too sleepy to see the screen.

*****

She still hadn't heard from Richard after three days. The fact that he hadn't even called to find out where she was showed just how little he cared about her.

On her fourth day in the city, Dee had to go shopping for some essential items at the local supermarket, a short distance from the hospital. She was walking past the information kiosk at the hospital when she heard her name being called. She looked around.

"Phillip?"

Phillip Mason smiled at her. "I thought that was you."

"What are you doing here?" she asked.

"Visiting a friend. He's a patient." He peered interestedly at her. "I was just going to ask you the same thing."

"My dad," she said, gesturing toward the bank of elevators. "He had a heart attack."

The man's expression immediately changed to sympathy. "Oh, I'm so sorry. Is it bad?"

She nodded. "Yeah, it's pretty bad. I …" She felt a lump in her throat.

He took her hand. "Would you like to get a coffee with me?"

"Oh, I don't know. I …"

"It's just coffee, Dee. You look like you could use a break."

She sighed. "You're right. Okay. But just coffee."

Together they walked to the café which was a few metres away from the information kiosk. Phillip ordered them a coffee each and they sat at a table.

"I take it the prognosis isn't good?" Phillip asked gently.

"No, it's not. He almost died when they first brought him in and they're keeping him sedated. It's been four days."

"Does Richard know?"

"I left a message with his assistant," she said.

"And I take it he hasn't called. Insensitive bastard."

She shrugged. "I guess he has a lot on his plate. Some kind of business deal."

"You're far too generous," Phillip responded. "He should be here. At your side."

"I don't know. I mean, I would have thought he'd have called by now, just to see where I am."

"Well, if you were my wife, I would have dropped everything just to be here with you.

Family is more important than anything."

She caught a hint of regret in his voice.

"Sounds like you know something about that," she said.

He shrugged. "Well, my father wasn't really much of a father, to be honest. When he wasn't working, he was cheating on my mother."

She grimaced. The last thing she wanted to do was think about her suspicion that Richard was cheating on her. With her mind focused on her father's health troubles, she hadn't given any thought to what she was going to do once she had to return home. She knew she had to walk away from her marriage, but the question was, would Richard even let her? She knew enough about domestic abuse to realise he wasn't going to let her go that easily.

She continued to ponder the problem that night in the motel, going over everything that had happened since the day she'd met Richard. Had she perhaps done something to encourage his behaviour? Maybe there was something wrong with her, she thought. Why else would he feel the need to see someone else while he was still married to her? Why else would he hit her?

She slept late the next morning and grabbed the jeans she had worn the day before, pulling out a cotton top which was creased from sitting in the overnight bag for several days. She dressed and left the motel. She was just about at the information kiosk in the hospital when she was confronted by a familiar face. Julia Carter.

Richard's mother had a face like thunder. She was an attractive woman but the anger in her expression was almost ugly.

"So, this is where you disappeared to," the woman said. "Do you know my son has been calling all over trying to find out where you are? Look at you. For God's sake, do you have no pride, girl?"

Dee tried to get past the woman, but Julia thrust a hand out, grabbing her arm.

"Let go of me."

"You think I don't know what you're doing, you stupid girl? You think I don't know about you seeing other men behind my son's back?"

"I don't know what you're talking about," Dee told her coldly. She wasn't going to ask the woman what she was doing so far away from her own home.

"Don't pretend innocence with me, you little slut!"

"Excuse me?" she said, staring at the woman incredulously. "My father happens to be a patient in this hospital! And if you don't mind, I'd like to get up there and …"

"I picked it, you know. I told him you were only after his money. Now here you are."

"Here I am. At a hospital!"

"I saw you. Yesterday. With that 'friend' of Richard's."

"Having coffee."

"Don't think I don't know what else you were up to. You and him. At that motel."

Dee huffed noisily. "How dare you accuse me of cheating on Richard when he's the one doing the cheating!" The other woman's eyes widened. "Yeah, I saw. I know he's been sleeping with another woman."

Julia slapped her hard across the cheek. Dee glared at her.

"Well, I guess I know where he gets that from," she spat.

She spotted a security guard coming toward them. At the same time, her phone began to ring. She dug in her bag for it, but Julia slapped it away. It landed on the tiled floor but fortunately didn't break.

"Don't you answer that. I bet it's your boyfriend."

"Ma'am, is there a problem here?"

When Julia spoke, her tone was full of derision.

"This little slut is my daughter-in-law and I'll thank you …"

The security guard ignored her and spoke to Dee, picking up her phone and handing it to her. The ringing stopped.

"Ma'am, I saw this woman attack you. Are you all right?"

"I'm fine." She looked at her phone. It beeped, indicating she had a voicemail. While Julia began arguing with the security guard, Dee listened to the voicemail. It was the nurse in the ICU, asking her to come up to the ward as quickly as she could.

She turned back to the guard, who told her she could press charges on the assault.

"Thanks, but I'll let it go." She glared at her mother-in-law. "You stay the hell away from me! As for your son, I did tell him I was here. I left him a message and I've called his assistant. So, don't try and tell me he doesn't know where I am, and he's worried about me. I haven't had a single call from him. Not one. Now, if you don't mind, I need to go find out what's happened to my father."

She walked away from the hateful woman. She was breathing hard, so angry at the woman's accusations it took some time for her to calm down. She was still practically snorting like a raging bull when the elevator doors opened on the floor for ICU. The orderly who had been in the lift with her shot her a questioning look as they walked out together.

"Are you okay, miss? You look a bit upset." He was probably her father's age or older with grey hair and a kind face. Dee saw his enquiry was sincere.

"I will be," she said, offering a smile of apology. "Thanks."

"No problem. I saw that woman yelling at you. What a bitch, huh?"

"Yeah. She's my mother-in-law. She's never really liked me." He immediately looked contrite and apologised.

"I guess I should think before I open my big mouth."

"Oh, no, don't apologise. She was being, well … anyway. Thanks for the concern."

"Is there anything I can do to help?"

"No. I'm just here for my father."

He nodded. "I hope things get better for you, miss. I never like it when I see pretty girls looking so down."

"Thank you," she said, blushing at the compliment. "Take care."

She followed the corridor to the Intensive Care Unit. The nurse at the station quickly came out from behind the desk.

"We tried to call you," she said.

Dee immediately had the feeling the news wasn't good. There was an odd buzz of activity in the unit. "I'm sorry. I was … unavoidably detained. What's happened?" she asked, opting not to explain about Julia. It wasn't important. The woman wasn't worth the trouble.

"I'm so sorry, Dee," the nurse said. "Your father passed away a few minutes ago. It looks like he had another heart attack. They tried to revive him but …"

She stared at the woman, an odd buzzing noise in her head. She felt dizzy and sick at the same time. For a moment it felt like the walls had closed in on her. She couldn't see anything. It was as if her sight had suddenly gone and everything was muted.

When Dee regained her senses, she found herself sitting on a vinyl-covered bench. The nurse who had been talking to her handed her a cup of cool water.

"You fainted," she advised.

Dee frowned at her, confused. "I did? I've never fainted before."

"Well, it was a bit of a shock." She put a gentle hand on Dee's shoulder. "You look like you're getting your colour back now."

The woman suggested she check Dee's blood pressure and Dee submitted to the exam. As expected, her blood pressure was a little high, but not so high as to warrant a stay in the hospital.

Over the next day or so, she had to spend time making arrangements for her father's funeral and notifying everyone. She decided to leave the motel and spent those days in the small house that had been her home since she was fifteen. The landlord gave her time to sort out what meagre belongings were in the property, although there wasn't much. She found his bankcard but no statements and nothing to enlighten her about his financial status. Or whether there was a will.

*****

By the time she drove back to the house she shared with her husband, she was exhausted. She'd been gone a week and had not heard from him once. She had no idea what kind of mood he was in and wasn't willing to find out. She hesitated at the door, keys in hand when it was flung open. He had clearly been watching for her.

"Where the hell have you been?" Richard growled, stalking toward her, and slamming the front door closed.

"Didn't you get my message?" she asked. "I rang your assistant and told her to tell you. I've been in Wellington for the past week."

"I've been in meetings all week," he replied, still angry. "You went to see him, didn't you?"

She frowned at him. "Him, who?"

"Mason."

"He took me for a coffee, but that was it. Why didn't she pass on the message?"

"Just tell the truth, Deanna. Are you cheating on me?"

"What?"

He grabbed her with both arms, his grip bruising as he shook her.

"Tell me the goddamn truth!"

His breath smelled almost fetid. He had obviously been drinking, probably far too much than was good for his liver, and smoking cigars. His eyes were bloodshot.

"You're hurting me!" she said.

"I'll do more than that if you don't tell me what you were doing."

She tried pushing him away, but his grip was too strong. She remembered what had happened the last time they had been in this position, and there was no way she was going to let him do that to her again. She managed to get a knee between them, applying enough pressure on him to make him ease his grip.

"Let me go!"

"Tell me!"

"Why don't you go ask your assistant?" she shouted back at him. "She's the one you should be yelling at, not me. Or are you too busy sleeping with her to get your messages?"

He let her go, clearly shocked by her accusation. It was difficult to tell whether he was shocked at the thought that she had found him out or that she'd accused him.

"What did you say?" he asked.

She used the opportunity to back away from him and felt for the door handle, pulling it open. He saw what she was about to do and put his hand on the door as if to close it.

"You're not going anywhere," he asserted.

"You're drunk," she responded.

"Deanna, I'm warning you!'

"What are you going to do, Richard? Hit me? Lock me in my room? Get the hell away from me, you bastard!" She had no idea how, but she managed to push him away hard enough, so he stumbled and fell to the floor, landing on his backside.

She pulled the door all the way open and looked down at him.

"By the way, I was there to see my father. He was in the hospital."

"What?" He stared up at her, his eyes looking glazed.

"Go ahead. Go confirm it when you sober up. If you remember any of this."

He still appeared confused. "Your father?"

"He's dead, Richard. He had another heart attack in the hospital."

She didn't give him time to respond, walking out the door and shutting it behind her. The tears began to fall as she got back in the car. She had no idea what she was going to do or where she was going to go, but none of that mattered. All she knew was that she had to get away from him.

She was still crying hard as she drove along the main road toward town, thinking she should try to find a hotel room for the night. She knew she had some decisions to make but there was no way she was going back to him.

The rain, light before, became heavier, making it even more difficult for her to see where she was going. She activated the windshield wipers, the green of the traffic light shining into the car, creating odd patterns on the raindrops on the glass. Just as she began to cross the intersection, another vehicle came out of nowhere, smashing into her side. She was aware of a brief pain before passing out.

Chapter Fourteen

Waking up was difficult. Her eyes felt heavy and her head swam, making her feel as if the world was spinning. She could vaguely hear voices speaking but couldn't make out what was being said. Then for just a moment, everything came into sharp focus and she heard someone say: "She's lost the child."

All she could think was, child, what child? Confused and fighting sleep, she let the darkness take her down once more.

When she woke again, she slowly realised she was in a hospital bed. She was flat on her back on what felt like a firm surface, with very little give. The last time she had been in a hospital bed, she had been maybe ten or eleven and they had to remove her appendix.

Dee turned her head, but her vision was so blurry she wasn't sure what she was seeing. It just looked like some kind of blue screen. She guessed it was a curtain of some kind.

"You're awake!"

She turned her head in the opposite direction and realised Richard was sitting beside the bed. Even with her blurred vision, she could see he looked haggard. He was unshaven, his hair mussed as if he had just crawled out of bed.

"Wh …" Her mouth felt like sandpaper. She tried clearing her throat before speaking again. "What …"

He leaned over her. "No. Don't try to talk. Just lie still. I'll call the nurse."

Frowning, she could only lie there as he stood up and reached for something over her head. She still felt muddled and disoriented. There was a vague sensation of something being not quite right, a dull ache that she couldn't name.

She had no idea how long she lay there with her husband sitting beside her when the curtain moved, and a woman came in.

"Look who's finally awake," she said cheerily. She was wearing what seemed to be scrubs - a white top over trousers. Dee frowned at her as the woman began chattering, wheeling some sort of machine over and pressing buttons. She felt something tightening on her arm and realised it was the cuff of a sphygmomanometer. The cuff began to feel too tight, almost as if her circulation was being cut off. It stopped suddenly as the machine beeped, then slowly released. Dee felt a slight tingling as the blood began circulating. The nurse picked up a chart and made some notes before pulling at the Velcro keeping the cuff wrapped, pulling it off.

"All right. That's looking good. How are you feeling, Mrs Carter?"

"Um, I ...I don't know."

"That's all right. You're probably feeling a little disoriented. We'll get the doctor around to you soon to have a look at you."

The nurse continued to ask her questions. Was she hungry or thirsty? What were her pain levels and so on? Dee did her best to answer the woman, even though Richard tried to interject. As if he could answer for her, she thought.

The nurse left after a few minutes, giving Dee the chance to look at her husband. She made a quick decision not to mention the argument unless he mentioned it first. The last thing she wanted to do was throw accusations at him while she lay in a hospital bed.

"What happened?" she asked.

"You don't need to know."

She tried to prop herself up on her elbows and looked at him.

"Tell me."

"The police think the other driver ran a red light. They're checking the dashcam footage." He had a camera installed in the car when he'd bought it.

The other car had gone through the intersection, against the traffic light, and hit her vehicle side-on, smashing into her door. It had hit hard enough that she had to be cut out by emergency workers. She had suffered multiple contusions, although she was lucky not to have broken any bones. They had initially been concerned about a head injury, but the worst was that she had suffered a miscarriage. She had been heavily sedated overnight.

Dee stared at him. She hadn't even known she was pregnant. He continued talking, saying she was still young and healthy and could still have a child. His tone was almost flat and matter-of-fact as if her losing a child so early in the pregnancy was something they could just ignore and pretend had never happened.

He didn't appear to remember anything he had said to her last night, expressing what seemed to her to be confusion as to what she was doing driving into town so late. He hadn't even known about the accident until he had woken up that morning to several messages on his phone from both the police and the hospital.

Dee thought she could write it off as him having been too drunk to remember anything that had happened and that he'd possibly been drunk enough not to have heard the phone if it hadn't been for his whole attitude. His demeanour toward her was cool. He didn't appear to show any concern unless someone was around. Even when the doctor was around asking her questions about how she was feeling, he tried to answer for her. The doctor walked away after examining her and he followed. Dee could see the two men exchange a brief conversation before Richard returned to her bedside.

"The doctor says you're going to be fine," he said.

That told her nothing, she thought. He refused to tell her anything else. Not even when she could go home. After a few minutes, he made moves to leave.

"I have to go," he said. "I just wanted to make sure you were all right." She had the impression he had been putting on some kind of show of being concerned about her but, for whose benefit, she had no idea.

She was left alone. Dee still had no idea how long she had been unconscious, and Richard had refused to answer any of her questions. A nurse came in a little later to check on her and take her blood pressure again, opening the curtain so she could see into the ward. There were three other women in the room with her.

"Where are my glasses?" she asked the nurse.

"I'm afraid they were smashed in the accident, ma'am. Did you need something?"

"Did my … did Richard say anything about getting me new ones?"

"I don't know. I just came on shift."

With a heavy sigh, Dee returned to looking out the window. She couldn't read since she couldn't see and couldn't even watch any television. The other patients received visitors but no one else came to see her. There was nothing for her to do but sleep.

When she woke up it had already turned dark outside and she heard the rattle of trolleys up and down the corridor. It wasn't long before a woman came in carrying trays. Dee tried to sit up and looked hopefully over to the door, watching as the other patients were served their food. The third patient got her dinner and the staff member went out again. Dee looked anxiously toward the doorway, wondering if she had been somehow missed. She was starving.

To her relief, the woman came back in with a tray for her. Dee reached for it eagerly. The tray had two little plastic cups which looked to her like ice-cream and jelly. A dinner plate, covered with a plastic lid, sat in the middle of the tray. A bread roll was placed on a smaller plate with a small packet of butter. Dee picked up the roll. It was rock hard. Disappointed, she dropped it back on the plate and picked up the plastic lid. Even without her glasses, the dinner looked unappetising. It was a meat stew with a greyish-looking gravy. The meat was stringy and the only vegetable they had included was sliced carrot.

Deciding she had to at least try to eat something, Dee grasped her fork and took

some of the stew. The first mouthful was horrid. Whoever had made the gravy used too much salt and pepper, and the little cube of meat stuck to the roof of her mouth. She couldn't even chew. Revolted, she pushed it away.

She lay back, returning to staring toward the window. Richard still hadn't come back, and she doubted he would. She sniffled, tears prickling her eyes. She had never felt more alone. Her father was gone. Her mother had returned to wherever she had been before Dee had got married. She had no idea if any of her friends knew what had happened.

"Are you all right?"

She looked up. One of the other patients had got out of bed and come over to her. She was only a few years older than Dee, at a guess.

"I heard you crying," the woman said.

"I ..." She sighed. "I don't know."

"Where is your husband? Is he the man who was here this morning? Why isn't he here now?"

She shrugged. "Work, I guess."

"Oh no, that's not right. He should be here. Taking care of you."

That was the whole point, she thought. He wasn't there. Did he even care about her? For a man who claimed to love her, he was conspicuous by his absence.

The other woman, who introduced herself as Florence, came to sit beside her. Dee found herself confiding in her, voicing all her doubts about her husband and what had happened before the accident.

"Oh, honey, you need to leave him," Florence said.

One of the other patients spoke up from the bed. "Flo's right, babe. This guy sounds like a total tool. I mean, if I'd lost a baby, my boy wouldn't leave my side."

"I sure as hell wouldn't tolerate my guy cheating on me," the girl opposite her interjected.

"But … I don't have anywhere to go," she said.

"What about your friend?" Florence asked. "The tv reporter?"

"I can't …" she began, thinking she couldn't ask Meg for help. Her friend had her own life to lead.

"If you can't depend on your friends," the second woman responded, "who can you depend on?"

Richard still hadn't turned up by the next morning. The doctor came in on his rounds but didn't mention her husband at all. His manner was cool, as if he was talking to a broken-down car rather than a human being with real feelings.

"Now, you've had a miscarriage so you may experience some vaginal bleeding for a few days. It should be no more than a heavy period. I would advise avoiding any sexual activity for the next couple of weeks, just to prevent any infection." She wanted to ask him how he'd known about the miscarriage when she hadn't even known she was pregnant but he didn't appear to be the type to welcome questions. He looked at the figures on her chart and told her she was fit enough to go home, but she would have to take it easy.

Dee didn't want to go home, back to that house. That wasn't her home. Even after more than a year, she still felt like a stranger there.

She got out of bed with difficulty. While she hadn't felt more than a dull ache for most of the day before, her head had pounded most of the night and she had felt a few aches and pains in her torso from all the bruising. The doctor had at least told her that it would take a few days to heal.

The clothes she had been wearing the night of the accident had to be cut off her so she had nothing to wear. The nurse had told her the police had managed to get her bag from the wrecked car and she had a spare set of house keys, along with her purse, so she would be able to take a taxi home, but didn't know what to do about her clothing.

Resigned to leaving the hospital in the gown they had given her, she was stunned when she heard Jenny's voice in the corridor.

Jenny appeared in the doorway, her face registering shock. "Oh my god. Look at you!"

"Jenny? How?"

Her friend smiled, telling her the hospital had called the house, looking for Richard, telling him that she was able to be discharged. The news that there had been an accident had come as a shock to her friend, but Jenny assured the nurses she would take care of it. Once again, Dee thought, you've come to my rescue.

"Thank you," she said quietly.

Jenny wrapped an arm around her. "I brought some of your clothes." She held up a pair of loose pants and a long-sleeved shirt, explaining it was pouring with rain and it was one of those days where they would experience a sudden change in temperatures, despite it still being summer.

Dee struggled to dress in the clothes, relieved that she didn't have to leave the hospital in one of their gowns. By the time they were ready to go, the nurse had brought in the discharge papers, along with instructions for Dee to rest for a few days.

Jenny looked at the woman. "Can you leave instructions that her husband isn't to be told anything about this? All he needs to know is that she's been discharged."

The nurse nodded knowingly. It appeared that, despite Richard's efforts the previous day to make himself look like the caring husband, the staff weren't fooled. Dee wondered if the nurse had seen something she hadn't been aware of herself. "Of course. Be safe, my dear."

"Good luck, hon," the other women called out.

Jenny walked slowly with her downstairs, leaving her in the café so she could get her car.

"I can walk," Dee said in protest.

"No, you can't. Just stay put until I come and get you. Hear me?"

She tried to aim a glare in her friend's direction. "Did anyone ever tell you you're bossy?" she asked.

She heard a snicker from someone sitting at another table and figured they had caught the tail end of the conversation. Jenny just grinned.

"Yes. Now stay put."

Dee waited, realising her friend was right. Despite her protests, she was exhausted from the short walk downstairs. Her whole body was aching and stiff. She figured she was bruised all over. By the time her friend returned, she wasn't sure if she would be able to walk out to the car by herself.

"It's just out front," Jenny said. She helped Dee to her feet and continued to support her as they walked outside. A man dressed in a security guard's uniform nodded at Jenny as they made their way through the automatic doors, out through the main door and around to Jenny's Suzuki.

"What's that all about?" Dee asked.

"You're not supposed to just leave the car here, but I wasn't going to make you try to walk by yourself. You look like death warmed up, love."

"At least I'm alive to tell the tale," she said, wincing as the effort to sit in the passenger seat jolted every nerve-ending.

Jenny helped her get settled in the car and buckle her seat belt before getting in the driver's side.

She drove down the slope and stopped the car, waiting for traffic to clear.

"Are you hungry?" she asked, her gaze still on the approaching vehicles.

"A little. I didn't eat much dinner last night and I didn't feel like breakfast this morning."

"Do you want to go home, or do you want to stop somewhere? No, you're probably too sore."

"That isn't my home," Dee told her. "Not anymore."

Her friend glanced at her before turning to drive down toward the traffic lights.

"Are you sure?" she asked. "It's a big step."

"No. I'm not sure of anything. I just know I can't stay there."

"What about your stuff? Your clothes? Your passport?"

"I'm scared he'll be there. I don't want to go back there, Jenny. I'm afraid he'll do something worse to me, or he'll try to manipulate me into thinking he's done nothing wrong. He knows I know about his cheating."

Maybe he hadn't cheated with his assistant, she thought, but there was still Kylie. What hurts the most was that he hadn't even cared to visit her in the hospital or be there to take her home when she was ready to be discharged.

Jenny seemed to make a decision. "I'll take you to my place. It's small, but you can stay until you decide what to do. Maybe your friend Meg can help."

She nodded. That was probably the best plan. She knew she wasn't up to even a two-hour drive, since Meg usually lived in Wellington. Dee had called her friend when she'd been staying in the city. Meg had offered the use of her apartment but Dee had felt she needed to be closer to the hospital. She hadn't known her way around the city and was afraid she would get lost driving back and forth between Jenny's place and the hospital.

"What about your job?" she asked. "If he finds out …"

"Don't worry about that. You're more important. Besides, I handed in my notice as soon as I found out what a lying, cheating dick he is."

Dee sighed softly and looked out through the windscreen at the road. "Thank you. I don't know what I did to deserve a friend like you."

Jenny reached out and gently patted her knee. "You didn't have to do anything. You're a good person, Dee. Don't ever think that you don't deserve good things in your life."

Jenny drove her to the small two-bedroom home she shared with her two boys. It was almost the same style as the house Dee's father had rented. While it appeared to be a little cluttered with dozens of little knick-knacks, it had a welcoming feel to it ... far more welcoming than the home she'd spent her teenage years and early adulthood in.

Jenny made her a hot drink and warmed up some soup, keeping up a steady stream of chatter. Dee was grateful to the other woman but having had so little sleep the night before, it wasn't long before she was struggling to keep her eyes open.

She woke up to find it was dim inside the house. She could hear something playing softly in the background and realised it was the television. A boy was sitting on a couch opposite her. Dee blinked the sleep out of her eyes and sat up slowly, all too aware of the aches and pains she'd experienced earlier just from moving.

The boy looked up. "Oh, hey. Mum's out but she said if you needed anything I could get it for you."

Dee stared at him. She hadn't met Jenny's sons and wasn't sure which one was the eldest. All she remembered was that one was about sixteen and the other had just turned twelve. Jenny had told her that both boys were tall for their age.

"I'm Nat. Nathan," he said. The older boy, she thought.

"Oh." She winced as one of the bruises on her side made its presence felt.

"Are you okay?" Nat asked. "Mum said you had an accident."

"I'm all right," she said. "Just very sore."

"I can make you a cup of tea if you like. Gray's in our bedroom. He wanted to play his games out here, but Mum told him you were asleep and she didn't want him to wake you." He rolled his eyes in exasperation.

"A cup of tea would be nice. Thank you," she said.

He got up from the couch. "Don't move. I'll go make it."

"I can ..." she began, trying to get up. The boy shook his head.

"No, Mum said you needed to stay put. It's like when she got sick. She wasn't able to get out of bed for days and there was nobody to help her except me and Gray."

She nodded but didn't make any comment, not wanting to embarrass the boy. He cared about his mother. Jenny always spoke fondly of her first-born.

Nathan made them both a cup of tea and sat down once again, but didn't turn back to the television.

He asked her what happened in the accident.

"I don't remember much. Just this car coming out of nowhere."

"Were the cops chasing him?"

"I don't know, Nat. Maybe."

"Well, I hope he gets thrown in jail. Mum's always saying a licence is a privilege, not a right."

"She's correct," Dee told him.

He was quiet for a few minutes, sipping his tea. He looked at her again.

"How come you didn't want to go home?"

"Uh, I don't know if I …"

"Is he a bad man? Your husband, I mean? Mum says he's not a nice person. My dad's like that too. Mum thinks I don't remember, but when I was little, he hurt her badly. Put her in the hospital and everything. I was scared because she was going to have Gray … Graham then, and my grandma … she's dead now … she told me that Mum could have lost the baby. I hated my dad for that. I mean …"

Dee suddenly felt very strange. The hand holding her cup was shaking almost uncontrollably and she began to cry. Nat got up and sat beside her, wrapping an arm around her and patting her shoulder awkwardly. It was clear he didn't know what to say or do, but the effort was appreciated all the same.

She was still sobbing when Jenny came in.

"Nat, what happened?"

The boy explained to his mother that he'd just been chatting when Dee had begun crying. He got up, letting his mother sit down in his vacated spot.

"Sweetie, what is it? What's wrong?"

"I lost the baby," Dee told her, barely able to control her crying.

She felt Jenny's arms around her. "Oh, honey, it's okay. Just let it out."

It took a long time before Dee felt calm enough to talk to her friend. Nat had left the room and returned with a box of tissues.

"I didn't even know I was pregnant," she said. "Why do I feel like this? I mean, how can I miss something I didn't even know I had?"

"Well, I'm not a psychologist but I think that it's a completely normal reaction. Especially with everything else going on."

"Am I being punished?" Dee asked.

Jenny frowned. "Punished? Why would you think that? You didn't do anything wrong."

"I don't even know if I want children. Richard … He wanted me to have a baby. I think he knew. That I'd lost it, I mean. Is that why he was so cold to me in the hospital?"

Her friend shook her head. "You know the answer to that," she said gently. "This is nothing to do with you and everything to do with him. Don't do this to yourself, love. You have nothing to apologise for." She was quiet for a moment. "As I said, I don't know much about psychology, but I think in some way you're feeling a little guilty. But honey, having a baby, especially Richard's baby, is the last thing you need right now. I know that might sound a little insensitive and I'm sorry, but you'll understand in time. You just need to give yourself time to process everything right now."

She knew her friend meant well. On some level, Dee knew she was right, but she couldn't help feeling the loss anyway. Maybe she hadn't wanted to have a baby, especially not when she'd been so unsure about her marriage, but she still felt horrible for the child that could have been.

"I'm sorry," she said, glancing at Nat.

The teenager shook his head. "It's all good."

"Thank you for keeping me company and making the tea."

He smiled. "Anytime." He got up from the couch. "Mum, I'm gonna go do my homework."

"Okay, kiddo."

Dee turned to her friend with a smile as the boy left the room. "He's a good kid."

"Yeah, he is. So, how are you feeling?"

"Sore. Tired. I feel like I could sleep for a week."

Jenny nodded. "I stopped by the house and got some more of your things." She handed Dee her spare pair of glasses.

Dee looked at her with concern. "Richard ..."

"He wasn't there," her friend told her. "But there were bottles everywhere. Looks like he's been on a bender."

She couldn't even feign surprise. She'd seen him drunk a couple of times, apart from that night in Melbourne, and both times he'd got a little too amorous for her taste. Then of course was the other night when she'd come back after taking care of her father's affairs.

"Anyway, there was a message from Carol on the voicemail. She heard about your father."

"I guess I should give her a call. She'll be worried about me."

"Why don't we wait until after dinner," Jenny suggested. "You need to eat something."

She nodded. Her friend was right. She had eaten very little when they'd got back from the hospital and she'd barely eaten anything since she'd woken up in the ward. She had some decisions to make and couldn't do it on an empty stomach.

Jenny cooked a vegetarian meal for them. While Dee wasn't a big fan of vegetarian meals, her friend was good at making something that was not only nourishing but tasted great as well. Dee got to meet the younger boy who seemed a little reticent. Either that or he was just sulking, his older brother told her. He appeared to resent the fact that they had a guest as it interfered with his gaming time. At least Nat seemed to have a good head on his shoulders, she thought.

While her dinner settled, she decided to call Carol and tell her what had happened. When the older woman answered, she sounded a little off.

"Richard called, looking for you," Carol said. "He told me about the accident."

He'd been in a foul mood, accusing Carol of having done something or said something. It was odd that the first person he'd thought of calling would be the woman he'd often said was nothing but a gossip. Not to mention that he'd continually tried to discourage the friendship between them.

When Dee told her that she'd left Richard, the other woman didn't sound surprised.

"You're coming to stay with us and I won't hear a word of argument," she said. "Not one word, Dee. You need someone to look after you while you're recovering."

As much as Dee wanted to figure things out on her own, she knew she needed time to recover before she could stand on her own two feet. Her world had turned upside down in a matter of days and it wasn't something she could just automatically bounce back from. As wrong as it sounded, it felt good to have that decision taken out of her hands. At least for now.

"Okay," she said.

Chapter Fifteen

Carol arrived the next day with Stewart. While Carol went to talk to Jenny in the kitchen, Dee got a chance to talk to the older man. She quickly apologised to him, saying he didn't have to put his day on hold just for this.

"Nonsense," he said. "When Carol told me you had left Richard and that you were coming to stay with us, I wasn't going to let you try to talk her out of it." He was grinning to show he meant no offence but she stared at him anyway. Stewart had always struck her as kind of a quiet man who didn't say much, but when he did, he meant every word he spoke.

"I just …" She didn't know what to say in response. The man looked at her kindly.

"Dee, I have to tell you, I'm no fan of Richard's. I never have been. Frankly, I think the man is arrogant and, well, excuse me for saying it, full of shit." He grimaced. "Don't tell my darling Carol that I said that because she'll threaten to wash my mouth out."

Dee chuckled. It was the first time in the last few days she'd found any humour in anything.

"May I be candid with you, Deanna? Sorry, Dee. It suits you much better than your given name, I must say."

"Please."

"I always thought you were much too good for that jerk. And that's the nicest way I can put it. Richard is what many of us would like to call a man-child but in the worst possible sense of the word. Don't get me wrong. I have a very close friend who behaves like that sometimes, but he's one of the nicest guys you could ever meet. I have been concerned about you, love. I knew you were unhappy with the situation but Richard had you so tightly under his thumb that I had no idea how to broach the subject with you. That was why I was so glad you and Carol became friends."

"Me too," she said. "And I do appreciate everything you said. It's just … well, what if he …"

She had spent the night going over everything in her mind. Part of her knew she was just trying to find ways to excuse her husband's behaviour. There had, after all, been times when he had been good to her. Even almost loving. It made her think that perhaps she had read the situation completely wrong.

"No," Stewart told her when she voiced her doubts. "This is what people like him do. Trust me on this. He'll play the hard-done-by victim and put all the responsibility for everything on you."

Jenny and Carol came in. Her friend had her cell phone in hand.

"You've got a few missed calls," she said, explaining she'd switched it off to ensure Dee got as much rest as possible. Not that it had made much difference.

Dee looked at the list of missed calls. Most of them were from Richard. There was one from Miranda. The other woman had sent her a text message asking if she was okay.

Just as they were about to leave, the phone rang. Dee glanced at the screen. Richard. She looked at her friends.

"What do I do?" she asked.

"Ignore it," Stewart advised. "You're not ready to talk to him."

She nodded, switching the phone off and putting it in her purse. Carol picked up her bag and went with Stewart out to the car. Jenny hugged her.

"Keep in touch," she said. "Call me if you need anything."

Dee looked at her friend. She felt a little guilty that Jenny had given up her job as Richard's housekeeper because of her. The other woman seemed to interpret her expression.

"Don't," she said. "Don't ever think you're responsible for me giving up my job with Richard. He's not worth it, honey." They walked outside together. Dee was still feeling a little stiff and sore and needed a little support from her friend.

"But what will you do for money?" Dee asked.

Carol approached them. "Jenny and I had a little chat while you and Stewart were in the other room. I know someone who is looking for an assistant. I've already contacted them and they think Jenny would be perfect for the job." The two women smiled at each other. "It's not what you know, it's who you know. As soon as they heard she'd left her job with Richard, they were keen to meet with her. They figure if anyone can put up with him for more than two years, they have to be good."

Jenny laughed. "Well, let's not nominate me for sainthood just yet."

"All right, you three," Stewart called out. "Time to hustle." He opened the back door and gestured for Dee to get in. She felt a little apprehensive. The SUV was a little higher off the ground than Jenny's little car and with her bruises, she wasn't sure she was going to be able to get in. He seemed to sense that and helped her up.

Once settled, she felt comfortable enough to drift into a doze as they travelled.

*****

She had no idea how long she had been sleeping when she woke again to find they were approaching the city limits of Whanganui. She turned her head to gaze out the window as the vehicle continued along a busy road. She realised they were travelling west toward the coast. She remembered Carol had told her that they had a house in what was considered the wealthy side of the city.

After what she guessed was about fifteen minutes, Stewart turned down a narrow street. From the way the grass looked on each of the properties, Dee guessed they were fairly close to the ocean. It seemed to be the same kind of grass that grew in sandy soil. She could remember trying to walk barefoot through something similar as a child and complaining that her feet hurt. She'd always had sensitive feet and had never liked the feel of walking on rough ground.

Stewart helped her out of the SUV and walked with her to the house. From the outside, it appeared to be a fairly large house with a contemporary design. One of the exterior walls was a different shape which to her looked rather odd. She had never been a big fan of the angular design but she wasn't about to say so to her friends.

She was led inside to a large room with two overstuffed couches in tan suede. There were two armchairs set perpendicular to the couches in a similar design with a contrasting colour. Stewart took her bag and disappeared through another door.

"You just make yourself comfortable, love," Carol said. "I don't know about you, but I could do with a cuppa."

Dee nodded. "Some tea would be great." Carol nodded and left the room through a large doorway.

She sat down on one of the couches. She had thought she would be uncomfortable with the way the couch was designed but she immediately relaxed. She found herself drifting off once more, all the tension she hadn't realised she'd been feeling leaving her body.

"Here you go."

She looked up, surprised to realise Carol had brought out a tray with mugs of steaming hot tea and a plate of biscuits. Dee wondered if she'd dozed off again and sat up.

"Sorry," she said.

"For what?" the other woman asked.

"I don't know. I just … for the first time in days I feel like …"

Carol added sugar and milk to the tea and handed her a cup. "Like what, sweetie?"

"Like I can relax, I guess. Let go."

"Is there some reason why you think you shouldn't?" the other woman asked kindly.

"I don't know," she said with a sigh. "It's just … when I got back, after Dad … before that, even, I just …"

"Let me guess. You were always on tenterhooks. Waiting to see if he was going to do something. That's a natural reaction, Dee."

She bit her lip, wondering exactly how much Carol knew.

"Did you know Richard's ex-wife?"

Carol frowned. "Miranda? I only met her once or twice. She seemed like a lovely woman, but we didn't get much chance to talk. Richard was rather possessive of her, even then." She sipped her tea. "Stewart probably knows more about Miranda. She and Richard separated not long after Stewart and I got together." She looked in the direction Stewart had disappeared in. "Hon?"

Her partner appeared. "What's up?" he asked. "I was just getting Dee's room ready."

Carol grinned at him. "You are a treasure, love. We were just talking about Richard's ex."

"Oh, yes. Miranda." He came in and sat down next to Carol on the other couch. "I met her a few times at Richard's place. He held a few parties at that house," he added, saying they were mostly so he could show off to his business contacts. "When they first got married, she would look at him as if the sun shone out of him. Completely besotted. Then about, oh, right about the time we got together, I was at this dinner and I heard them fighting. I didn't hear everything, but it looked like she was accusing him of cheating on her. The poor girl seemed devastated."

Dee nodded, remembering that Miranda had told her she had loved Richard. She felt even more sympathy for Richard's former wife.

"I saw him with another woman," Dee told the couple. "It was the night before I went down to Wellington. I even met her once," she added, explaining about the day in the café.

"I'm so sorry," Stewart said. "I don't hold with things like infidelity. The trouble is Richard was brought up to believe that he could do what he liked and get away with it because he's rich. Julia was the same. Richard's father cheated on her and she seemed to think that gave her licence to do the same. That poor sod she's married to puts up with it. I'm at a loss as to why."

Again, Dee nodded, remembering Al, who did seem too nice to be married to someone like her.

"I don't understand people," she said. "I mean, why would he stay married to her if that's what she's like?"

"Sometimes I think it's a case of opposites attracting," Carol said. "People tell me I'm bossy and ask Stewart why he puts up with it."

Stewart looked at her with a smile. "You're not bossy," he said. "Sure, you like things a certain way but what's wrong with that? Besides, you have to be assertive to do what you do. I sure as hell couldn't teach teenagers."

Dee sipped her now lukewarm tea and smiled at the older couple as they exchanged looks of deep affection.

She found herself telling them about her meeting with Miranda at the Melbourne Cup and what had happened afterwards. Carol looked shocked and Stewart looked as if he wanted to punch something.

"You really should think about pressing charges," he advised.

Dee frowned at him. "Why?"

"Because what he did to you was rape. Dee, this isn't forty years ago when such things were never even considered illegal. Forcing intercourse, even with your spouse, is still rape." He glanced at Carol. "I think we should talk to Tom."

"Who's Tom?" Dee asked.

"Tom Harding. He's a lawyer," Carol explained. "He's also a close family friend." She looked at Stewart. "Do you think he'll take on the case?"

Stewart nodded. "He's dealt with someone like Richard before." He turned to look at Dee. "We're not going to let Richard get away with this."

Dee went to bed that night thinking over everything the couple had said to her. She had never even considered that she could press charges against Richard for what he'd done to her that night. She wondered if the police would even believe her since she hadn't reported it after it happened. She had read enough to know that some women chose not to report any cases of abuse for fear they would be blamed for the abuse. As wrong as it was, it was still fairly common, from what she'd heard.

She lay on her back, staring into the darkness above her. She couldn't help going over everything in her mind. She'd spent most of her life trying to be what everyone else wanted her to be. Her father had tried to control her life and she'd defied him to marry a man who, in the end, had been just as controlling. Even though he'd claimed to love her.

Yet at the same time, she felt guilty. That perhaps if she'd been a better wife, like being more social and more confident, Richard might not have done the things he did to her. She knew she was trying to justify his behaviour, but the failure of her marriage still hurt. Part of her wondered if she'd been more loving toward her husband, if she'd truly loved him, then things would have been different.

She found herself thinking about the baby. Richard had wanted to have a child with her. Even with her doubts about her husband, she couldn't help thinking the loss of the baby had been some kind of punishment. That somehow fate had decided to right some kind of wrong she'd done her husband by taking away the one thing that might have changed everything between them.

She cried herself to sleep that night.

When she got up the next morning, she could tell from the looks between Stewart and Carol that they had heard her the night before. She ate her breakfast without saying anything to either one of them. Stewart got up from the breakfast bar and put his dishes in the sink.

"Sorry, I have an early meeting. The CEO wants to talk to the execs about the restructuring."

Dee frowned. "Restructuring? Is your company in trouble?"

Stewart shook his head. "Not that I know of. And I should since I'm the one in charge of the finances. No, I think it's just looking at where some divisions could do with some changes. Upgrading. That sort of thing." He smiled at her. "Anyway, Tom's number is on the notepad by the phone." He shot Carol a look and she nodded. "See you tonight, love."

Dee looked at Carol, seeing the serious look on the older woman's face.

"Finish your breakfast, sweetie. And then I think we should have a little chat."

She bit her lip but nodded. She finished her toast and grabbed her cup, following Carol into the other room.

"How are you feeling?"

"Okay. It's getting better."

Carol nodded. She was quiet for a few moments before speaking in a gentle tone.

"We heard you last night."

Dee bit her lip again. "I guessed that from your faces this morning. I just … I kept thinking about things. Going round and round in my head."

"Like what?"

She shrugged. "I don't know. Maybe if I'd been …"

"No, you don't," Carol replied, interrupting her before she could say any more. "Don't think I don't know what this is about. You're trying to justify his behaviour. Dee, honey, nothing and I mean nothing you could ever do could justify what he did to you." She paused. "Do you think Stewart tries to control me? Manipulate me?"

"No, but …"

The older woman shook her head. "No buts. Believe me, we've had our fights. But he's never done anything to hurt me. He's never hit me. Even when I've made him angry. Let me tell you something about Stewart. He's no wimp. Sure, he can act like an idiot at times. But then, so can I. And he's never afraid to call me on it. So I don't want to hear that maybe if you'd done something he wanted you to do then he wouldn't have hurt you the way he did."

"He wanted me to have a baby," she said. "We'd never even talked about having children and he …"

Carol gazed at her. "Who made all the decisions in your relationship?"

"Um, he did."

"Who decided where you would go and what you would do?"

She didn't even need to think about it. Every social event they'd gone to had been something Richard had either been invited to or he'd planned it himself. Every trip they had taken had been something he'd instigated. The only time they'd done something she wanted to do was the night they'd gone out with Meg and her boyfriend. Even then, Richard had been the one to choose the restaurant where they'd gone to dinner.

All the gifts he'd given her - the flowers, the clothes - they had all been used as just another way for him to manipulate her into getting what he wanted.

She told Carol what had happened in the hospital and her suspicions that Richard had only been there for show.

"I think he was angry at me for losing the baby. I didn't even know I was pregnant."

Her friend nodded. "I'm assuming that it was still fairly early in the pregnancy."

"But why didn't I know? I mean, surely I would have at least started to suspect something."

"One of the women I worked with at the school. She was a few years younger than I, but she had fertility issues. She had been feeling off for weeks but didn't know why. Then she went to the doctor and was told she was four months' pregnant. She had no idea."

Dee sighed. "I don't know. I still think I should have known. Like there should have been signs." Yet how had the doctors known?

Carol started to say something but was interrupted by the phone ringing. She picked it up.

"Hello?" She quickly glanced at Dee and shot her a cautionary look. "Richard. No, I haven't heard from her. Excuse me? Don't speak to me like that. I told you I haven't seen Deanna or heard from her. Why would I lie? I'm just as worried about her as you are. Fine. You do that."

She hung up the phone and looked once again at Dee. "Well, that was …pleasant."

"What did he say?"

"He called me a liar and threatened to call the police."

Dee shot her friend a half-smile. Technically she was lying but it was for a good cause.

"What were you going to say before the phone rang?"

"Just that I imagine the doctors would have ordered blood tests after the accident and your blood might still have shown the presence of some pregnancy hormones. I've never done any medical training, but I think it would be standard procedure."

"Do you think they would have … I mean, how would they have known about the miscarriage? If I was only a couple of months along …"

"I think that's something you'd have to ask your doctor, honey."

"I don't know. I mean, it bothers me. Why am I so upset about this? I didn't even know so how can I be sad for something I didn't know existed?"

"I'm guessing, but for one, I think your body might still feel pregnant. Besides, why shouldn't you be upset? You're allowed to grieve. It's not just about the baby you lost. It's everything."

That made sense, she thought. She was grieving for her failed marriage, for what could have been. They continued to talk about what had happened both before her marriage and afterwards.

"Do you think he ever loved me?" she asked.

Carol looked thoughtful. "I don't know. Perhaps he did, in his own screwed up sense of it. Like your father. He said he loved you and I think he did but in a suffocating way. I don't know if it's a male thing. But with Richard, I feel he still has a very backwards view about women and their place in the world." She scowled. "That man seems permanently stuck in the Dark Ages."

"I guess."

"Honey, I know you're hurting, but you've done a good thing by walking away. If you hadn't, I fear things would have gotten much worse. Imagine if you hadn't miscarried!"

She hadn't thought of that. What if she had ended up having the baby and was still living with Richard?

"This is just a theory, but I think Richard planned to get you pregnant and make sure you could never leave."

Dee frowned at her friend. "What do you mean?"

"Well, I'm not an expert on these things, but one of the hardest things for women in violent relationships is the fear that one day their husband, partner or whatever will eventually take their issues out on the children. Or that if they try to leave, hubby will use the children against her."

"Do they really do that?"

Carol nodded. "I taught this girl. Her parents were in the middle of a bitter divorce. Her mother told the court he beat her. He threatened to kill her and their daughter if she didn't go back. The poor child was living in fear of her father finding them and carrying out his threat."

Dee felt sick. Imagine, she thought, if she had stayed in her sham of a marriage, had children with him and then tried to leave him several years later. As much as she had wanted to deny it in the beginning, she wondered if Richard would have become much worse as the years went on."

"It takes a lot to walk away. Maybe what happened with your father, and then with the accident, was the wake-up call you needed."

"Maybe it was," she said. "I still should have known though. I mean there were so many times he acted like …"

"Don't," Carol said gently. "Don't do that to yourself. There is nothing wrong with wanting a little security. Besides, many women go through this. They'll talk about red flags they've seen or things they might have done that provoked their partner's reaction. The truth is, some women do see those things and think that maybe they can fix things."

"You sound like you know a lot about this stuff," Dee told her.

"Well, I'll let you in on a little secret. Stewart knows, but no one else does. Not even Helen. I was in that kind of relationship once, but like you, I dared to get out before things got any worse. And I did think I could change him. Save him. I went to a support group and I found out that many women felt the same way I did. Some of them didn't get out in time." She smiled. "We're the lucky ones, Dee. We had our eyes opened before things got any worse."

Dee was grateful to her friends for their support, but as her body recovered from the accident, she began to feel she couldn't continue to impose on them forever. Carol, however, wouldn't hear of her leaving.

"You can't go back to Petone," she said. "Your father's gone and the house has probably been rented to someone else."

Dee realised her friend was right. She had nowhere else to go. She had already met with the solicitor who had written up the separation papers. It was unfortunate that the process of law was rather slow and she had to be legally separated from her husband for two years before she could divorce him.

"It's hard, I know," Miranda told her over the phone one morning. "Richard tried to fight me over the separation and I was so worried it would delay things."

Dee sighed. "Tom said even if I could prove he cheated, he could say anything he liked about me in court and get away with it."

"Yeah, I know. Unfortunately, he's of the ilk that believes money can get him anything he wants. What about what Julia did to you at the hospital?"

"That still doesn't prove the abuse from him," Dee pointed out. Stewart and Carol had offered to provide witness testimony, should it ever come to that. "I don't know, I ..." She stopped, hearing loud voices in the hallway.

"Where is she? I know she's here and I demand to see her!"

"Oh, God. He's here!"

Miranda gasped. "How did he even know where you were?"

"I don't know. What should I do?"

The answer was taken out of her hands when the door to the family room crashed against the wall. She looked up and stared at the face of her husband. It was red with anger, almost ugly with the intensity of his emotions.

"Deanna!"

He strode over, his hand reaching out as if to grab her. She dropped the phone and quickly backed away.

"Don't you dare, Carter!" Stewart called out from the doorway behind Richard. "If you so much as lay one hand on her, I'll be calling the police."

Dee stared at him. She knew if she looked away, he would win.

"Stay away from me, Richard," she told him quietly.

"Deanna, don't you know I've been calling all over trying to find you. You disappeared from the hospital, you weren't answering my phone calls. Darling, I've been so worried about you."

"Stop it," she said. "Don't try to manipulate me. It won't work."

"I don't know what you're talking about. Deanna, please, this has all been some kind of mistake. Someone has been telling you lies about me."

"Really? So me seeing you with … whatshername? Kylie? That was a lie? I saw it with my own eyes, Richard. How long have you been playing me, huh?"

"I don't know what you saw, but it wasn't me. I've never …"

She glared at him. "Really? Never? What about the perfume on your clothes? The only way that could get there would be if you were getting up close and personal with someone. And don't try to lie your way out of it, or tell me it was my perfume. I would never wear anything like that."

He appeared to have no answer to that.

"So, that's it? I've been tried and convicted without a single chance to defend myself?"

"You were so quick to believe I'd been cheating on you, even though I told you I'd been at the hospital for days with my father."

"My mother saw you with Mason."

"And you automatically assume that means that I was lying to you about my father?"

"I never …"

"Never what? Three days I tried calling you. I left messages, but you claim you never got them."

"I didn't. I don't know why …"

Yet his gaze faltered and she knew he was lying.

"How is it you were so quick to believe your mother, someone you claim to hate, yet you wouldn't believe me, someone you claim to love?" she accused.

"I'm sorry. My mother …"

"I don't care about your mother, Richard. The woman assaulted me and, because of her, I never got the chance to say goodbye to my father."

"Your father never cared about you," he said.

"I don't care. Leave, Richard. You have no right to be here."

He reached for her again, but she thrust her arm out, pushing his arm away and again told him to leave.

"You heard her," Stewart told him.

He glowered at her. "So, that's it? You're not even going to give me a chance to defend myself, are you?"

"Nope," she said shortly.

"You'll change your mind. Just remember that you signed a prenup, Deanna. That means you get nothing. You hear me?"

"I don't want anything from you," she said.

Two more people appeared in the doorway. Dee realised they were police officers. One male, one female.

"Sir, you've been asked to leave," the woman told Richard. "Unless you would like to leave in handcuffs, I suggest you comply."

He turned to glare at her but seemed to quickly realise she meant business. The other constable spoke to Stewart.

"Your wife called us," he said. Stewart didn't bother correcting the man about Carol and just nodded.

"Thank you. I suppose Carol explained everything?"

"Yes, she did," the woman explained. She turned once more to Richard. "What's your response, sir?"

"All right. I'm leaving," Richard said with a growl. "But don't think this is over, Deanna. I will fight this divorce. You can count on that."

As soon as he was gone, Dee felt all the breath she hadn't realised she'd been holding leave her body. Stewart hugged her.

"You were great," he said. "I'm proud of you for standing up to him."

She pressed a shaking hand to her suddenly pounding head and smiled gratefully at the older man, telling him she probably wouldn't have been so brave if he hadn't been there. Who knew what Richard would have done to her if they'd been alone?

Chapter Sixteen

Richard continued calling over the next few days. While he made no further attempts to get into the house, Stewart told Dee his car was parked on the road and he was watching, clearly waiting for any opportunity to try his luck once more.

Dee's solicitor advised her to apply for a protection order. Especially after he heard what had happened in Melbourne. The lawyer appeared before the judge on her behalf, which was a relief as Dee hadn't wanted to face Richard in court.

The judge had read the application and granted the order, Tom told her. She was safe where she was and it meant Richard couldn't set foot on the property. He was also expected to attend a domestic violence programme.

"What happens if he refuses to comply with the order?" Dee asked, speaking with Tom over the phone.

"He still has a chance to give his side of the story. Given what you've told me and what I've heard from others, he won't have much of a defence. If he refuses to attend the programme, he could face jail time."

She had a feeling that wouldn't change anything where Richard was concerned. He had always acted as if mud wouldn't stick because he was rich. She figured his lawyer would try to get him out of the compulsory programme.

"No. I know," Tom said when she voiced her doubts. "But at least Carol's looking after you. Now, what do you plan to do about money?"

"Um, I don't know. I guess I'll have to apply for the benefit," she said. She explained to Tom that she had some money invested in retirement savings but Richard had taken control of that.

"I'll sort that out," he replied, telling her he would sort out the benefit as well. "Have you talked to your father's lawyer about the estate?"

She frowned. As far as she knew, there had been nothing for her father to leave. She hadn't got around to talking to his bank, since the accident had happened within days of his death and she hadn't been able to sort out all his affairs.

"I don't think he had a lawyer," she said. "I found his bank card, but no papers or anything. I don't even know if he left a will." She sighed. "What with everything else going on, I just haven't had a chance to do anything about it."

"Well, let me look into that for you. There should be something filed with Public Trust, at least. You realise that if he did have any assets, but no will, it could be very complicated."

She nodded. "I know. But I don't think there's anything I can do about that."

"What about your mother? Would she know if your father left anything?"

"I asked her about that, but she and my dad hadn't talked in years, so she didn't know anything."

"Well, I'll follow up with her. In the meantime, sit tight."

She sighed, quietly confessing to the lawyer that she felt guilty for the fact that her friends were doing everything for her and she had no way of paying them back. The lawyer told her not to worry about that. As far as Carol was concerned, there was no expectation for Dee to pay anything back and that the best thing for her to do was just get her life together. The cost of supporting her for a few weeks was worth it if it meant she was away from Richard.

After a month of living with her friends, she began to feel strong enough in herself to think about her future. While she wasn't getting very much in the way of a benefit, she was able to pay something toward her living expenses and save the rest. She hadn't heard anything from the lawyer but hadn't expected any news on that front. The separation papers had been filed and the protection order was in place.

Dee sat curled up on the window seat in the conservatory, her bare feet propped up on the cushion as she looked over the garden. Some of the trees had begun to drop their leaves, those remaining having turned a golden brown. The sun was still bright, a golden haze seeming to drift over the foliage. It was peaceful.

"Here you are," Carol said brightly, entering the room. "I thought you'd like a cup of tea."

Dee smiled at her friend. "Thank you."

"What have you been doing?"

She glanced at the book she'd left open on the table beside her. She'd begun reading the works of Jane Austen but just couldn't seem to get into it.

"I've just been sitting here, contemplating. It's so pretty right now."

"I love autumn," Carol said with a happy sigh. "Early autumn, anyway. Summer's wonderful but there's something almost magical about the colours when the leaves start to turn."

Dee stirred her tea, moving to sit upright. "I've been doing a lot of thinking. I probably can't afford it right now, but I was thinking about maybe trying to enrol in a course. I've had a lot of time to think about my life, what I want to do now I'm on my own. For the first time in my life, I'm not beholden to anyone."

She'd thought a lot about the way she'd grown up. Everything she had done was always for someone else. She had got a job at the fast-food restaurant to get time away from her father. She had taken the job at Carter Tech to please him. She had then resigned the job to please Richard. Maybe she had married Richard to defy her father, but that had been exchanging one bad situation for another.

"I want to do something for me, you know?"

"Have you thought about what you want to study?"

She nodded. "Photography," she said.

"I'm so proud of you, Dee. I think it's wonderful."

"I have to do some research. Figure out where I want to go. I don't want to go back to Palmy. Not if there's a chance I could run into Richard."

"No, you're right. I have a friend who runs a course in photography at Wintec. You might be able to get into the second semester."

"Wintec. That's in Hamilton, isn't it?"

Carol nodded. "You'd have to find a place up there. How would you get around?"

"I guess I could always go and stay with Miranda. She did offer."

"Sure, but they live south of Cambridge. It's a long way to go if you don't have a car."

That was true, she thought. While the car Richard had given her was insured, the lawyer had told her the man had already claimed the insurance and she was unlikely to get anything from it.

Since there were at least three months before the second semester began, Carol suggested she continue to research and, in the meantime, she would talk to her friend and see what he thought.

A few days later, Tom came to the house with some papers in hand. He was smiling.

"I thought you'd want to hear the news in person," he said.

"What is it?" Dee asked as Carol went to make them all a cup of tea.

"Your father's life insurance," he said. "It took a while. Your father's papers were a mess. My assistant pretty much hates me right now," he added with a wry grin. "But we found the policy and contacted the company. Now, the issue is, we were unable to find a will. The law requires anyone appointed as an executor to investigate and we put a notice in the local paper. That's why it's taken so long to get back to you."

"So, what happened?"

"No one came forward. It looks like your father died intestate." Dee had heard of the term but didn't know what it meant for her.

"Which means?"

"The court appoints an administrator. In this case, that would be you or your mother. There's one small kink."

"What would that be?"

"Richard's solicitor has applied to the court to act as administrator on your father's estate."

She stared at him. Was Richard trying to get control of whatever assets her father had?

"How can he do that?"

"He's trying to claim that because you were married at the time of your father's death, it's community property. Don't worry," Tom said, gesturing with his hands. "I've already filed a counter-claim with the court and given them a detailed account of what's been going on in your marriage. He has no right to it. Now, while the insurance policy isn't a substantial amount, it's still a good amount of money to give you a little breathing room. The only problem is that even once the court has made a decision, there's a waiting period of about six months." He explained it was to ensure that no one else tried to make a claim on the estate.

He seemed fairly certain Richard had no claim whatsoever to the money from her father's insurance policy, given the separation had occurred around the same time. Not to mention, Tom added, that because of the waiting period, the claim wouldn't be valid.

"Well, that's good, I guess."

He did have some other news. He had applied for control of her retirement funds to be returned to her control. She could withdraw them or transfer them to another account so Richard couldn't try to regain access.

"I talked to a friend of mine in the police and they suggested sending an investigator to talk to the hotel in Melbourne."

"How is that going to help prove what he did to me?"

"Well, it won't, necessarily, but the staff might have heard something or they might have seen Richard's behaviour toward you. You did say he'd been drinking heavily that night. I know it's not much consolation but it will still help your case. And don't worry about the expenses. Stew's picking up the tab on this." She wanted to protest, thinking it was going to cost an awful lot of money, between the settling of her father's estate, the divorce and hiring an investigator, but Carol insisted it was fine.

As grateful as she was to her friends for helping her, Dee knew it was time she learnt to stand on her own two feet. That night, during dinner, she broached the subject with them.

"I've decided I need to find a job and get a place of my own," she said. "At least until I can enrol full time in a photography course."

"Are you sure?" Carol asked her. "You know we haven't minded helping you."

"I'm sure," she said, even as Stewart placed a gentle hand on his partner's arm.

"Sweetheart, she's right. She needs to learn to stand on her own two feet."

Dee nodded. "I've been thinking a lot about this. I did everything to please my dad and then I did everything to try and please Richard. I realise now that nothing was ever going to please either of them." She told the couple she hadn't made any firm decisions on where she was going to go, but she still had time to do a little research on the courses available and choose what suited her best.

She was surprised, a couple of weeks later, when Stewart handed her a box. To her delight, she saw it was a DSLR camera. It looked a little beaten up but it had everything she would need to begin learning the basics of photography.

"A friend of mine works as a professional photographer," the older man told her. "When I told him about you, he gave me this. It was the best model on the market at the time and he learnt his trade with it. He's more than happy to pass it on."

"Thank you," she said with a smile. She hadn't given much thought to buying her equipment but realised she would need it during the course.

Stewart told her his friend had a studio in Hamilton, not far from the inner city campus of the Waikato Institute of Technology.

"If you're interested, he's more than happy to give you some pointers. He also has a few contacts if you're thinking about moving up there."

Dee had done a little bit of research and decided the Wintec course was her best option. She'd also found a place to live. She would be sharing a house with three others, but they were all close to her own age and were students. The house had been let fully furnished so she knew she wouldn't have to worry about trying to find her own furniture. Best of all, it was only about ten minutes' walk from the campus.

She'd applied for a couple of jobs at retail outlets. She was yet to hear about any interviews but figured it was something she could worry about once she got up there. She had enough money saved to be able to pay a bond and any extras she would need until she could start earning an income.

A week later, Dee packed her meagre belongings and left the guest room. She walked out to the kitchen to find Carol looking as if she was about to lose her best friend.

The older woman sighed. "I know why you have to go, sweetie, I just …"

"I know," Dee said softly. "But it's not like I'm going to drop off the face of the Earth."

"I've loved having you here."

"I've loved being here," Dee responded. "Thank you," she added, hugging her friend. "For everything."

She glanced at the clock. "It's time to go. My bus leaves in an hour."

Stewart nodded, picking up the keys. "Come on, girls," he said. "You can say your goodbyes at the bus depot."

The drive into town took roughly twenty minutes. Dee sat quietly in the back of the car. Part of her didn't want to say goodbye. Carol and Stewart had been amazing and she knew no matter what, they would always be there for her.

A small group of people were waiting at the depot when Stewart pulled up and parked the car. They got out, making their way to the small shelter. A cold wind was blowing from the riverside, which was just a few short metres away, making them shiver. Dee pulled her jacket around her and shifted the strap of her bag.

Carol turned to her, helping her with the heavy bag.

"Have you got everything?" she asked.

Dee nodded. "Yes."

"Dee …"

"Carol, I … Just thank you. I don't know what I would have done without you. Both of you," she added, smiling at Stewart.

"You're a survivor, Dee. Don't ever believe anything different."

Stewart nodded. "You'll find a lot of people like Richard in this world. The point is, you didn't let him wear you down. You decided you didn't have to put up with his bull, and I'm proud of you for that."

Dee could see a bus approaching. "I think that's my bus," she said.

"Now, remember, we'll be up there in a couple of months," Carol told her.

She nodded. They had made plans to go up for a small charity event and had promised to drop in on her at the same time.

The bus pulled in and the driver got out. He disappeared inside the information centre.

"You don't have to wait," Dee told the couple. "It's freezing. I don't want you both to get chills."

"All right." Carol hugged her. "You take care of yourself."

Stewart grinned and embraced her. "You be good, kiddo."

She brushed her hair behind her ear. "I'm always good," she told him with a laugh.

She watched them walk away, telling herself not to get emotional as they got in the car. They waved at her before Stewart pulled out and drove past the parked bus, beeping the horn as he did so.

A few minutes later the driver emerged from the depot and waited by the bus with his passenger list. Dee lined up and got her name checked off the list then boarded the bus to her new life.

Chapter Seventeen

Three months later.

"Dee?"

She turned from where she had been dusting shelves to look at the man who had called her name.

"Phillip?" She looked at him in surprise. "What are you doing here?"

"I live here," he said. "More to the point, what are you doing here?"

"I live here," she said. "Well, not here," she added, canting her head as if to indicate the shop. "I'm working here, part-time."

She had managed to get a part-time job in a camera shop, thanks to one of her flatmates who had told her about the position.

"I didn't know you had moved here," he said.

She nodded. "Three months ago. I decided to start studying for an art degree at Wintec." She glanced over, hearing the manager clearing her throat. A customer was perusing the display cabinet and the woman was glaring in her direction, sending the message that she should be working, not chatting. "Uh, I really should ..."

Phillip smiled apologetically. "I'm sorry. I was just passing by and I saw you. What time do you finish work? I thought you might like to have a coffee with me."

She had enjoyed the last time she had had coffee with the man, although she remained wary, knowing he and Richard used to be friends.

"We close at twelve on Saturdays. I have a few things I have to do after closing, so twelve-thirty?"

"Great. I'll see you then."

She watched him walk out of the store and resumed her cleaning. The manager, a dumpy woman in her late forties with what appeared to be a permanent frown, waited until the customer had left before sidling up to her.

"Who was that?"

"Just … a friend," Dee said, not wanting to give the woman any more information. She had told the shop's owner her circumstances and what had made her move but as far as she knew, the manager didn't know any of that.

"Well, tell your friend that you shouldn't be socialising in work time."

"I'm sorry. He said he didn't know I'd moved here."

"Just in future."

Dee nodded and turned back to her dusting. In the month or so she'd been working at the store, she had seen the manager chatting to friends and thought it was rather hypocritical of the woman. She wasn't about to point that out, however.

An hour or so later, they closed the shop and finished their closing duties. Right on twelve-thirty, Dee left the building. Phillip was standing leaning against a car, watching the storefront.

"You know, that could almost look like stalking," she said. "The way you're staring."

He laughed. "Maybe to the untrained eye. Ready to go?"

She nodded. He opened the car door for her and ushered her inside.

The car was fairly modest, unlike the Porsche Richard had picked her up in on their first date. Dee felt comfortable almost immediately.

"This is a nice car," she said as Phillip pulled out of the park.

"You sound almost as if you were expecting something more, I don't know, pretentious, maybe?"

"Well ..."

"I'm sorry. Maybe I should have dragged out the old Porsche."

She looked at him askance. "You have a Porsche?"

"No," he said, chuckling. "I'm not that arrogant. I'll leave that to the Richards of this world. So, do you have any plans this afternoon or ..."

"Actually, I have a photography assignment. But I just have to go take some photos at the lake." She had taken her camera to work with her, intending to walk up to the lake before heading back to the flat.

"Well, how about I take you to lunch first and then we can drive up to the lake."

She smiled and nodded. While she was a little unsure about trusting him, she realised that all the times they'd talked, he hadn't appeared to be anything but a nice man. He hadn't shown any kind of romantic interest in her, that she could think of and she didn't want to read more into it.

Phillip drove to a café a short distance from the lake. It was a sunny day but a cold breeze was blowing in over the water. Dee shivered a little as she got out of the car and waited for Phillip. He activated the central locking and joined her on the path.

"It's a bit nippy," he said.

"Yeah, I noticed."

"Then let's not stand around here freezing our asses off," he said with a cheesy grin. He propelled her forward before opening the door to the café and ushering her inside.

The interior of the shop was warm and quiet. There were only a few customers. It seemed, despite the sunny day, no one was brave enough to take their chances with the cold.

Phillip pointed to the board above the counter and Dee perused it, quickly deciding on toasted sandwiches.

"You need to have more than that," he scolded.

"It's fine. Honest. I like toasted sandwiches. Especially on a day like this."

He nodded and gave their orders to the girl on the counter before leading her to a table by the window.

"Well, no one could ever mistake you for a gold-digger," he remarked as they sat down.

She looked askance at him. His tone suggested there was more to the remark than a casual joke. "Let me guess."

He shook his head. "He's been trying to convince us all he's the injured party. Frankly, I couldn't give a shit … excuse me," he added, grimacing. "Sorry, you don't deserve that."

"The swearing? I've heard worse. Especially around campus."

"Still, I shouldn't be so rude." He snickered a little. "You hear kids these days come out with stuff I wouldn't have dared say to my mother. Not if I didn't want my mouth washed out with soap."

"I always thought that was some kind of old wives' tale," Dee told him.

"Trust me, my mother threatened to do it on more than one occasion. I certainly gave her reason to."

"Oh, you couldn't have been that bad, surely?"

"I was a little brat," he assured her. "Until I was about six, I guess. Then reality set in."

She frowned at him. "What does that mean?" she asked.

"I watched my father beat the crap out of my mother. I swore then and there that I was never going to be like him."

Their coffees were brought to the table and Dee took a moment to study the man opposite her. He'd spoken matter-of-factly but she guessed he had gone through a lot of pain in his life.

"So, what happened?"

"When I was twelve, Mum ended up in the hospital. Broken ribs, broken arm, two black eyes and a fractured eye socket. I told her to leave him. The social worker at the hospital told her to leave him. He told her if she left him, she would never see me again." He sighed heavily. "He won. She stayed."

"How could he do that?"

"Because like it or not, when you're rich and you know people in high places, you can get away with anything. Even murder."

She stared at him, hearing the bitterness in his tone. Was he suggesting that his father had … Phillip must have seen her expression and shook his head.

"No, he didn't. After she got out of hospital and went back to him, I confronted him. Told him he better leave my mother alone or I'd make sure he met with a very nasty accident. He laughed in my face but, the next time he tried to beat her, I knocked some sense into him."

Dee looked at him in sympathy. A twelve-year-old boy should never have had to deal with something like that. He'd missed out on his childhood, trying to protect his mother.

"Where is he now? Your dad?"

"Six feet under, pushing up daisies," he said. "He went out one night, drunk as a skunk, wrapped his car around a tree. I wish I could say I'm sorry he's dead, but …"

"You're not."

"Mum told me I needed to forgive him but, in all honesty, I don't think I ever can. You remind me of her, actually."

"Your mum?"

"Yeah. She's a good person. You'd like her, I think."

The food was brought out and Dee regarded her companion silently while she ate. Phillip had ordered a quiche for himself. He finished his meal quickly and sipped his coffee.

"So, I know what Richard's been saying, but what really happened?"

She told him everything, from how she had met Richard to what had happened to make her leave.

"I guess you could say it was the proverbial straw," she said, after relating what had happened in the hospital.

"I'm thankful it wasn't any worse than that. I mean, I'm sorry for the accident, and that you lost the baby, but ..."

She hadn't thought about the miscarriage in weeks. As much as it had hurt in the beginning, she had realised it was somewhat of a blessing in disguise.

"Carol's always saying things happen for a reason and I guess in a way it worked out for the better. I wasn't ready to have a child and I wouldn't have wanted to raise a child in that mess. I mean, if what happened in Melbourne was any example, then I could have ended up just like your mum."

He regarded her silently for a few moments.

"I have to be honest with you, Dee. I did want to warn you about him but I figured you wouldn't have believed me."

"Maybe if you'd said something before Melbourne, I might not have," she said. "But after that ... even when part of me thought I should give him the benefit of the doubt, it was like I was always walking on eggshells. I had to be so careful in what I said or did. After what happened with my dad and then the accident, it was the wake-up call I needed." She chewed on her lower lip. "What happened between you and Miranda?"

"What do you know?"

"Richard tried to tell me she cheated on him with you, but she told me she loved him and nothing ever happened. I mean, he was the one who cheated."

"Yeah, the funny thing about cheaters. The first thing they do is accuse their spouse of cheating just so they can cover up any residual guilt they might have." She remembered him telling her his father had also cheated on his mother. She wanted to ask if he was talking from experience but chose not to.

"I don't think he feels any guilt at all. I'm not sure what he feels."

"If anything," Phillip told her.

"I guess that's true."

"But back to Miranda. The only thing I ever did for her was to provide a shoulder for her to cry on. I also introduced her to John."

Dee nodded. She'd been out to Miranda's property near Cambridge a few times since she'd moved to Hamilton and had seen just how happy her friend was. The other woman had given birth to a boy a couple of weeks earlier. The couple were thrilled to be parents at last.

"So, you helping Miranda, was that why you're not friends anymore?" she asked.

He shook his head. "I saw Richard's true colours years ago, but at the time we were working together on a business deal. I hate to admit it, but the deal was too important. So I maintained the illusion for a while until the deal was signed."

They moved on to talking about what she was doing. Phillip seemed interested in hearing about her course and what she planned to do with it.

Dee had been thinking about what she wanted to do with her newfound skills. She had looked into what sort of job she could do once she finished her studies, but photographing weddings and doing studio photography wasn't something that attracted her. She loved being in the outdoors, learning to take artistic shots and telling stories through her photography. Even her teacher told her she had an aptitude for it.

She had considered travelling to distant countries and working for a charity, hoping to use her skills to tell stories of those in developing countries through photographs. That took money that she didn't have.

Chapter Eighteen

It felt almost like déjà vu as she walked into the hotel ballroom. More than a year earlier she had walked into another hotel ballroom, feeling like a fish out of water. While she had been to a few more social events since then, this was the first she had been invited to since she'd left her husband.

This time, instead of the capital city, the event was being held in Hamilton. Phillip had invited her, saying it was something he saw as an obligation as a member of one of the so-called pioneering families. She'd learnt much about her new friend in the weeks since he'd discovered her working in the camera shop. His family had been one of the original board members of the New Zealand Company, a company from England that had established many of the first settlements in the early part of the 19th century.

Phillip was rather cynical about his family's roots, especially the fact that it had been on his father's side. His mother's family hadn't been quite as well-established, since they'd arrived in New Zealand more than a century later. According to a history that had been written on his family by a distant cousin, Phillip's family had been part of the aristocracy but he cared little for titles. Richard, on the other hand, had envied it, as his own family had no such lineage and wanted to cash in on what he saw as a distinct advantage. In many ways, Phillip had realised that his friendship with

Richard had been more about his ancestry than any kind of actual interest in friendship.

They'd met in high school. Phillip's mother had wanted him to get a decent education so she'd sent him to a private boys' school in Wellington. Julia Carter had sent her son to the same school.

Dee sighed. It had been sweet of Phillip to invite her to the event, but she wasn't sure about facing some of the other guests. From what he'd told her, there were a few who had been mutual acquaintances of both him and Richard and some of them had taken Richard's side over the divorce.

She glanced over towards the assembled guests, looking for a dark blond head.

Phillip reached for her hand. "He's not coming," he said. "He wasn't invited. Serving on the committee does have its advantages." He looked her over. "By the way, you look beautiful."

She nodded. She'd chosen a cocktail dress in a cream colour. The scoop neckline was lace, while the rest of the dress was chiffon. The skirt was asymmetrical, with the front hemline ending just past her knees with a slightly longer back. Dee had pinned her long hair up into a loose knot, emphasising her long neck. Her flatmate had told her the effect was elegant and perfect for such an event. As much as she was flattered by the compliment, having had so few of them, she had no idea what the appropriate response should be.

Phillip led her to the bar so he could order them some drinks. Dee noticed some of the guests were staring at her but as soon as they saw her looking back at them, they turned away and began whispering to their companions. She recognised one of them as a woman Phillip had pointed out to her the first time they'd met.

They circulated but Phillip appeared to be steering her away from certain members of the group, perhaps to avoid any unpleasantness. Dee was pleased to see Miranda with her husband and smiled in greeting as the other woman joined them. Miranda kissed her cheek.

"I'm so glad you came!" she said. "You look wonderful!"

"So do you," Dee told her. Miranda was wearing a sleeveless dress in forest green. The colour suited her dark hair and fair complexion.

Her friend grimaced a little. "I don't know. It still shows my tummy a little."

John nudged his wife. "Honey, you just had a baby two months ago."

"You're right," she said, smiling at her husband. "Ignore me, I'm being silly."

"No, you're not," he told her. He looked at them. "That old bitch Bella had the nerve to criticise her weight. Hypocritical, if you ask me."

Phillip nodded. "We all know she's had more than a little nip and tuck." He had once cynically told Dee that most of the older women with money to burn tried to defy ageing with cosmetic surgery and often resorted to the same thing when they gained unwanted weight.

"Anyway, who cares about your tummy?" John continued. "Our son is the reason for it and that's the greatest gift you could ever give me."

Miranda smiled lovingly at her husband. "Aww, how do you always know the right thing to say?"

"Just lucky I guess," he said modestly.

"Well, I think you look amazing," Dee told her friend warmly.

They chatted for a little while about life in general. When the two men began to talk business, Miranda rolled her eyes before giving her husband a teasing grin.

"Let's leave these two to talk shop," she said, her hand on Dee's arm. "I could do with a bit of fresh air."

They walked out to the balcony, still chatting. Miranda admitted she'd had a little difficulty leaving her infant son, even for just a few hours.

"So, who's looking after Daniel?" Dee asked.

"John's mum. She's so good with him and I love her to bits. She's nothing like Richard's mum. You know, when John and I first started dating, she told him he better hang on to me." She continued to gush about her mother-in-law who sounded the complete opposite of Julia Carter.

"She sounds wonderful."

"So, what's going on between you and Phillip?" Miranda asked.

"We're just friends," Dee told her.

She wasn't sure where her new friendship with the man was going. She did like him but was wary. He was kind and had never shown any inclination to behave as Richard had done but, in many ways, Dee was gun-shy.

A husky voice caught her attention.

"Did you see the way she was all over Phillip Mason? Seems like she couldn't wait to get her hooks into someone else."

"Of course, since her little scam with Richard failed."

An expression of annoyance showed on Miranda's face. She turned to look for the source of the voices.

"How dare you?" she accused.

Dee saw it was the older woman Phillip had once claimed had a lot of cosmetic surgery.

"How dare I? Look at her. She's not showing even an iota of remorse for what she did to poor Richard."

Dee glared at the woman and spluttered, barely able to keep her anger in check.

"Poor Richard? That man is nothing but an abusive, manipulative, narcissistic jerk and I'm glad to be rid of him."

"Well, of course, you would say that," the woman replied. "Don't even try to look innocent when you're nothing but …"

"But what?" Phillip asked, appearing behind her. "Tell me, Bella. What exactly are you accusing Dee of doing? The only thing she ever did wrong was trust a guy like Richard, who we all know isn't as innocent as he tries to make himself out to be. The man is a lying, conniving snake. The only reason you take his side at all is you're afraid Julia will bad-mouth you and make you look bad."

John had also joined them, wrapping an arm around his wife's shoulders.

"I think, Bella, you need to apologise to Dee."

"I'll do no such thing," the old woman scoffed. "I tried to warn him about her. I said she was nothing but a gold-digging …"

"Bella, shut your mouth or leave!" Phillip told her.

A woman with short, greying blonde hair moved to interject.

"Bella, there you are." She turned to look at them. "I'm so sorry. I invited Bella here. I didn't think she would cause so much trouble." She turned back to the older woman. "Bella, sweets, we talked about this. You can't go around accusing someone without knowing all the facts."

She led the older woman away, quickly defusing the situation. A tall man stood watching as the two older women walked off.

"I'm sorry," he said. "Bella happens to be an old friend of Mum's. I think if Mum had known she'd act like this, she wouldn't have invited her."

Phillip nodded. "It's okay, Nick." He turned to look at Dee. "Nick Sloane, this is Dee Hargreaves." He smiled at the other man. "Where's Kate tonight?"

"It's nice to meet you, Dee. Officially, that is." He quickly explained that he'd been a long-time acquaintance of Richard's but he'd met her briefly at an event in town that Richard had taken her to. He turned back to Phillip. "Kate's at home. The doctor told her she shouldn't be travelling this late in her pregnancy." He grinned, clearly a proud husband and soon-to-be father. "She's having a boy." He appeared to be excited for the impending birth of his son.

"How's business?" John asked.

"Oh, you know. Same crap, different day. It's all good," he added with a grin.

She couldn't remember meeting him until he reminded her that the event Richard had taken her to had been the opening of an exhibition at the museum where Kate, Nick's wife, worked part-time as an assistant. She'd helped put together the exhibition and had been acting as hostess that evening. Nick had gone along to support his wife. She recalled Richard had made some kind of caustic remark about Kate working when her husband could support her, implying that her 'place' was taking care of the home, not working in something she obviously enjoyed.

Dee listened as the men chatted. From their conversation, she gleaned that Nick was not a fan of Richard's behaviour and that the only reason he had anything to do with the man was that they had mutual business interests.

During dinner, they sat at the same table with Miranda and John. It felt almost as if the other couple had 'adopted' her, but she didn't mind. Her friends ensured that anyone who had taken Richard's side was informed of the truth of the situation. It was obvious that not every person was going to believe her side of the story, but she could live with that, she thought.

Phillip drove her home afterwards, stopping his car at the kerb beside the house.

"I had a good time tonight," she said.

He smiled at her. "I'm glad. Trust me, these things can get so boring sometimes. It was good to have some company. Especially such lovely company."

She smiled bashfully, ducking her head at the compliment, feeling her cheeks warming. She reached for the door handle.

"Thank you for inviting me," she said softly. "Good night, Phillip."

"Good night, Dee," he replied.

She walked up the pathway to the house. The outside light was on so she could see the step. She reached up to unlock the door before turning to look around. He was still parked on the road, clearly waiting until she got inside. She waved at him and entered the house, softly closing the door behind her.

It was well after midnight but she couldn't sleep, too wound up from the evening. All she could think about was how differently Phillip had behaved toward her, compared with Richard. Her ex-husband had often ignored her to talk to anyone else at any social event they'd gone to, but Phillip had gone to great lengths to ensure she didn't feel neglected. Even when he was chatting with some of his business acquaintances, Miranda or another friend of Phillip's was there to include her in the conversation. It was a huge contrast.

She didn't want to fall for the man but there was something very special about Phillip Mason. Maybe he wasn't as handsome as Richard, but if there was one thing she had learnt from her marriage, it was that good looks didn't mean good character. Phillip was funny and smart and never sounded like he was just telling her what he thought she wanted to hear. If it was true that a man could be judged by the way he treated others, especially those who were less well-off, then it appeared that Phillip was a kind and decent man who wasn't interested in the trappings of wealth.

The next morning, one of her flatmates asked how the evening had gone.

"Oh, it was good," she said.

"Just good?" Alison asked her.

"Well, more than good."

"Your friend, the one who picked you up, he seems nice."

"He is," Dee told her.

Alison frowned. "Why do I sense there's a but?"

"I don't know. I mean, I thought my ex was a good guy, but …"

She'd told her flatmate everything about her marriage. Alison was studying her Master's degree in psychology at Waikato University and was interested in the effects of abuse.

"Well, let me unpack this for you. When you were going out with Richard, did he ever do anything that set off any alarm bells?"

"You mean, like being mean to a waiter, or …"

"Anything. I mean even an offhand remark that comes off as an insult."

She nodded. There had been plenty of times he'd done that. If it wasn't her looks or her weight, it was how she behaved. In his mind, it had probably been constructive criticism, but, to her, it had been more than a little offensive.

"So, this guy, Phillip. Has he ever said anything like that?"

"No. He's been brutally honest. And I've never seen him be mean to anybody." That wasn't strictly true, she thought since he'd joked about Bella and her cosmetic surgery. Then again, he'd made it fairly clear that he didn't tolerate people who pretended to be something they weren't. While someone else overhearing his remarks might think he was being offensive, Dee had realised he only said such things about people who deserved it.

After dinner the night before, Diane Sloane had brought Bella over, saying the older woman wanted to apologise for her behaviour. It was obvious from the other woman's expression that the apology was half-hearted and hadn't been Bella's idea at all. It was also just as obvious that she still believed Dee to have been the villain in the situation, rather than Richard. It appeared nothing was going to change her mind.

Alison listened as she related what had happened.

"Well, I get why you might be a little concerned about the way Phillip talks to these people but … didn't you say he had an abusive father? It sounds to me like he kind of sees himself as a white knight."

"I don't see that."

Her friend frowned. "Don't you? Ever since you met the man, he's been there to help you in some form. You did say he stayed to talk to you that first time."

That was true, Dee thought. Even all the other times they'd met during her marriage, he'd said something to defuse the situation or he'd kept her company.

She bit her lip and sighed. "Do you think maybe Richard was right about … I don't know."

"What? To accuse the two of you of flirting?" Alison paused for a moment, looking as if she was carefully considering what she was about to say. "I'm not saying you were. I mean, I honestly think you don't know how to flirt. But I do think that Phillip has liked you from the start. Is he attracted to you? I haven't seen enough of you two interacting to be able to determine that. But from the way he acts toward you, I think it's possible. The question is, how do you feel about him?"

"I like him, but I'm just not sure … I mean, there's something about him. It's not just that he makes me laugh. He makes me feel like … I know it sounds dumb, but, he makes me feel like I matter."

"That's not dumb, Dee. That's how it's supposed to be when two people care about each other. Where your ex was concerned, as much as he claimed to love you, he never made you feel it. The man was sexist, misogynistic, manipulative and completely self-centred. That isn't the behaviour of someone in love. That's the behaviour of someone who enjoys power too much. You know, most intimate partner violence has an element of power about it."

"But Richard only hit me once. Maybe a couple of times."

Alison shook her head. "Domestic violence isn't just about physical abuse, Dee. What he did to you was emotional abuse. He belittled you; he acted like a condescending jerk and he was using you. This is the reason so many men get away with this kind of behaviour, Dee. Because people consider emotional abuse as having less of an impact than physical abuse. I mean, just because the scars are psychological, doesn't change the fact that they're there."

She stared at her friend. Alison was clearly passionate about the subject.

"Sorry. I'll get off my soapbox now," the other woman replied.

"It's okay. Honest. I've just always thought … well, it doesn't matter what I thought."

She continued to think about it over the next week or so and decided to read up on the subject a little. Alison had lent her a book written by a psychologist who had interviewed others who had escaped abusive relationships. Both men and women. While they each had slight differences in their stories, it helped her to understand just how lucky she had been to walk away when she did.

Chapter Nineteen

As the end of the semester approached, Dee was kept busy completing several assignments. Her photography tutor had given her some feedback on a photo essay and she had been using Alison's desktop computer to do some editing on it.

She heard Phillip and Alison talking in the hallway and glanced at the clock on the computer. Phillip had promised to take her out to Miranda and John's for dinner that evening. She frowned. It was still early.

Phillip came in, still chatting to Alison. Dee turned her chair around to greet him.

"Hi," she said. "Am I late or are you early?"

"I'm early," he said with a slight shrug. "I had to get out of the house. Fumigating," he added. "Cockroaches." He shuddered visibly. "God, I hate those things."

Dee would have laughed at his reaction if she hadn't shared the same feelings of disgust at the pests. They'd had the same problem a month or so earlier but their landlord had refused to do anything about it.

"Would you like a drink, Phillip?" Alison asked.

"Thanks. Sparkling mineral water if you have it. Heard the cops will be out with their checkpoints tonight." He didn't owe Alison any explanations but Dee knew that, with his father's history of alcoholism and subsequent death, Phillip drank very little alcohol, especially if he was driving.

"Sensible," the other woman replied. She went to the fridge and poured him a glass, offering the same to Dee, who took her drink with a smile.

Alison left them alone, saying she was going to go talk with her boyfriend on Skype on her I-pad. Jeremy was in the army, deployed on a training mission in the Middle East.

Phillip grabbed a chair and placed it so he could sit facing its back and watch her work. Dee resumed her editing. It was a scene from the lake. As summer slowly approached, many people were out enjoying their free time. She'd managed to get a shot of someone sailing against a backdrop of the setting sun.

"That looks nice."

Dee grimaced at the image on the screen. Even to her inexperienced eye, it looked a little out of focus. The scene was just a little too generic. Her tutor had told her to take shots that stood out; were unique. Yet, judging from Phillip's reaction as he looked at the photo, he didn't notice its flaws and imperfections.

"It's not very good," she said with a sigh.

He swivelled the chair around so she faced him.

"Why do you do that?" he asked, frowning at her.

"Do what?" she asked, confused by the question.

"Put yourself down like that?"

"I didn't realise I was," she told him.

"I've noticed. Believe me, I've noticed. You do it a lot. You'll say something negative about yourself. If you say anything at all. You're not very good at taking compliments, you know."

"But I just … I mean, it's not me. It's the photo," she said, gesturing toward the computer.

"It's not just the photo. And, look, I'm not a photographer. I couldn't take a decent shot if my life depended on it. I don't have the … what do you call it?"

"Artistic eye."

"Yeah, that. But I know what I like. And I like the shot."

"I'm sorry," she said, sighing again. "Richard never ..."

"Since when did his opinion matter?" Phillip asked.

"I ..." She had no idea how to respond to that. Phillip huffed as if he was angry.

"I hate that man," he muttered bitterly. "I can't stand anyone so full of themselves that their opinion is the only one that matters. As if he's an expert on everything. And he treats people like they're this big," he added, holding his thumb and forefinger a few centimetres apart. Dee snickered. "I'm serious!" Phillip told her.

"I know. It's just ..."

"No! Not just! Did he seriously never tell you?"

"Tell me what?"

"Just how amazing you are?"

She thought for a moment. That kind of description of her had never passed that man's lips.

"No. I don't think he did," she said, remembering all the times he would criticise her.

"Well, you are. I mean, my mother never had the strength to walk away from my father even when things got really bad. Even the times he'd put her in the hospital. But you did. You decided you weren't going to put up with his bullshit and you walked. And don't tell me you had help, or that it was because of the accident. Sometimes the strongest thing you can do is ask for help when you need it. And as far as I'm concerned, you're far better than him. Like ten times better. He might have money and all that, but he's still a douchebag. I mean, how can you not know how beautiful you are? And, by the way, this isn't a come-on in any way, shape or form, but you're fantastically gorgeous and sexy as hell. But it bugs the hell out of me that you don't know it. It's not just your looks. It's who you are. You've had to deal with so much in your life, yet you're the most compassionate, kindest woman I've ever known. And ..." He stared at her. "Why are you crying?"

A single tear had rolled down her cheek at his passionate speech. No one else had ever spoken to her in that way before. No one … no man, at least, had ever spoken with such passion. It was overwhelming.

"I don't know," she said quietly. "But that is the most beautiful thing anyone's ever said to me."

"I meant every word," he replied.

"I know you did," she told him before standing up and kissing him on the lips. It was just a brief peck but when she started to pull away he caught her arm in a gentle grip, his eyes darting from side to side as he gazed at her. For a moment it was as if she forgot to breathe as they stared at each other. Then he pulled her into his arms, his lips taking hers in a hard, passionate kiss.

When they finally parted, she could only stare at him in wonder. It had just been a kiss, but that one action had confirmed, in an instant, everything wrong in her marriage. She'd known it but had shrugged it off, thinking that all the things she had read about passion were highly overrated.

Phillip frowned at her. "What's wrong?"

"He never really loved me, did he?"

He shook his head. "No. I don't think he did. I think he wanted you to believe that so he could control you. Look," he said, running a hand through his dark curly hair. "I'm no psychologist. I bet Alison could probably give you some insight there. But I think guys like Richard are very good at knowing just how to push those buttons. Give you just enough so you think he'll follow through on his promises to take care of you. I think he knew the way your dad was toward you and thought that was a weakness he could exploit. This is just a theory, but I think maybe he chose you because you were so passive. That you just went along with what everyone wanted instead of fighting for what you wanted. He just wanted someone who would be the 'little woman'."

It made sense in a lot of ways.

"My dad was like Richard. He wanted a wife who would stay home, take care of the house and the kids. He was a big believer in the whole love, honour and obey thing. As long as it only applied to the wife and he didn't have to follow along with it.

"I talked to my mum about this a few years ago and she said in the beginning, the only time he would hit her would be when she hadn't done something, or if she dared to talk back to him. Then it just escalated to the point where he would smack her if she opened her mouth." He looked down. "God, I hated him. Heaven help me. I mean, if I believed in God or whatever, I'd probably go to Hell for saying this, but I'm glad he's dead. I can't ever forgive him for the way he terrorised Mum."

He looked back up at her, his eyes glistening with tears. No matter what he said about his father, it was obvious the pain was still raw.

"When Miranda came to me and told me she'd found out Richard was cheating on her, I was afraid for her. I once saw him punch a girl he was dating because she had the nerve to accuse him, rightly, of cheating. Mind you, I also saw Julia smack him around a time or two when he was a kid. I'm not making excuses for him, but he is the way he is because of her. Because he was never taught any better."

Dee nodded. Richard had intimated as much in the few times he'd talked about his mother and after she'd left him, she'd realised that was where a lot of his behaviour had stemmed from.

"You know, the night we met, I wanted to tell you to just get out of there. Run as far as you could from Richard."

"Why didn't you?" she asked.

"Because I didn't think you'd believe me if I told you what he was really like. I knew you had to learn that for yourself. It was the only way you'd ever be able to break free of him. And you did. You surpassed even my expectations, Dee. You've got this amazing strength that I don't think you even realised you had."

From the way he spoke, she sensed he was being totally sincere. She'd got to know him well enough in the past two or three months to know that he never said anything he didn't mean, especially when it was a compliment. Yet a part of her couldn't help but hear her father or even Richard telling her not to trust her instincts. That the only reason Phillip was telling her any of this was because he wanted something from her.

She remembered one of the last fights she'd had with her father before she'd left him for good.

"You think he wants you for yourself, Deanna?" Jack had told her. "He's a man and all men are just animals. All they care about is their own gratification."

She could understand her father's cynicism, given his past, but it still made little sense. It meant he was saying the same thing about himself, yet even after her mother had left, he had never shown any interest in dating someone. The only thing he had been interested in was going to the local pub. Except he hadn't been going to drink and socialise. According to the private investigator the lawyer had hired, the truth about her parents' divorce had come out. The reason they'd fought a lot over money was that he was spending it all on gambling. They'd lost the house because he had spent the money they would have paid on the mortgage and the house had been a mortgagee sale.

Her lawyer, Tom Harding had contacted her a month or so earlier and told her the estate was now settled and she had inherited a lump sum of just under $100,000. It had been all that was left of her father's life insurance policy after taxes, funeral costs and his debts had been settled. It was still more money than she had ever seen, even during her marriage, Richard had only ever provided her with an allowance and she'd never had access to the accounts. She'd opted to leave her retirement savings in an investment account since her part-time wages and student allowance was enough to pay her living costs. The money from her father's estate was also invested.

As Phillip drove them to Cambridge, she talked about her parents' marriage. He glanced at her before returning his gaze to the road. The highway from the city was now a four-lane expressway, but some parts of it were still being worked on.

"Don't take this the wrong way, Dee, but I think your mother was wrong too. She left you with your dad and, from the sounds of things, didn't even sue for custody. She just went off and started living her own life."

"Well, I guess I can see it from her point of view. I mean, I was only a kid and she thought my education was more important than dragging me halfway around the world."

"Except she left you with an abuser."

Dee frowned. "I don't see that." He glanced at her and she could tell he was a little puzzled by her response.

"Don't you? Why? Do you think abuse only counts if it's physical?"

She shook her head. "No. It's just, I don't know. I think he was trying his best."

"Okay, then let me point out a few things from what you've said. He spent most of his money and expected you to support him. Am I right?"

She shrugged. So her father had asked her to help pay for expenses, but that didn't mean … Then again, he'd forced her to get a job rather than follow her dreams of further study.

"He did get me the job at Carter Tech."

"Which put you directly in the line of sight of another abuser. Dee, I'm not saying you're naïve, but I think you're not seeing your father for what he was. He was just as much trying to control your life as Richard was. I mean, I know your father made sure you continued your schooling, right up until the end of high school. But did he ever encourage you to pursue the subjects you wanted or did he control that too?"

She had to think about that for a moment. He'd suggested practical subjects beyond the core subjects, like economics and geography. It was only when one of her teachers had told him at a parent-teacher meeting that she had an aptitude for art that he'd allowed it. Yet every time she talked about what she was studying in art, he'd said something disparaging, suggesting that she would never make a good living in it.

She realised now that when he'd say something about how smart she was, it had all been designed to manipulate her. He'd wanted her to get a job that would pay well enough so she would continue to support him, while he spent his money elsewhere.

Phillip turned into the gravel driveway of Miranda and John's property and slowed before coming to a complete stop. He looked at her.

"Dee, I know this isn't something you want to hear, but I care enough about you to be completely honest with you. All your life, you've let other people control you. Tell you what to do, how to live your life. The only way you're ever going to get past this is to stop making excuses for them."

She frowned at him. "How am I meant to do that? I don't even know who I am without them."

"And that's half your problem. That's what I was talking about earlier, Dee. I think you're an incredible woman, but you shy away from that idea. I'm not saying you dismiss it, but I think deep down you just don't believe that about yourself and that's what keeps you from moving forward."

"But I am moving forward," she said. "I'm studying photography."

"That's not enough." He glanced toward the house. Miranda was waiting on the steps for them. "Look, let's not talk about this tonight. But I don't want to just let this lie, Dee. The question is, do you trust me?"

"Yes," she said quietly. It was true. She trusted him more than she could remember trusting anyone. He nodded.

"Okay. We'll talk about this tomorrow. All right?"

Part of her wondered exactly what he was going to say. Even if he was trying to be honest with her, she wasn't sure she wanted to hear it.

Chapter Twenty

Phillip picked her up just after lunch the next day. He hadn't told her where they were going and she didn't ask, thinking he would tell her when he was ready. She watched as he turned onto the expressway and drove north.

He didn't seem to want to talk, connecting an MP3 player to the car's electronic system. She sat back and listened to the music. It wasn't quite to her taste, being hard rock, but it was better than Richard's. He'd only ever played classical music, claiming the more contemporary selection was low-class and poor taste.

She stared out the side window, not knowing what to say to break the apparent tension between them. He didn't seem to be in a bad mood but he was in what she thought was a broody one. He continued to drive, keeping his gaze firmly on the road in front of him. She still had no idea where they were going when they reached the motorway into Auckland. She could only sit back and watch in confusion as he turned off the motorway and headed east. She tried to make sense of where they were going but the few times she had been in the city had been when Richard had taken her on a business trip or he'd used one of the corporate suites at the sports stadium. She'd never seen very much of the city.

Finally, about two hours after they'd left Hamilton, he stopped the car in a car park a few metres from the beach. Dee stared out over the white sand. She could remember going to the beach a few times where she grew up, but there it tended to be grey sand and the view wasn't nearly as pretty. The landscape on Petone beach was mostly beach grass and very few trees. Here, the trees bordered a large expanse of lawn. Young children were running all over it, playing tag or whatever games children played at that age, she observed.

"Want some ice cream?" Phillip asked. She stared at him.

"What?"

He got out of the car. She followed suit and frowned as he pointed. She turned around to look in the direction he was pointing and saw there was an ice cream parlour across the road.

"This place makes the best ice creams," he said. "Well, they don't make the ice cream on site. That comes from overseas. So, you want some?"

"Um, sure," she said. She followed him to the shop. It was busy, being a warm, sunny day and it took a while for them to be served.

"Hi, what can I get you?"

Phillip looked at her. She bit her lip. "Um, I haven't decided yet. You go first."

He nodded. "I'd like a rum and raisin. In a waffle cone. Two scoops."

Dee looked up at the board, then down at the selection of flavours, quickly deciding on salted caramel. She gave her order to the server.

Phillip paid for the ice creams and guided her out of the shop.

"Let's go sit over here," he said, walking back across the road and along the path toward the beach. There were wooden benches lined up along the edge of the sand.

They sat eating the frozen treats. Phillip watched the waves washing along the shore.

"I come here sometimes when I just need to de-stress," he said. "My grandparents lived here, many moons ago. Back before it got too expensive for them."

"Your mum's parents?" she asked.

He nodded. "Good people. They tried to talk my mum into leaving dad when things got really bad, but ... well ..." He shrugged and sighed. "What about your grandparents?"

"I only knew my Grandma, on my dad's side. Mum's parents didn't figure in my life. I'm not sure why."

"Dysfunctional families," he replied. "How's your ice cream?" She was nonplussed at the sudden change in the subject but nodded. The ice cream was sweet and the flavours could be a little overpowering, but it was very creamy and had a nice texture. It was a lot richer than the locally-made dessert.

"It's nice," she said. "Very rich, but nice."

"Yeah. My grandma introduced me to it when I was a kid. I always liked chocolate, but then I got a taste of this and that was it."

They finished the ice creams in companionable silence. Dee sat back and studied the beach. A few people were sitting on the sand while others were in the water. Someone was out further on a wind-sailing board.

"I should have brought my camera," she said. "I could get some great shots."

"Next time." He reached for her hand. "Want to go for a walk?"

"Uh, okay," she said.

They began walking along the path, dodging to avoid other pedestrians and the odd cyclist.

"Phillip, why did you bring me here?" she asked.

"I wanted to continue our discussion from last night."

"I get that, but why now? We could have talked in the car. Or at my flat."

"This wasn't something I wanted your flatmates to get in on," he said. "Dee, what I said last night, I didn't mean it as a criticism. The thing is, I think you want something from me that I can't give you."

"What do you mean?"

"Something has been happening between us during the last few weeks. I know you've noticed it."

How could she not? They'd spent a lot of time together and the more she had got to know him, the more attracted she was. He was nothing like Richard. Her ex-husband had overwhelmed her. Made her feel she had to go along with whatever he wanted.

"Okay, you're right. I do feel something for you. I think it's worth exploring."

He stopped walking and looked at her.

"What do you want from me, Deanna?"

She crinkled her nose. She hated her birth name. Richard had always sounded so condescending when he used her proper name and she hated to hear it from anyone else. Especially from Phillip. It felt almost as if he was trying to put her at arm's length.

"Don't do that," she demanded.

"Do what?" he responded.

"Push me away."

He frowned. "What makes you think I'm trying to push you away?"

"You never call me Deanna. Only Dee. Richard would only ever call me by my proper name. He knew I hated it. Dad knew I hated it. And I think you know that."

"I don't mean to make you feel like I'm pushing you away," he said.

"Then why do it?"

He huffed. "I don't know." He looked away for a moment before turning back and shaking his head. "Don't fall for me, Dee. It'll only end badly."

"What do you mean?"

"I mean, I'm not good for you. You'll only end up getting hurt."

"You can't control how I feel, Phillip."

"No, I know that. But I think you want something you're not ready for."

She grabbed his hand, thinking somehow the physical contact would force him to look at her.

"I'm not just going to walk away because you're afraid."

He inhaled sharply, giving what she assumed was meant to be a half-laugh, but ended up coughing a little.

"Afraid? What do you think I'm afraid of?"

"Maybe of becoming like your father."

"Well, they do say the apple doesn't fall far from the tree."

"Your mother had nothing to do with it, I suppose?" she accused.

He looked almost angry. "Do you know what he said to me the day I confronted him and told him to leave my mother alone? He told me I was just a weak little boy. That my mother had made me weak. Then he laughed in my face."

"That doesn't mean he was right, Phillip."

"Doesn't mean he was wrong, either. Dee, please believe me when I say that I care about you too much to hurt you that way."

She stared at him. "Seriously? You say you care about me and you see that as a weakness?" He looked almost taken aback, shaking his head vehemently.

"No! God, no, I just … this is coming out all wrong. I just wish you could understand. I don't want to make you do something you don't want to do. I don't want to be like Richard."

"You're **nothing** like him," she told him fiercely. "Richard was all about control. I always had to go along with whatever he wanted. The only time he ever asked me what I wanted was when he was trying to manipulate me into thinking he cared about me."

"I know," he said. "He used you."

"And that's something I'll never understand," she replied. "But that's neither here nor there."

They resumed walking, a palpable silence between them. Dee noticed other people giving them looks and wondered if they'd heard the argument. She chewed on her lower lip, thinking over everything that had happened in the past few weeks. Phillip had taken her out many times but he'd always made sure it was something she wanted to do. She'd mentioned a film she'd wanted to see at the local cinema and he'd taken her, even though it hadn't been his kind of film.

If he was so afraid of being like his father, or like Richard, why would he do something that wasn't really to his taste, but because it was something she wanted?

"Why did you kiss me yesterday?" she asked.

He stopped walking once more and turned to her, his eyes dancing.

"If you don't want whatever this is," she said, "then why?"

"I don't know," he said. She could tell from his tone that he was trying to be honest with her. "I guess because I feel something for you too. And that's what makes this so hard."

"Phillip, I don't know where this is going, but I do know I want to explore it. I'm not asking for a lifetime commitment."

"But you will."

"Don't do that. Don't tell me what you think I might want down the line. Neither of us knows what the future holds."

He shook his head. "You will. They always do."

She glared at him. "Will you stop? And who are 'they'?"

He bit his lip. "Every woman I've ever dated," he said.

"That isn't a good enough reason, Phillip." She huffed. "God, you're so infuriating. Why are you so adamantly against this? Why can't you just accept it for what it is right now?"

"Because, I ..." He looked away from her, staring out over the ocean. "Because you're right. I'm afraid. Of you."

She scoffed. "Me? What could you possibly have to be afraid of with me? I'm not anybody special."

"See, there you go again, putting yourself down. And you are special, Dee. The fact that you don't even know it is what makes you so special. And dangerous."

She laughed incredulously. "What? How could I be ..."

"The moment I saw you, I knew you were different. I never believed in love - or even attraction - at first sight, but that night I saw you standing there, looking so lost and I just knew. I even told myself that I shouldn't approach you, knowing what I was feeling."

She remained silent, still not able to wrap her brain around the idea that she was a danger to him. He turned to gaze at her.

"In a sense you were dangerous. To my sense of self-preservation."

She had to laugh at his expression. It was goofy as if he was trying to pretend he was just an innocent boy experiencing his first crush.

"You're incorrigible," she said.

He laughed. "I am. It's true. But I never say things I don't mean."

They turned to start walking back to the car. Phillip sighed. "I have to be honest with you, Dee. It bothers me."

"What does?" she asked.

"That you keep putting yourself down as you do. It's like your father and Richard wore you down so hard that you just don't know who you are."

"I don't," she said. "But I don't see what any of that has to do with us."

"I don't want to be the kind of man who tries to make you into something you're not. I can't change the way you feel about yourself. Only you can do that."

"I'm not expecting you to," she said. "But my wanting to explore what I feel has nothing to do with what my dad or Richard did to me. I felt something for you before I even left Richard. From the moment we met. I tried to make myself believe it was nothing."

Maybe they had only met half a dozen times during her marriage, but they had always been memorable. Phillip had always made her feel like what she said was worth listening to. There had always been something about him that she'd liked, without really knowing why. Now that she had time to examine all those feelings, she'd realised it was attraction.

"Those few times we talked, I never felt like I was just being … patronised, I guess. Richard always tended to monopolise the conversation and, even when I was talking, I never felt like he was listening to me."

She wasn't sure she was explaining herself very well. She wanted him to understand there was a major difference in the way he made her feel as opposed to her ex-husband.

She wasn't sure if she loved him, or even if it was the kind of love that she'd always thought would mean marriage, but it was the kind that made her feel almost gooey inside. She laughed at herself for thinking of it in those terms, but she couldn't think of any other way to describe it. She felt warm and even a little tingly when she was with him. Most of all, though, was that he did make her feel she was valued. Unlike Richard, who had only ever seen her as a possession.

"I hate that guy," Phillip muttered.

"I get that, but hating him isn't going to change anything he's done. I mean, you can't make him take responsibility for his actions. At the end of it all, he's the one who is going to have to live with himself. Hating him is just wasted emotion."

"You get that from Alison?" he asked with a sardonic grin.

"She's been kind of practising her counselling skills on me," she admitted, laughing. "But she's right. As much as I hate how I fell for his manipulations, that is my issue. And that's something I have to work on."

"You're better than me," he said. "Every time I see him I want to just …" He held up one hand and made a fist with the other, punching his open hand. "You know, he might have been born with a silver spoon in his mouth but there's one thing being raised with money can't teach, and that's class. You may not know much about my world, but you've ten times the class he has."

"Then teach me your world," she pleaded.

He frowned at her. "What?"

"I can get an education at the finest university in the country, but a degree won't give me life skills. If you're so concerned about the way I see myself, then I think you're the best person to show me at least a part of the real world."

"I don't think that's the way it works," he said.

"I'm not suggesting you 'Eliza Dolittle' me."

He laughed. "What? I think you've got the whole concept of the movie wrong. Wasn't Henry Higgins the teacher?"

"You know what I mean! I'm not some street waif who can't speak the Queen's English, or however the story went. I'm just asking you to show me more of your world."

"How is that going to help?"

"You said it yourself. When you met me, I looked lost. And I felt it. I felt like a fish out of water. If I can learn to fit in your world, then maybe I can fix myself along the way."

He shook his head. "You don't need to fix yourself," he said. "You just need to believe in yourself."

She understood that, but she didn't think it was something she could do alone. She tried to explain that to him.

"But why this way?"

"Because that's the world you know. I'm not asking you to teach me how to make billion-dollar deals or anything. Nor am I asking you to take charge of my life. That's not what this is about. I just think that if I can fit in your world, I can do anything I set my mind to."

Maybe it sounded illogical, but it was the one thing he could help her with. She thought if she could learn how to fit into that world, make people believe she belonged there, she might just gain some confidence while she was at it. It wasn't as if they were all that different from anyone else. While many of the members of this 'elite club' did come from money, she knew from Carol that some of them worked nine-to-five jobs and weren't exactly well-off.

Chapter Twenty-One

"Sweetie, you know I adore you, but is this really what you want?"

Dee looked at her friend. Miranda had rung and suggested they go shopping at the big complex on the north side of the city to pick up some summer outfits. Now she had lost the baby weight, the other woman was keen to replenish her wardrobe. They were looking through outfits in the air-conditioned mall, standing on opposite sides of a clothing rack.

"I don't know any other way to do it," she said. "I read this book years ago. It was something like 'Fake it 'til you make it.' Besides, if I can learn to handle someone like Faye, then I figure I can handle anyone."

She'd had a run-in with the older woman at a dinner party for John's birthday. Faye was skinny as a rail, which Dee thought was unhealthy considering the other woman was at least 75. She had congratulated Miranda on losing weight, but Dee had overheard her insulting Miranda while talking with another woman.

"I do not know why she is even here," Faye was saying. "In my day, you wouldn't see me until the child was weaned. She's a new mother. She should be home taking care of her child, not …"

"Not what?" Dee asked. Faye turned and looked at her, making a face like she'd tasted a lemon. "Not joining her husband in celebrating his birthday? I suppose you think we should go back to the way things were a hundred years ago when women weren't even allowed to vote."

The older woman pointed a bony finger at her. "You should learn to be quiet, young lady. You should have stayed with that husband of yours and just opened your legs."

"So I should have just let him attack me?" she asked. "Let him treat me like a possession?"

"If you were doing what you were told, you'd be having babies, not wasting your time with this photography nonsense."

"It's not nonsense, Faye," Phillip said, coming to stand at Dee's side. "Dee happens to be very talented. You, on the other hand, are nothing but a bitter old bitch. It's no wonder your husband fooled around on you. God forbid he expected you to be anything but a mindless drone."

"How dare you speak that way about my late husband?" Faye accused.

"We both know the truth, Faye, so why don't you get off your high horse."

Dee smiled a little at the memory. She hadn't needed Phillip's help to put the old lady in her place, but it had been nice all the same.

"I think if I can handle someone like Faye …" she repeated, thinking that might help her eventually do the same to Richard.

"Yes, but Faye is a dyed-in-the-wool snob." Her friend shook her head. "Besides, no one takes her seriously."

Dee raised her eyebrows trying to figure out exactly what the other woman had just said.

"Dyed-in-the-wool?' What does that mean?"

Miranda gazed at her for a moment. "Uh, you know, I don't really know. But it sounds like Faye, don't you think?"

Dee laughed. "You're terrible, Muriel." Miranda had recently made her watch a classic Australian movie about a girl who obsessed about weddings. The line had become famous in pop culture.

They both giggled, drawing the attention of one of the shop assistants.

"Can I help you ladies with anything?" she asked, looking Dee over with almost a derisive look. It was a hot day and Dee was dressed in shorts and a light cotton top that was hardly 'haute couture.' Not in this particular shop, which looked as if it catered to the more 'upmarket' dresser. It was still at least better than some of the clothes Dee often saw young teenage girls wearing. By comparison, her outfit would be considered conservative.

Miranda must have spotted the look as she sniffed haughtily. "No, thank you. My friend and I are quite happy browsing." She made sure to emphasise the 'my friend.' The assistant shot her a dirty look but walked away.

"Bitch!" Miranda muttered. Dee tried to look scandalised but all she could do was laugh. Her friend didn't curse much but when she did it was entertaining.

They walked out of the shop, having found nothing that piqued their interest.

"Let's go get something to eat," the older woman said. She pointed out a casual dining restaurant near the entrance with tables outside. She chose a small table in the corner underneath an umbrella so they could get some shade. "They make this great spicy beef salad. I haven't had one in ages. Not since the baby, anyway." She chattered on about having tried a spicy dish while she was pregnant, only to suffer from indigestion all night. There was a pause as they gave their orders.

"I'm sorry," she said. "Here I am prattling on about the baby."

"I don't mind," Dee told her.

"You don't talk about it much. The miscarriage, I mean." She'd learnt about Dee's losing the baby through the grapevine. Richard had been shooting his mouth off, suggesting the loss of the baby meant more to him than it did to Dee. The worst of it was he'd implied she'd known about it all along and had deliberately chosen not to tell him so she could get rid of it. Even though the evidence had been clear, he had also tried to suggest that Dee was the one who had been responsible for the accident, instead of the other driver.

Dee looked at her friend. "To be honest, I don't think about it much. I know that sounds kind of cold, but … I mean, sure, when I found out, yeah, I felt rotten for a few days, but I now think it was kind of a blessing in disguise. Goodness knows I wouldn't have wanted to bring a child into that marriage." She sighed. "It would have been just another way for Richard to control me."

"That's true. You're amazing, Dee. You sound so strong."

"I've had my moments of weakness, believe me. I mean, there've been times when I've wondered if I made a huge mistake. That maybe I misjudged him. Then Phillip reminds me of all the things Richard did and I realise I was right to get out when I did."

"Uh, speaking of Phillip … Like I was going to say, this idea you have. Of him teaching you."

"It's not exactly teaching," she said. "It's more … guiding, I guess."

"Sure, but hon, you know as much as I adore him, he's got a lot of issues."

"So do I," she said. "I can't explain it. There's something about him that … I don't know, it sounds so cliched, but I'm kind of drawn to him. It's not just that he makes me laugh. He makes me feel like I matter." She sighed and shook her head. "That sounds so weird."

"No, it doesn't," her friend told her. "Your dad never made you feel that way and Richard just used you. I felt the same way when I fell in love with John. I mean, don't get me wrong. We're far from the perfect couple, but he makes me feel like I'm not just in this relationship by myself. We really are partners. I did love Richard, but I never felt like he felt the same way."

Their meals came out and they ate without talking. The one thing Dee liked about her friend was that even though she and her husband had come from more wealthy backgrounds, Miranda never treated her as if she was beneath them. She had once told Dee that she had been raised to be respectful to everyone, although she'd admitted to being something of a brat in her teens. When she'd first begun dating Richard, she had realised just how bad her behaviour had been.

"So, how are things going with you-know-who? Have you heard anything?"

Dee nodded. She'd had a call from the solicitor who had told her Richard had been ordered to appear in court after he'd refused to attend the domestic violence programme, saying he was far too busy with work and he hadn't done anything wrong. It was the usual story of him refusing to take responsibility for his actions.

"So, what happened?" Miranda asked. "Did the judge hold him?"

"His lawyer managed to get him another chance, but Tom says he doubts Richard's going to comply with the order. I think he said that if Richard still won't go, he'll be held in contempt."

"The man certainly knows how to make an ass of himself," her friend commented.

Dee huffed. "Even if he does go to jail for a couple of days, I don't think it'll change anything. He still claims he did nothing wrong, even though Tom's got one of the staff from that restaurant in Melbourne testifying about his behaviour that night."

"John would say something like Richard thinks his shit doesn't stink. I work around horses and I can tell you … That stuff stinks to high heaven!"

Dee laughed at her friend. "You're weird," she told her. "Works for you, though."

"So, when does Pygmalion start his lessons?" Miranda asked once they'd finished their meals. Dee almost rolled her eyes at the reference. She had related a little of the conversation between her and Phillip and her friend had laughed at the My Fair Lady quip, reminding Dee of the Greek legend which had inspired the play.

"It's not like that," she told her. "I mean, sure, Phillip's going to guide me on what to say and stuff, so I don't come off sounding like a total idiot, but it's not like he's going to make me hold a mouthful of marbles."

"Well, no, that would be rather silly. I just don't get what you think you need to improve. It's like you see rich people as a whole different world."

Dee shook her head. "Look, I get it. People who come from wealthy backgrounds are pretty much the same as everyone else. I mean, you can still be poor and be spoiled. I understand that. But even you have to admit that you get treated differently from me."

Miranda frowned. "You mean, like that girl in the shop just now? There's a little secret nobody ever tells you. They're trained to judge someone on appearances. I mean, there's nothing wrong with what you're wearing, but unless you walk in those places smelling to high heaven of expensive perfume, wear expensive clothes and jewellery, they're always going to look down their noses at you."

Dee looked at her. Miranda wasn't exactly wearing high fashion either, but the short pants she was wearing were tailored linen that looked expensive. Her blouse looked equally expensive.

When Dee pointed it out, Miranda offered her what she'd often called her 'Mona Lisa' smile. It was enigmatic and almost mischievous.

"What?" Dee asked.

"I didn't buy these at some expensive fashion boutique. I made them."

She looked at the other woman, eyes wide. "You're kidding!"

Miranda shook her head. "Before I married Richard, I studied fashion design. I was going to open up shop as a fashion designer. Only he wouldn't hear of it."

"Oh, my god. I didn't know that about you. Do you make your own clothes?"

"I used to. But with the baby and all, I haven't had much time to devote to it. And the farm keeps me busy as well. Sometimes when we're away at the races or when I have some down time I'll sketch something and think about making it, but that's usually about as far as I'll get." She gestured to her outfit. "These I made while I was pregnant. Sort of an incentive to lose the baby weight."

"Wow! That's so amazing! I could never do that."

"I couldn't take such beautiful photographs," Miranda told her. "We all have our talents, I guess."

"What does John think about it?"

"He loves it. He encourages me to work on the designs and I will when I have time."

Dee envied her friend a little. Miranda had not only found someone whom she loved and loved her in return, but he also appeared to see them as equals, encouraging her to pursue her own passions. It was something Richard had never done.

"Anyway, what was I saying? Oh yes, something about being treated differently. The point, that I lost somewhere down the line, is that you don't need to change to fit in. Do you think Richard chose you because he thought he could manipulate you? Or rather, that it was the only reason he did so?"

Dee frowned at her. "What do you mean?"

"You're special, Dee. You may not see it, but we do. Even snobs like Faye. I think if you had a mind to it, you could fit in anywhere. No matter where you go. That's what Richard saw in you. That's what Phillip sees in you. If you could just see it in yourself. It's not about how you look or what you wear. Or even how you carry yourself. It's … I don't know what it is, but you have a way of drawing people to you. It's not like you act like you want saving." Her friend shook her head. "I'm not explaining this very well. I mean, I know you're not looking for a white knight to save you, but at the same time, I don't think you're fully aware of who you are, or that you don't need saving."

"That's why I need to do this," Dee told her.

"Going to parties and being around people who you perceive as being better than you because they come from a different world isn't going to change that."

"No, but it's the only thing I could think of. I mean, it's not like Phillip's a world-famous athlete coaching me for an Olympic event or anything. This is the world he knows. It's the world you know. You've been around it all your life."

"Sweetie, I understand. I do. But do you think we judge you because of your roots? If anything, we love you because you don't act like anyone we've ever known. If we hadn't known your background before we met you, we wouldn't have even thought for a second that it was where you were from. You have a way about you that … oh god, this sounds so pretentious in my head, but you defy stereotypes. But you don't even know how amazing you are. And I think that's what attracts us the most."

Dee could only stare at her friend. She had never known anyone saw her that way. Phillip, of course, paid her compliments all the time. When she talked to Jenny, her friend was always saying the same thing. Yet there had always been a part of her that wondered if they were being truthful.

She called Jenny later that day, once Miranda had dropped her off at home.

"Is there a reason you think you shouldn't believe it?" Jenny asked.

"I don't know."

"Sweetie, loving someone doesn't mean you're blind to their faults. It also doesn't mean they're going to lie and tell you something they think you want to hear. You need to stop listening to the past and start seeing what's right in front of you. I don't know if this idea of yours is going to work, but I can kind of understand what you're trying to do." She paused, speaking to someone in the background. "Ugh. My coworker just told me you-know-who's here. He keeps trying to get me to tell him where you are. I've told him a dozen times already to leave me alone."

"He hasn't been to your house, has he?" Dee asked anxiously.

"A couple of times. The boys have run him off." Jenny chuckled. "I used to hate the fact the boys were getting taller than me. Now their height comes in handy."

"He better not try anything," Dee told her fiercely.

"He keeps trying to make it sound like it's all been a big mistake. He wouldn't dare threaten me around the boys. Can't have any witnesses," she added darkly.

"Don't talk like that."

"It's nothing I haven't been through before," her friend told her. Dee had learnt more about Jenny's situation and her ex had done far worse.

"You shouldn't have to go through this at all."

"Well, don't you come rushing back down here. You need to focus on yourself." Jenny paused. "I'm proud of you! It took a lot of courage to walk away."

Dee shook her head, thinking that what she had done to escape her marriage had been nothing compared to what her friend had gone through. She still had her doubts at times, but everyone she knew had told her she'd done the right thing.

It seemed, however, that Richard was still trying to manipulate her through her friends. He must have thought he could get to her by stalking the people she cared about. Even Carol had mentioned a couple of altercations. Dee had got onto her lawyer who had made submissions to the court asking for the protection order to be extended to her friends but it seemed that the police wouldn't do anything unless he physically attacked them. She didn't want things to go that far.

"I don't like that he's still trying to manipulate me through you."

"I can take care of myself, hon. Don't let him do this to you."

"I wish the police would do something. It's not fair that they can't do anything unless he physically attacks you."

"Yeah, but unfortunately that's the way it is. I know you're worried, but I meant what I said. Richard knows he can't do anything to me. Not without the serious threat of jail time. That won't help his business."

Dee wondered what that meant. "Do you know something?" she asked.

"Just something I heard on the grapevine through my boss." Jenny's job was working in administration for a small tech consulting firm. It was nowhere near as big as Carter Tech but her boss knew a few people in the same circles. "Listen, I have to go. You-know-who's making a huge fuss in reception."

"Okay. Let me know how it goes."

"Will do."

Chapter Twenty-Two

Dee was exhausted. It was almost Christmas and the shop had been so busy she had been working more than full-time hours. While she was grateful for the extra pay, the ten-hour days were taxing. She was on her feet for most of it, talking to customers on the shop floor, ringing up their purchases or generally just tidying up the stock. If she got a moment to sit down, her manager would be on her back, telling her to get back out on the shop floor. The store wasn't that big and it was located in a part of town that, while not unpopular, generally didn't get a lot of pedestrian traffic. Most people looking to buy camera equipment or get photos enlarged from the shop were serious photographers. Others tended to shop at the huge complex on the north side of town.

She didn't like her manager. The woman seemed to have a permanent sour expression and claimed her job title meant she only did paperwork and nothing else. In her initial interview, Dee had been told the manager's job was to provide back-up if it was busy and otherwise help keep the shop tidy. She did none of that.

The store had been opening a little later as the holiday approached. Being summer, it was light until late into the evening but, by the time Dee had walked through town to her flat, the sun had set. She couldn't wait to kick off her shoes and soak her aching feet in the bath. Part of the shop's dress code was that she had to wear heels and, after nine hours of standing, her feet were often sore and rubbed raw.

As she slowly made her way along the darkening street, she saw a car parked on the kerb. The car looked to be fairly low to the ground, reminding her of the car Richard had picked her up in the first night he'd taken her out. She could remember having a little difficulty getting into the car in her skirt and heels.

She was too tired to examine the vehicle more closely, walking down the path to the front door. She was startled when the door was flung open. Richard stood there, his face like thunder.

"It's about time you got home," he told her. "I've been waiting for you."

She stared at him. "What are you doing here?"

"I came to take you home," he replied. He reached for her and she pulled away before he could grab her arm.

"I'm not going anywhere with you," she said. "Do the words 'protection order' mean nothing to you?"

"Deanna, you will stop this ridiculous nonsense!" He grabbed her wrists and pulled her into him forcefully. "You're coming back with me and that's final."

"Get your hands off me!" she screamed.

"I'll do anything I like," he screamed back. "You're my wife!"

"I'm not your wife. Not anymore," she returned. "And that doesn't give you the right to manhandle me!" She struggled in his strong grip but he wouldn't let go.

"It's my right!" he said.

"I'm not your possession!" she yelled. "Get away from me!" She tried again to pull away from him and felt a sharp burning pain in her wrist. The next thing she knew was a stinging in her cheek and a dizzying sensation.

"You little bitch!" Richard was saying, his voice as cold as ice. "You think I was just going to let you walk away from me? I own you! You're nothing without me. You hear me?"

Dee lost all sense of what was happening. All she was aware of was the man's hands all over her; hard, rough, bruising hands of a man determined to show her just how insignificant she was.

Her ears were ringing and she was sure he had hit her again at some point. It felt almost surreal as if she was floating above her body.

"Dee? God, baby, I'm sorry."

She felt herself being lifted and a soft voice crooning in her ear. "I'm here. God, I'm so sorry. I should have been here earlier."

She opened her eyes a little to see lights flashing. Blues and reds, mixing in together; another light in her eyes, making her flinch in pain.

"Sir, we need to take her to the hospital."

"Yes, of course. Dee, love, they're going to get you checked out. All right?"

She could only nod, still confused by what was happening. Her head felt as if it had been wrapped by a steel band, squeezing hard enough that she thought it was going to pop. She felt people around her, heard voices, but none of it was making much sense.

She was barely aware of being lifted onto a stretcher before being loaded into the back of an ambulance. A man sat beside her, doing … something.

"We're just taking you to hospital, love," he said. She again nodded.

"My name's Eddie. Can you tell me your name?" he asked after an expectant pause.

"Deanna," she said softly. She licked dry lips, tasting something metallic. "Dee."

"Dee. That's a nice name. I've got a cousin called Dee. In Aussie. Well, it's Deirdre, but she always hated that."

"Me, too," she whispered. It hurt even to breathe.

She could feel his hands on her. Even though she knew he was just examining her, part of her felt dirty. She flinched and tried to pull away.

"It's okay. We just need to make sure you're not bleeding internally, love. You took a pretty big whack."

"Where … where is … he?"

"The guy who did this? The cops got him, love. Your boyfriend was pretty freaked out. I think if he hadn't been so focused on you, he might've killed the guy. Can't say as I blame him." There was another long pause. "We're here. Sit tight, hon. We'll have you out of here in a mo."

About a minute later, the stretcher was being wheeled out of the ambulance and down a corridor. Dee lay there, watching the light panels on the ceiling as she passed them. The stretcher collided with something and she winced as it reverberated through her head.

She could vaguely hear the sounds of a busy emergency department but could do nothing but lie still. It hurt to move. Her chest felt like it was on fire. Every breath seemed to burn.

She had no idea how long she lay there. She was aware of what she thought were nurses coming in to check on her but not how much time passed between visits.

"Ms Hargreaves?"

She blinked and looked up at the older man. He was about 60 with close-cropped white hair. She saw he had a clipboard in his hand.

"I'm Dr Carson."

She flinched. The name was too similar to her ex-husband's. She barely listened as the doctor told her what he was going to do.

"So, we'll get you down to x-ray and see what we're dealing with," he said. He patted her gently on the arm. "I promise. We'll take good care of you."

Getting an x-ray was an exercise in torture. The radiologist was kind enough but didn't seem to realise just how difficult it was for Dee to move. The pain had become a deep, throbbing ache through her whole body. She was terrified of making things worse by one wrong move.

She couldn't help thinking over what had happened and wondering if there was something she could have done differently. She should have defended herself, she thought. Done something. Anything to stop him from beating her. Why had she just taken it? Was she that weak?

Despite the pain in her head, or perhaps because of it, she began sobbing. Great, heaving sobs that left her feeling drained, her chest still burning.

"It's okay, sweetheart. I'm here."

Gentle hands stroked her face, wiping her tears away with a tissue. She opened her eyes, to be greeted with a blurry vision of Phillip beside her bed.

"You're safe, now," he said softly. "I'm not going anywhere. I promise."

Dee drifted off to sleep, encouraged by the gentle, loving tone of the man beside her.

When she woke, sunlight was streaming in through a window. She blinked and tried to sit up, but the moment she moved, she could feel a heaviness in her chest.

"Shh, don't try to sit up," Phillip said softly. She felt his hand on her arm and turned her head on the pillow to look at him. She felt sore on one side of her head and her left eye felt almost watery. She tried to blink away the sensation.

"You've got one hell of a shiner," he told her. "The doc said it was lucky your eye socket wasn't fractured. He thinks El Douche might have kicked you in the head at one point."

"El Douche?" she asked softly, wondering why he'd chosen to use that particular term.

"What would you prefer? Dickhead? Arsehole? He's in jail, by the way. The cops told me they're opposing bail."

He went on to relate what had happened. He'd been planning on picking her up from work but had been late getting to the shop and it had long been closed for the night. He'd then driven to her flat, hoping to see her on the way, arriving just in time to see Richard about to rape her. He'd very swiftly seen red, grabbing the other man by the shoulder and pulling him off before punching him hard enough to send her ex-husband flying backwards.

She looked him over. He was cradling his hand, which appeared to be badly bruised. He must have seen her look as he shrugged. "It was worth it," he said. "I'd do it again in a heartbeat to get that animal away from you."

"How did he even know where I was?" she asked.

"I don't think you need to worry about that right now," he said. "You need to focus on healing. You've got bruised ribs and a concussion. You're lucky he didn't break your wrist," he added, pointing to the bandage on her wrist.

He told her she'd been admitted to a private room and the hospital had asked security to make sure any visitors had to sign in. "The doc wants you to stay put for a couple of days at least." He visibly shuddered. "I wish I'd got there sooner. I swear, Dee, when I saw you lying there … I thought he was going to kill you. It just … I remember what my mum went through and I …"

"I'm sorry," she said.

"You have nothing to be sorry for. It's that bastard!"

She could sense the anger rising in him. "Don't," she said. "Don't waste your energy on him. He's not worth going to jail for."

Phillip looked at her, his eyes widening. "Do you think I would go that far?"

She chose not to answer that, remembering what he'd told her about his father. She did think Phillip would go that far, given the right motivation.

"I'm just saying. Don't sink to his level. If you do that, he wins."

The man sitting beside her smiled suddenly. "You're right. You're right. I know you're right."

She would have rolled her eyes if it hadn't hurt. She'd once told him about one of her favourite romantic comedies and he liked to tease her about it every so often.

Phillip had to leave when the doctor came in to talk to her. He did so under protest, saying he would be back as soon as he was allowed. He'd stayed all night, refusing to leave her side, even to go home and get some sleep.

After the doctor had left, Dee lay back, wishing she could take her own advice about dealing with Richard. She hated the man. As uncharitable as it was, she wished he would get a good dose of Karma. To know what it was like to feel helpless as blows were rained down on him.

She fell asleep but her sleep was disturbed by dreams of Richard screaming at her, his words insulting, calling her various names, suggesting she had been cheating on him all along. Part of her recognised the dreams as memories of the night she'd returned to her husband after her father's death. Other dreams had him not just screaming at her but striking her hard enough to make her see black specks in front of her eyes.

She woke suddenly with a gasp to find Phillip had returned. He was sitting beside her bed on the vinyl-covered chair which seemed to be ever-present in hospitals. Dee could remember long hours sitting on such a chair by her father's side in Wellington hospital.

"Sorry if I woke you," he said. "I came back as soon as they let me."

"You didn't," she said. "Wake me, I mean." His look was sympathetic.

"Bad dreams?"

She nodded, not wanting to give him the gory details. She shifted in the bed, her body aching from having stayed in one position for too long. The movement jarred her ribs and set off a percussion in her head, making her feel as if the room was spinning.

"I called the shop and told them what happened," he said. "That woman didn't seem to give a damn whatsoever. She told me if you didn't show up to work, you'd be fired."

"She doesn't have the authority to fire me," Dee said.

"Yeah, after I got off the phone with her, I got in touch with the owner. He sends his regards, by the way. He told me to tell you to rest up and not worry about your job. He'll find someone to take over for you until you're back on your feet. He's also going to deal with the manager. I get the impression he's not happy with her over a few things."

A nurse approached the bed. "I'm sorry to disturb you," she said quietly. "A policewoman is wanting to speak with you. If you're up to it."

Dee nodded her assent. A minute later a woman in police uniform came in. She was pretty, with olive skin and a Maori tattoo on her chin.

"Ms Hargreaves, I'm Constable Mahia. Are you up to talking with me about last night?"

"I can try," she said.

Phillip got up from the chair and offered the constable the seat. She nodded and smiled, thanking him as she sat down. He remained standing, leaning against the window.

"So, I understand the man who attacked you is your ex-husband?"

Dee nodded. "I had a protection order against him."

"Has he been violent with you in the past?"

"A couple of times. I think there's already a court record. Do you know how he found out where I was?"

The woman shook her head. "I'm sorry. No, I don't. If you can, please take me through some of the background just so I can get a clear picture of your relationship."

Dee slowly explained everything, from the moment she'd met Richard to her decision to leave. The constable nodded, interjecting occasionally to ask questions. She glanced down at her notes.

"You said his mother also hit you?"

"Once. In Wellington. The security guard saw it. Julia's never liked me."

"Yes. I understand." She closed her notebook, saying she had enough information. Dee looked at her questioningly.

"How did the police …"

"Your flatmate called us," she said.

"How did he even get in the flat?" Dee asked, remembering Richard had stormed out of the house.

"I can answer that," Phillip said quietly. "He convinced your flatmate he just wanted to talk to you." He added that her flatmate, Steven, had called the police as soon as he heard Richard screaming at her.

He looked at the officer. "What's going to happen now?"

"Mr Carter appeared in court this morning. Unfortunately, he was allowed bail, but he was put on a plane back to Palmerston North and told if he even set one foot in Hamilton before the case comes up on the court docket, he'll be arrested for breach of bail conditions." His car had been impounded and would be towed back to the city.

"That won't stop him," Dee said.

"No. I know," she said sympathetically. "This incident was particularly nasty, not just because of your injuries, but for the way he managed to not only find your address but talk his way into seeing you. From what you've said, he strikes me as one of the worst kinds of abusers. Of course, that's my opinion. I'm just sorry you had to go through this."

She quickly explained the process from there. Richard would have to appear in court again to answer to the charge of breaching the protection order and on the assault charges. That would be at least two or three months, although the delay was more to give Dee time to recover from her injuries. Richard was looking at a jail term as well as heavy fines. What those would be was up to the judge.

"What do I do now?" she asked.

"You let me worry about that," Phillip said. "You can't stay in that house. Not now he knows where you live."

"Doesn't he know where you live?" she asked.

"Yes, but I can get security cameras installed outside and I can get the gate modified so it can only be opened with a remote."

Constable Mahia nodded. "That's a good idea."

"There's plenty of room," Phillip told her. "If you're worried about your personal space."

She felt her cheeks grow hot. "I'm not worried about that. I trust you."

His expression was odd but she didn't comment on it. She wondered if he was already regretting the offer.

"Will I have to testify?" Dee asked the officer.

"I think so. If you don't want to face him in court, they may be able to make arrangements so you can testify by video, but you'd have to talk to the Crown lawyer about that."

Dee nodded. "Thank you."

The woman shook her head and smiled. "No. Thank you. I'm sorry this happened to you. We're going to do our best to make sure he never does this to anyone else. In the meantime, just rest and get well."

Chapter Twenty-Three

She was discharged from the hospital two days later. Phillip came to her room and walked with her to the parking building where he'd left his car.

"We'll need to pick up some stuff from your flat," he said. "I called Steven and told him to make sure someone was home."

Dee glanced at him. "Oh, yeah," she said. "Because I don't have my keys."

Phillip nudged her gently, taking out his car keys. "You can change your mind," he said. "Miranda offered ..."

She nodded. Miranda had visited her the day before, completely devastated at what had happened. Her friend had told her that her husband had been all for getting a flight down the island and beating the living daylights out of Richard. Dee had begged her not to let John do that.

"I haven't changed my mind. But I'm wondering if you have."

He sighed heavily. "It's not that I've changed my mind," he said. "But I worry that you trust me too much."

"You're not Richard, okay? Or your father, for that matter."

"If I hadn't been so afraid he'd killed you, I really would have done the deed."

"Don't talk like that," she said.

"It's true, though. He deserves it for what he did to you. Do you know, the moment I saw him standing over you, about to do something unspeakable, it was like a literal interpretation of seeing red. I was so angry, Dee. Angrier than I ever was, knowing my father was beating my mother and there was nothing I could do. I would have killed Richard and I wouldn't have regretted it for a moment."

"Yes, you would," she told him. "That's not who you are."

"You're wrong, Dee. That is who I am. Look where I came from."

She huffed, refusing to believe that he was even capable of such a thing. As much as she cared for him, his refusal to see himself as anything different from a man he hated was exhausting and she was still in too much pain to deal with it.

An hour or so later, Phillip turned his car in the driveway of his large home. It was fairly new. He'd sold the house he'd grown up in and had one built on a semi-rural property on the north end of the city. Dee had been there a couple of times and liked the rural outlook. She enjoyed the peace and quiet of the area, compared to the hustle and bustle of the city.

The gate slid smoothly open. It looked like Phillip had already had the new security system installed. She couldn't help wondering if he was thinking she should go somewhere else, why would he go to so much trouble to make sure she was safe?

He helped her out of the car and led her inside. The house was fairly modest, compared to the huge five-bedroom colonial villa the family had owned since Phillip's parents had married. His mother now lived in a small but modern unit on the east side of town.

The living area was open-plan, combining kitchen, living room and dining area. It was situated at the back of the house, which overlooked farmland. A sliding glass door led out onto the deck and a small pond.

"I'll go put the kettle on," he said. "Why don't you go and relax?"

She reached for his hand. "Phillip."

"I'm right here," he said. "I'll just be in the kitchen."

She let him go, watching as he walked into the kitchen, leaving her to settle on the couch. She sank into the comfortable cushions, her fingers brushing the cream suede fabric. The summer sun was shining through the glass pane, adding a warmth to her face. The house was temperature-controlled but the heat of the sun was pleasant. Dee hadn't been able to feel warm since the night Richard had attacked her.

Phillip came over with a cup of tea for her and what looked like a glass of scotch for himself.

"Really?" she said as he sat down, the glass in his hand.

"You don't approve."

"It's the middle of the day."

"It's one drink," he replied. "It's not like I'm going to be a barfly, is it?"

"That's not the point." She huffed. "Never mind. Do what you want."

He frowned at her. "Why the attitude all of a sudden?"

"Why do you keep backpedalling on me?"

"I don't know what you're getting at."

"You offered for me to stay here and then you acted like you immediately regretted it. Why?"

"Because I don't trust myself with you, all right? You have no idea how it felt for me that night. Seeing you. Seeing what he'd done to you."

"I would if you'd just tell me."

"What do you want to hear, Dee? You know what I want to do to that prick!"

"Stop it. This isn't you."

"What? Do you think I'd cry if he suddenly turned up dead in a ditch somewhere? He was going to rape you, probably kill you. All because he didn't want anyone else to have you. Do you know what the cops said to me the other day? That he'd been mouthing off, saying if he couldn't have you, no one could."

She remembered Richard screaming that he 'owned' her. There had been times when her marriage had felt like indentured servitude. Like he'd only ever seen her as something pretty he could put on a shelf and forget about.

"What did you mean when you said you don't trust yourself with me?"

Phillip put his glass down on the table and came over to sit with her.

"I mean, I don't want to do the same to you that he did. I want to wrap you in my arms and never let you go. I'm afraid, Dee. Of forcing you to choose between me and the life you deserve." He ducked his head for a moment, then looked at her. "I'm not good for you. I'll ruin you."

"Then why am I here?" she asked.

"Because I'm selfish," he said. "Because I wanted to protect you." He ducked his head. "And … because I'm in love with you."

She was a little taken aback by his admission. Was he expecting her to say it in return? She did care for him and had already told him she had feelings for him, but she had just been beaten by her ex-husband. Falling in love with someone else was the furthest thing on her mind.

She couldn't gauge anything from his silence.

"Phillip," she said softly. She reached for his hand. "Can you look at me, please?"

He lifted his head, his brown eyes practically boring into her. She felt a slight shiver. It was nothing to do with fear.

"Remember what I said that day we went to Mission Bay?"

She frowned, trying to recall the conversation.

"I said you were dangerous. And I was afraid. The fact is, what I feel for you, it terrifies me. Because it's like I said. I'm not good for you."

"Why? I mean, I know what you said about trying to change me, but is that really what this is all about?"

He sighed. "I don't know. I don't know how this works, Dee. I've been with plenty of women, but as soon as it looked like it was getting serious, I ran."

She had no idea what to say. She'd known he had these issues but hadn't realised just how deep-seated they were. He was so afraid of becoming the kind of man he hated, he would rather deny himself his own happiness.

"Look," he said when she didn't say anything. "This is my problem to deal with." She frowned. His feelings for her weren't a problem to be solved. She listened as he went on. "You're not ready for this," he said. "You just got out of the hospital. You need to heal."

*****

Meg was in full agreement. Her friend dropped in for a visit a few days after she'd been discharged. Meg winced in sympathy when she saw the still livid bruise on Dee's face.

"God, I'm sorry, babe. That asshole! If I'd known, I never would have let you marry him."

"You weren't to know," Dee told her. "Richard seems to be highly skilled at putting up a good front."

Meg shook her head. "I don't know, mate. I got bad vibes from him the night we had dinner with you guys. I wish I'd said something."

It was Dee's turn to shake her head. "Don't do that. Don't blame yourself. Even Miranda says he's a master manipulator."

"Still, we've been doing segments on this for our current affairs show. How these guys, and some women too, mind you, put on this respectable front, but they're monsters underneath. It's kind of a big deal." Her friend went on to relate some of the statistics she'd learnt in her investigation. As much as Dee loved her friend and knew she was just trying to share her own experiences, she didn't want to hear the statistics. She knew how lucky she was to have not only got out but survived Richard's attack.

Meg must have seen her face as she broke off.

"Oh, sweetie, I'm sorry. Here I am going on about this stuff when you've actually lived it."

Dee shook her head. "It's okay. I just want to put it behind me."

"So, when's the court case?"

"Tom says it'll probably be in March. The courts close down for Christmas and the court docket's already full. He even said I don't have to testify if I don't want to. The evidence against Richard is pretty solid."

"So what are you going to do?"

"I don't know. Part of me doesn't want to face him, but I think it might help if I do."

"How so?" Meg asked.

"I don't want to be afraid anymore, Meg." She bit her lip, taking a deep breath, hoping it would ease the lump in her throat. She'd already cried enough over the man and his treatment of her.

Her friend seemed to understand, moving over to sit beside her, wrapping an arm around her. "You want to know something? I look at you and I think about how strong you are. I mean, he could have worn you down, but you chose to walk away. You're so brave, you know? I wish I was as strong as you."

"I wish that were true," she said softly. "I hate him, Meg. I really hate him."

"I know. That's about how I feel too. But you're still the better person because you aren't letting it stop you from doing what you want. I mean, major props, my friend. You could have just buried yourself in misery, and you know, no one would have blamed you. But you're getting a degree. You're studying photography. Pursuing your dreams. That's something he can never take away from you."

She smiled weakly at her friend. "How do you know the right thing to say?"

"It's a gift," Meg said. She picked up her coffee cup and sipped, making a horrid face. "Ugh, this is cold. How about I go and make fresh cups?" She got up, taking both cups to the kitchen.

Dee chuckled. "Phillip says I shouldn't drink so much coffee."

"You've had how many cups this morning?" Meg asked from the kitchen.

"Um, that was my second."

Her friend made a sound like blowing a raspberry. "What does he know?" She turned to boil more water. While Phillip had a coffee machine, Dee preferred the sachets of instant latte or cappuccino. She watched as her friend opened up new sachets and put the powder in their cups.

Meg leaned on the counter while she waited for the water to heat up.

"So, tell me more about Phillip."

"What do you want to know?"

"Well, obviously he thinks the world of you. I mean, you're living here in his house."

"He's just trying to keep me safe," she said. She chewed on her lower lip and sighed. "I'm kind of worried, actually."

Meg was slightly distracted by the kettle. She took it off the stand and poured water in their cups, stirring the coffees. She returned to the couch with the fresh coffees.

"What are you worried about?"

Dee told her everything Phillip had said to her. Her friend nodded.

"You're right. The man's got more baggage than an airport carousel. My question, however, is this – Are you able to overlook this issue?"

"I don't know. That's the problem. I mean, I'm worried he's going to do something drastic. Like, go after Richard."

"Well, on one hand, I couldn't blame him for being angry enough to want to punish the guy but, on the other hand, he could wind up in jail himself."

"I told him that. I told him Richard wasn't worth going to jail for."

Meg looked thoughtful. "You know, I don't think it's about Richard at all. I think … I mean, I'm probably way off-base, but I wonder if maybe he's punishing himself. I know you said he tried to protect his mum from his dad. What if he was angry at himself for failing to protect her and punish his dad? What if he feels that history is repeating itself with you and Richard? Like maybe he feels he should have warned you earlier?"

Dee thought about it for a moment. It certainly sounded plausible.

"He needs to deal with it," Meg told her. "I know you said he's in love with you but, unless he deals with all that crap, you're always going to worry that he'll snap. Is that what you want in a relationship?"

She shook her head. "No." She realised that Meg had hit the nail on the head. She'd walked away from one bad relationship. While Phillip was nothing like Richard, there was always a part of him that she couldn't reconcile with the kind man that she knew. She was afraid that one day he would let that side of him take over.

"Do you love him, Dee?" her friend asked.

She didn't even have to hesitate. She did love him. Despite all her concerns, her feelings ran deep. Meg nodded when she answered.

"The thing you need to think about is, will it be enough? Being in love with someone doesn't make the problems go away. Goodness knows, Andy and I have our share."

"You do?" Dee asked.

"Yeah," Meg said. "When I went to take on the job as Europe correspondent. Andy wasn't sure he wanted to continue a long-distance relationship. There are just too many issues." She sighed. "He's not too happy with me at the moment."

"Why?"

"I didn't want to tell you this, but I'm going away again. For two years this time."

"What?"

Her friend nodded. "I got asked to take over as New York correspondent. It means a promotion, pay increase. Andy's kind of torn. I mean, this promotion means we'll be able to get the house we always wanted, but …"

"He thinks the distance will be too hard."

"Yeah. I mean Europe was a few months. This is for two years."

"Well, at least with his work, he can still visit you in New York. Or maybe you could both move there for the time being."

"That's always a possibility. We'll work it out. Part of being in a relationship is compromise. I mean, just quietly, I think the bosses are testing me to see if I'm ready to be a presenter."

Dee nodded. She could understand Andy's reluctance. Long-distance relationships over such a long period could make or break a relationship. Meg and Andy had been together a while and really cared about each other. It was just a question of whether they could handle two years apart.

She wondered, if that kind of opportunity ever came up for her, whether her relationship with Phillip would survive the distance. Somehow, she had the feeling it wouldn't.

Meg was right. Love wasn't enough. While she did feel safe with Phillip, there was always that small part of her that worried that he might continue to bury his issues. If he didn't deal with them, she worried that eventually, he would take it out on her. As much as he tried to fight it.

She didn't want to make the same mistake with him that she'd made with Richard.

The two men were worlds apart. For all Richard's claims that he'd loved her, she had never really believed him. When Phillip had told her of his feelings, she knew he was being totally sincere. It wasn't just the fact that the admission had cost him. It was the way he looked at her.

Chapter Twenty-Four

By the time Christmas came, Dee was sufficiently recovered to feel she could get out and about. She still had the occasional twinge around her ribs, but all the other bruising had healed.

Before Richard's attack, she had planned to go to a Christmas Eve party being held at a hotel in the city. Now that she was almost fully recovered, she decided she would still attend. She wasn't going to let her ex-husband bully her into hiding.

Phillip came home from work as she was dressing. He frowned at her.

"Why are you dressing up?"

"For the party tonight. Remember? Miranda invited us."

"I don't think you should go."

"Why?" she said. "Richard won't be there. He's restricted." Not that that would stop him, she thought, but then again, if he was arrested for breaching bail conditions, it would mar his image and that was something she doubted he would want to happen. He'd built his business on the mask he wore in the corporate world.

"You think it's wise?" Phillip asked.

"Don't get over-protective on me," she said. "I've been holed up here for the last three weeks and I'm not going to let him force me into hiding." She tried to make him understand that while Richard couldn't get to her if she was in hiding, he would still get what he wanted because she would never have a life. She was damned if she was going to let him keep on trying to control her.

Phillip didn't answer but he didn't try to dissuade her either. He disappeared to his bedroom to get ready for the party, leaving her to finish putting on makeup. She had chosen to wear a red sleeveless dress with a bodice that dipped just enough to show cleavage and moulded to her curves. The skirt came to just above her knees. It was modest, but not as conservative as the outfits she usually chose to wear. She wanted to send a clear message. That she wasn't as weak as some people thought she was.

She brushed her hair until it shone. Dee had decided to treat herself to a good cut and colour with a little of the money from her father's estate and her hair was now a honey blonde. It had grown past her shoulders in the past year. She'd also had contact lenses fitted. For the first time in weeks, she was beginning to gain some self-confidence.

"Wow! You look beautiful."

She turned and smiled at Phillip. He'd dressed in a pair of dark jeans topped with a white shirt and black blazer.

"Thank you," she said. She walked barefooted over to him and kissed his cheek.

"We should go," he replied, the keys to his car clinking in his hand.

"I need to put on my shoes," she told him, slipping her feet into high-heeled sandals. She held onto him for balance as she adjusted the strap.

"You know, you could have just sat down to do that."

"Where's the fun in that?" she quipped.

He snickered. "Funny. That's cute, really. I just think you wanted an excuse to touch me."

"Damn, you caught me out." She laughed as he pretended to huff.

"Come on, you. Before you get me into trouble."

"Oh, I think you can achieve that all on your own, Mr Mason," she replied, walking with him through the house to the garage.

"Takes one to know one, Miss Hargreaves."

An hour later, they walked into the lavishly-decorated ballroom. Dee looked around for her friend and was surprised to see Carol and Stewart standing talking to another guest. Stewart was the first to spot her. His eyebrows shot up and he wolf-whistled, prompting Carol to smack his arm before looking around. She too looked stunned.

The couple quickly came over to greet them.

"Wow! Look at you, Dee! You look amazing!" Carol kissed her cheek. Stewart grinned and kissed her other cheek.

"Thank you," she said, beaming at them. "I didn't know you were here."

"Miranda invited us," Stewart told her. "To be honest, we weren't sure you were coming. After what happened."

"I decided I wasn't going to let what happened dictate my life. I'm not going to become a hermit."

"Good for you," the older man said warmly.

Phillip touched her arm and murmured something about going to get them drinks. Dee continued to chat with her friends, who introduced her to the guest they'd been speaking to.

"Georgia's a business journalist."

"Actually, I'm an assistant editor now," Georgia replied. "My husband owns his own tech company."

Dee frowned. "Your husband?"

"Quinn."

"Wait. Quinn Masters? I used to work for Carter Tech. I remember something about a contract with your husband." She could vaguely remember having to type up the contract and get her boss to sign off on it.

Georgia nodded. "I'm not surprised you've heard of him, then. New Zealand's a small place when you work in similar industries." She leaned closer. "By the way, good for you for kicking Richard Carter to the kerb. As Quinn says, he's a good businessman, but a lousy human being."

Dee thought over what the other woman had implied. It appeared that those Richard had done business with were not as blind to his faults as she thought. God, she'd been so naïve to have been fooled by his manipulations.

She went outside to get some air a little later, sitting down at one of the tables provided for the guests. She let the cool breeze drift over her, closing her eyes for just a moment.

"You've got some nerve."

She opened her eyes to the sight of Faye Williams. The elderly dowager was glaring at her.

"Excuse me?"

The older woman scoffed. "I heard all about it. How you had your husband thrown in jail. I suppose you'll be going after his money."

Dee stood. Faye was a little shorter than her but the lack of height didn't seem to be a problem. She was clearly accustomed to talking down to anyone she considered her inferior.

"First, you might want to check your facts before you throw accusations. Secondly, I'm not the least bit interested in that bastard's money."

"How dare you? You little ..."

Phillip must have heard the woman's raised voice as he came out. Dee shot him a look, begging him not to say something he'd regret.

"You know, in my day ..."

Dee glared at the woman before she could say anything further.

"Well, this is the twenty-first century and treating women as property is very much frowned upon in this society. I'm sorry your husband treated you so badly that you have to take it out on everyone else, but I don't have to and I won't allow you to speak to me that way." She put up her hand before the older woman could open her mouth to berate her some more. "And save the speech about having respect for your elders. As far as I'm concerned, respect has to be earned and you have disrespected me from the moment we met."

She brushed past the older woman. As she reached Phillip's side, she turned to look at the woman.

"And by the by? Richard tried to kill me. So I didn't get him thrown in jail just because." The woman glared at her, obviously gearing up to berate her some more. Dee realised Faye was never going to learn her lesson, but she no longer cared. "I'm not going to run away like some scared little girl just because you believe I should have just let him do whatever he wanted to me. I'm not chattel and I won't be treated that way. So why don't you mind your own business?"

She let out the breath she hadn't realised she'd been holding as she walked away. Except for a very small group, everyone else was shooting admiring glances.

"Well done," Phillip whispered in her ear.

*****

Dee was tired by the time they got back to the house. Phillip escorted her to her room, stopping her from going inside with a gentle grasp of her wrist.

"I was so proud of you tonight," he said. "You really told that old bi… Faye, off."

"She won't learn anything."

"Maybe not, but there are a few people who were there tonight who saw you in a new light. I mean it, Dee. I'm really proud of you."

She looked up at him. The light in the hallway reflected in his gaze, making his eyes almost twinkle. She pressed a kiss to his lips, not intending for it to go any further. Phillip pressed the advantage, pulling her closer as his tongue darted forward, coaxing her to open up to him.

It was tempting, oh so tempting to want to invite him in, but somehow it felt wrong. As much as she cared for him, she couldn't help thinking of what she'd said to her best friend. It wasn't enough. There were too many obstacles in their way.

He must have felt her withdrawal as he pulled away.

"What is it?" he asked.

"It's nothing. I'm tired, that's all. Goodnight, Phillip."

*****

Neither one of them mentioned what had happened the next day. Christmas was over, New Year's came and went and Phillip went back to work. Yet they just seemed to carry on as if they were housemates, rather than potential partners.

News came from the solicitor toward the end of January. Richard had agreed to plead guilty to a lesser charge of aggravated assault.

"So, what does that mean?" Dee asked.

Tom explained that the guilty plea meant she wouldn't have to face Richard in court, but she would still be allowed to submit a victim impact statement which the judge would read prior to sentencing. Tom surmised that Richard's lawyer would probably submit something along the lines of the damage it could do to Richard's business and reputation to garner some sympathy.

"Let's hope the judge isn't sympathetic to him."

It remained to be seen whether Richard's interests would take precedence over her right to ensure he was punished appropriately for what he'd done. She knew he would never truly take responsibility for his actions. He still saw her as a possession.

Phillip seemed indifferent to the news when he returned from work.

"Well, I guess we'll see if the system really works or if, yet again, he gets off scot-free."

"Don't be like that," she remarked.

"You have no idea how it works, Dee. Guys like Richard think they're above the law. They think because they're rich they can get away with anything."

It was an old argument and she didn't want to go over old territory.

"What's wrong?" she asked.

He sighed, dropping his shoulders. "I don't know."

"Don't you?" she said quietly.

He turned, his gaze almost intense as he studied her. "No, you're right. The thing is, I've been doing a lot of thinking. About us. I don't think this is working."

She nodded, chewing on her lower lip. "It isn't," she agreed.

"I'm betting you know why."

"It's not that I don't love you, Phillip. I do. It's just … it feels wrong to start some kind of relationship with you when I'm afraid you'll just find a reason to push me away. You once told me that in the past you'd run away when things got serious. Yet somehow it seems like I'm different."

"You are. Dee, believe me, those other women …"

She raised a hand. "I don't need to hear it," she said. "The problem is not your feelings."

"I do love you."

"I know you do. But another man once told me he loved me too."

"I'm not Richard, as you keep telling me."

"No, you're not. Nor are you your father, but you also once told me you're afraid you'll become him. And the truth is, I'm afraid of that too."

"What are you saying?"

"I'm saying I don't think it's ever going to work between us. Not until you deal with your fears. I can't be with someone who continues to deny he has a problem. I don't want to make the same mistake twice."

"Mistake?" He looked confused.

"What I mean is, when things started going badly with Richard, I knew there was something wrong in our relationship, but I thought if I could just give him what he wanted, then he might change. I guess I thought I could save him. Then you swooped in, all white knight and I thought you were saving me. And I thought I could do the same for you."

"You can't save someone who doesn't want to be saved."

"No, I know that. When I asked you to help me learn to fit in your world, I thought that was the only way I was ever going to learn to love myself. I realise now I didn't need you to be my white knight. The only person who was ever going to help me change was me." She approached him and kissed him gently on the lips. "I do care for you. But sometimes loving someone isn't enough. And I need to find my own way before I can let someone else in."

He looked resigned. "Where will you go?"

"I don't know yet. School starts up again in a couple of weeks."

"I'll help you find a place," he said.

"Thank you, but this is something I need to do on my own."

"It's okay to ask for help," he reminded her quietly.

"I know. And if I ever need that help, I promise you'll be the first person I'll ask."

Chapter Twenty-Five

A few weeks after classes began, Meg called her through the video calling network.

"I heard about something I thought you might be interested in."

"What is it?" she asked her friend.

Meg held up some brochures for a school in New York.

"They accept applications from students all over the world but they only select one.

I think you should apply."

"I don't know," she said slowly. The school was known to be quite prestigious and some very well-known artists had studied there. She wasn't sure of her chances, considering the bar was set extremely high.

"You never know if you don't try," Meg told her. "You're really good, Dee. Besides, you'll already have your accommodation all sorted. You can stay with me."

Dee laughed. "All right. You talked me into it."

The application required her to obtain references from her teachers as well as a character reference. Miranda was only too happy to provide the character reference.

"Wow! This is a prestigious school," she said, waving the brochure Dee had printed out. "I bet you'll get in. You have an amazing eye, Dee. Brendan raved about the photos you did for him.

Brendan was another racehorse owner who had asked her if she'd like to earn a little bit of pocket money taking photographs of some of his horses. He had planned to use the photographs to advertise the animals for breeding. While she hadn't planned on that branch of photography as a career, it had been good practice for her.

She forgot about the application in the weeks that followed. Her life became filled with assignments and outings with friends she'd made through her classes. She was still working at the camera shop, although she was now the assistant manager and the owner had hired a young man to work part-time.

Her flatmate stopped by the shop late one afternoon with a package for her.

"It's from New York," Paul told her. "I figured it was important."

"Thanks," she said, tearing into the envelope. Inside was a thick prospectus and a letter had been attached.

"Dear Miss Hargreaves, we're pleased to advise …"

She'd got it. The judging panel had seen her portfolio, along with all her references, and decided she was good enough to enrol at the school in their study abroad programme.

The first person she thought of telling was Phillip. She still saw him for the odd lunch or dinner. When he called that evening suggesting dinner and a movie, she eagerly said yes.

"I have some news," she told him when he picked her up. He looked at her with wariness in his eyes.

"What is it?" he asked.

She showed him the letter. He read the contents quietly, his face almost expressionless. Almost. She knew him well enough to realise he was trying to hide his emotions.

"This is great," he said as he finished the letter. "Why didn't you tell me about this before?"

"Because I didn't think I would get it," she told him. "Meg told me about this weeks ago and I forgot about it until I got the letter."

"I've always told you that you need to do what's best for you. I'm proud of you, Dee. I know you're going to do great."

There was a hint of regret in his eyes. She knew what he was thinking. She still loved him, but this was something she had to do.

"I do love you, Phillip. But I wanted more from you than you were willing to give." She smiled and reached over to squeeze his hand. "Even if there was never anything else between us I'll always remember what you did for me."

"What was that?"

"You helped me learn to love myself. Because of you, I know who I am now. I'm not some doormat who lets someone like my dad or Richard decide how to live my life."

He sighed. "That's all I've ever wanted for you, kiddo," he said. "That's all I ever wanted."

It was a cold July day when Phillip drove her to the international airport in Auckland. He followed her inside, waiting as she checked in her baggage. He continued to wait with her until it was time for her to go through security.

"You can change your mind, you know."

She laughed a little and shook her head. "You know I can't pass up this opportunity."

"No, you can't."

She glanced at the screen above where they were sitting, just as the announcement came for the passengers on her flight to go through security. He stood up to walk with her.

"Be happy, kiddo."

"I will be," she told him. "Thanks to you."

He canted his head and offered a modest 'aw shucks' look.

"I didn't do anything."

He was wrong about that. He'd helped by reminding her that she was in control of her destiny.

The announcement came again over the speakers. "Attention passengers flying to Los Angeles on Flight 402, boarding will commence shortly. Please make your way through security to Gate 10. Thank you."

Dee tucked her long hair behind her ear. "That's me," she said.

He hugged her again before picking up her hand luggage. "Go on."

She took the bag, making sure her boarding pass was still tucked in the pocket, along with her passport. She started to walk away, then paused and turned. He was still there, waiting for her to go through security. He was clearly trying to hide it, but she could tell it was affecting him more than he wanted to let on.

Sensing her hesitation, he came to her, wrapping his arms around her one more time.

"You have to do this," he said. "For you."

"But you ..."

"I'll be fine. I'm always fine," he told her.

"I do love you," she told him.

"I know."

She heard the announcement a third time and knew she couldn't put it off any longer. He pushed her in the direction of the waiting border security agents who were pretending to be busy rather than watching them.

"Go," he repeated.

Dee nodded, sniffling a little as she took her bag and walked up to the security agent, handing it to the man to put through the scanner. As she walked through, she looked behind her once more. He was gone.

*****

Less than a week later, she stood above Niagara Falls, camera in hand. The wind whipped through her hair, tendrils flying in her face. She took a few shots, listening to the roar of the rushing water below. A few tourists milled about, chattering about the view, but she tuned them out. She let the camera dangle on its strap, lifting her face to the hot sun and closing her eyes, letting her other senses take in her surroundings.

As hard as it was leaving all she loved behind, everything in that moment told her it was the right thing to do. Her journey was just beginning.

Epilogue

Three years later.

The gallery was crowded. Her agent had been very enthusiastic about the exhibition.

"It's created quite a buzz on social media," Lisa told her.

It was her first photographic exhibition, displaying some of the photographs she had taken in her travels around the world. Her agent had decided to host a cocktail evening for her first showing. Many of the guests who had turned up had been old acquaintances, eager to see what she had made of herself.

Dee had changed in three years. Her hair was now down to the middle of her back, less out of vanity and more out of a lack of hairdressing facilities in some of the remote places she had visited. It was coloured an ash blonde, having been bleached naturally by the hot sun in those countries. She somehow looked younger than 31, her hazel eyes sparkling and her skin glowing with health and vitality.

The years away had been good to her. She held herself and spoke with confidence that those who had known her previously would never have seen before.

She was sipping champagne, watching the guests as they perused the photos.

"Absolutely stunning," a voice said behind her.

She turned and offered a smile. "Thank you," she told her friend. "Which photo's your favourite?"

Carol hugged her. "I wasn't talking about the photos, darling. I was talking about you. You look gorgeous. Well, more than you did before."

"I'll take that as a compliment. How are you?"

The older woman grinned, waving a hand. Dee could see a wedding band on her finger.

"So, you finally caught him, huh?" she said.

"And it only took eight years. Who woulda thunk it?"

Stewart came up behind Carol and kissed his wife on the cheek. "Talking about me again, I see?"

"Your ears burning, were they?" Carol shot back.

He just shook his head and grinned. "Hello, Dee. You're looking wonderful. Carol has kept me up to date with all your travels. I must say, your photographs are simply beautiful."

"Thank you, Stewart," she said.

The couple brought her up to date on everything that had happened in the years since. Her ex was out of jail but he'd lost everything. He had angered far too many people, not just Dee, but many of his business acquaintances. They had discovered he'd been involved with some local con men who had scammed lots of people out of money. It turned out that the racing syndicate he'd been included in had been part of the scam.

Dee was relieved to learn that someone had bought Richard's business when he'd been forced to put the company into receivership. He was completely broke and utterly humiliated. Her friends assured her there was no possibility of him looking for her. He'd left New Zealand for Australia and wasn't planning on returning. They suspected he had done so to escape criminal charges over the scam.

Jenny walked in with her two sons. Both towered over their mother as the group began looking over the photographs. Dee tapped her friend on the shoulder. Jenny's eyes widened as she saw her.

"Dee! I nearly didn't recognise you. You look amazing!"

"She sure does."

Dee turned to look at Phillip. He had changed a little in the years since she'd left. His dark hair had begun to grey at the temples. There were creases around his eyes that hadn't been there before. Signs of a man who had become more open to expressing his emotions, she thought. She wondered if he had ever sought the help he needed to deal with his past.

"Hey kiddo," he said, kissing her on the cheek. She took a moment to take him in. Even after three years, she still had stirrings of those feelings she thought she had got over long ago.

"Hey yourself."

He turned to glance at the display. "You did it, huh? You went out there and you showed the world what I always knew."

"Yes, I did."

Someone else stepped up to congratulate her on her work. She chatted with them briefly before turning back to Phillip.

"Thank you," she said.

"For what?"

"You need to ask?" she responded.

He shook his head. "No. I said it three years ago and I'll say it again. You did all this yourself. And I'm proud of you, Dee. You not only did everything you said you would do, you surpassed it."

"It took time," she told him, "but I did. I found myself. I learnt to love myself."

"And that's all you ever needed."

About the author

E M Richmond lives in Palmerston North, New Zealand. She is the author of several novels, including the Phoenix series and Amanda Steele, Private Investigator.

The name is a pen name.

For more information on this title or any others, visit: http://leannewarr.com.

www.ingramcontent.com/pod-product-compliance
Lightning Source LLC
LaVergne TN
LVHW020541100826
845148LV00010B/1559